A Houghton Mifflin Literary Fellowship Book

Looking for a Bluebird

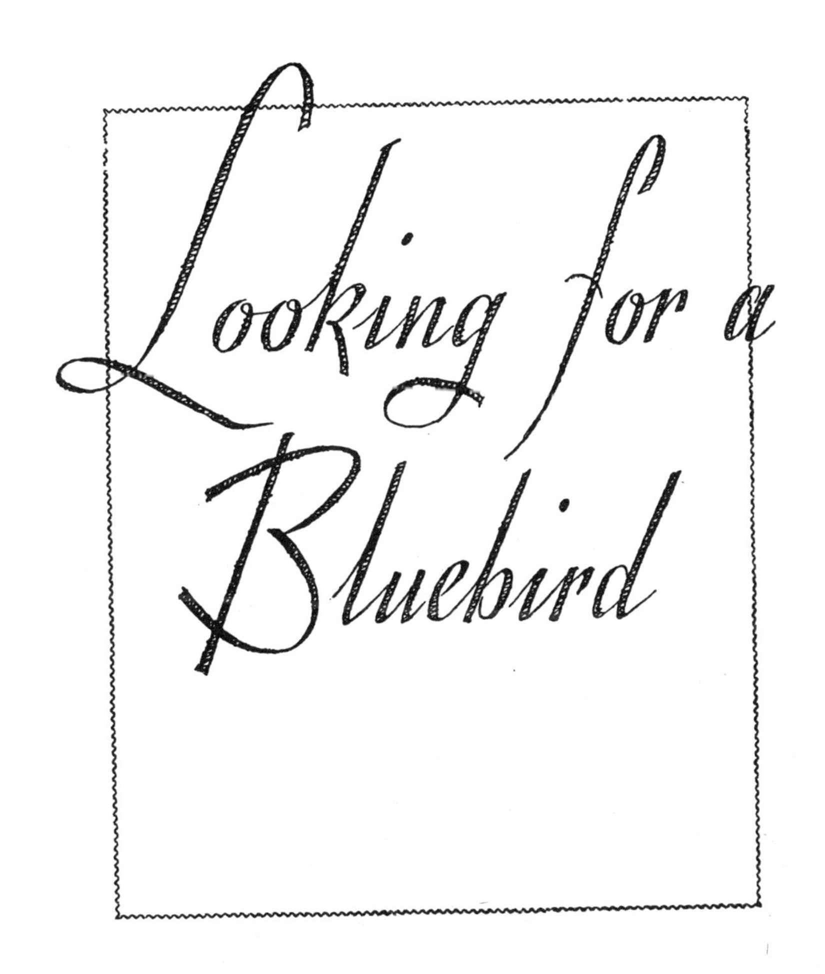

Looking for a Bluebird

BY JOSEPH WECHSBERG

Illustrated by F. Strobel

GREENWOOD PRESS, PUBLISHERS
WESTPORT, CONNECTICUT

Library of Congress Cataloging in Publication Data

Wechsberg, Joseph, 1907-
Looking for a bluebird.

Reprint of the ed. published by Houghton Mifflin, Boston.
1. Musicians--Correspondence, reminiscences, etc.
2. Wechsberg, Joseph, 1907- I. Title.
ML418.W3A3 1974 787'.1'0924 [B] 73-16801
ISBN 0-8371-7234-9

Originally published in 1945 by Houghton Mifflin Company, Boston

Reprinted with the permission of Joseph Wechsberg

Reprinted in 1974 by Greenwood Press, a division of Congressional Information Service, 88 Post Road West, Westport, Connecticut 06881

Library of Congress catalog card number 73-16801

ISBN 0-8371-7234-9

Printed in the United States of America

10 9 8 7 6 5 4 3 2

FOR

ANN

The author's thanks are due the editors of *The New Yorker* and *Esquire*, who first published some of this material.

Contents

Chapter 1

PIER 99

I FIRST saw New York early one morning in July, 1928, from the sun deck of a small, decrepit French Line steamer, *La Bourdonnais*. I was making my first transatlantic crossing, as second violinist with the ship's orchestra. All night long, while we were still far out at sea, there had been a reddish glow in the dark sky, like the reflection of a big forest fire.

'It took the *types* on the bridge eleven days to find Broadway,' Maurice, my orchestra leader, said. 'Hello, Broadway.'

I had been too excited to go to bed, afraid of missing the great moment. Now, as I stared through the morning haze, what had looked like the contours of a giant chain of mountains took on the shape of buildings, towers, roofs, and windows.

'C'est ça,' Maurice said, his flat hand outstretched like an innkeeper showing his best room to a prospective guest. 'The Skyline. Eau chaude et froide. Bains. Confort moderne. This is my hundred-and-eighty-ninth crossing, and it's nice seeing it again. Ecoute, mon petit, did you store the cognac bottles under my berth?'

I said yes, I had, and the six bottles of Veuve Clicquot were in the 'cello. In addition to being the orchestra leader, Maurice also played the 'cello. He played very well when he was sober. He had two instruments, one for playing, the other, with a detachable back, for storing laundry, certain photographs, and liquor bottles. Maurice was a short, rotund fellow with the healthy, pink complexion of many Frenchmen who have been brought up on pinard instead of mother's milk. He was forty-five and looked half his age. His rich, uncombed hair was always hidden under a Basque béret which he did not bother to take off while playing or even in bed. He seldom undressed himself. It was the duty of the first and second violinists to get him out of his clothes and the wine bottle out of his hands, and all the time he would be sound asleep. He was an Alsatian, his wife lived in Atlantic City, and his mother in Paris, Eighteenth Arrondissement. He had worked on many great liners of the day — the *Berengaria, Paris, Leviathan, Mauretania, France, Aquitania,* and *Ile de France.*

I often wondered what had made Maurice take a job aboard *La Bourdonnais,* which had but one funnel, no glass-covered deck, no swimming pool, no valuable oils in the music saloon, and carried no celebrities in de-luxe suites, because there were no suites. It took her eleven days — twice as long as the big liners — to cross the ocean. On that trip she had sailed from a dilapidated, open-air pier in Bordeaux, picking up more passengers at the Spanish ports of Vigo and Santander, going north-north-west to Halifax and then on to New York. The passengers, mostly Spaniards and Canadians, were kept apart in the dining-room. This clever bit of protocol eliminated many frictions. On the starboard side, where the Spanish group ate, there was much noise and animation. On the port side, home of the Anglo-Saxons, prolonged periods of silence were not unusual. There were only about sixty passengers, and the quête — the collection for the musicians, which is always made by a popular lady passenger on the last day of the trip — was poor compared to the princely tips which our colleagues aboard the *Ile de France* and *Paris* were getting from prosperous Americans.

We did not dock at Pier 57, berth of the great Compagnie Générale Transatlantique liners, at the foot of West Fourteenth Street. Our ship's officers said there was no room, the *Ile de France* and *Paris* being there. The fact was that the company officials, afraid of damaging the French Line's excellent reputation by disclosing such poor relations as *La Bourdonnais*, were eager to keep her out of the public eye.

We went way up to Pier 99, at Fifty-Ninth Street. They could not hide us farther away because Pier 99 was the last one. We docked without any cheers, reporters, or photographers. Ten people, the police and customs men, and three bored dogs were waiting. It was quite a letdown after what a first violinist from the *Ile de France* had once told me: 'You arrive on Forty-Fourth Street, almost in the heart of the big city. You walk over to Times Square. It's a great experience.'

I stared gloomily at the rows of walls, broken windows, factories, and a game of ball going on in the middle of the street, and then went down to our two connecting staterooms. Maurice and my colleagues were in the middle of great preparations, storing away wine bottles. As a rule we had our meals in the first-class dining-room, just before the regular service, together with the small children and their nurses. We were served two bottles of wine apiece with each meal, one white, one red. No one except Maurice ever finished the bottles, and he kept urging us to take them down to our staterooms. Two days before we got to New York, he had borrowed six hundred francs from the tourist-class bartender and ordered all the rest of us to get more money. Dimitrij, our piano-player, a pale man from Vladivostok, got five hundred francs from a sinister-looking sailor, at fourteen per cent interest. Lucien, the first violinist, who had a way with the ladies, borrowed eight hundred francs from Madame Marguerite, age forty-eight, the chambermaid and only female member of the crew, also at fourteen per cent. I secured five hundred from the chief steward, at eleven per cent.

All the money was carefully counted and written down, then Maurice went to the first-class and tourist-class bars and bought bottles of cognac, Byrrh, Scotch whiskey, Dubonnet, gin, Bénédictine, champagne, Pernod, beer, rum — all at the fifty per cent discount which we musicians were allowed at the ship's bars. By the time *La Bourdonnais* entered the territorial waters of the United States and the bars were closed, our two staterooms were beautifully stocked with large quantities of liquor and beer and over eighty bottles of red and white wine. To get more space, we knocked out closets, threw out life-belts, and thoroughly rearranged our staterooms. This was easy. There were few nails left on *La Bourdonnais* and everything was in a loosely jointed state.

We got our debarkation cards after the ship docked and were free to leave. Maurice gave me a list of telephone numbers and told me to go to the nearest drugstore and call them up. 'You say, "Hello, *La Bourdonnais* is in port," and that's all.'

I pointed out that I was Czechoslovak, had never been in America before, spoke only somewhat limited English, and had never talked on the telephone to an American. I was afraid they might not understand me.

Maurice chuckled, in a half-amused, half-pitying way. 'They will understand no matter how you say it. Get going, mon petit.'

I called the numbers from a drugstore near Columbus Circle. Maurice was right. Nobody seemed to have any trouble in getting my message. The simple words appeared to cause unanimous delight to all the people on the other end of the wire. Most of them uttered cries of joy and said they were coming right over and assured me of their everlasting friendship.

I went over to Broadway and down to Times Square and had a chocolate soda and a shoe-shine. When I came back to Pier 99, early in the afternoon, Lucien was going aboard with two dignified-looking citizens. It was very hot and he wiped his forehead.

'Those gentlemen are friends,' Lucien said to the customs men near the gangway. 'They've come to visit with us.'

Dimitrij was standing in the corridor leading to our staterooms. He looked tense and businesslike. 'Where have you been?' he said to me. 'Maurice is waiting for you. There is work to do.'

There were fifteen strangers in our staterooms. Most of them were bald, and all had the look of prosperous, busy men, happy to get away from the office for an afternoon. It was very hot down in the cabins, and they were sitting in their shirtsleeves, fanning themselves with their straw hats. Because it was so hot, they were thirsty, and each one was holding a glass in his hand. They were sitting on the berths, on the floor, on the 'cello case, on piles of sheet music, on chairs, drinking highballs and wine and beer and gin and Dubonnet and cognac and everything mixed. Two men were squatted in the bathtub, their legs crossed in Brahmin fashion, but their faces were red and happy and they seemed quite comfortable.

Maurice was standing before the washbasin, which had been turned into a bar, mixing drinks, opening bottles, and stuffing money into his trousers pockets. He told me to raid the adjoining staterooms and bring all the mouthwash glasses. Dimitrij came in and helped us wash glasses. The gentlemen shook hands with me and said I must come and have lunch with them tomorrow.

At dinnertime, Maurice went to the dining-room above and took four guests along. We were allowed to have dinner guests while the ship was in port, provided we paid for their meals, but the regulation about payment was seldom enforced, since so much food was wasted aboard ship anyway. Maurice and his friends came back from the dining-room, each happily carrying two bottles of wine. Next, I was dispatched to the dining-room with another party of four. Two of them were, they explained to me, a railroad executive and a corporation lawyer. The others preferred vaguely to mention their 'downtown offices.' All were in high spirits and very amiable, and the corporation lawyer offered me a job.

'What kind of a job?' I asked.

'Oh, any kind of job,' he said. 'What kind of job do you want?'

The food aboard *La Bourdonnais* was excellent, but my four guests ate very little. The chief steward came to say hello and the railroad executive shook hands with him as though he were an old friend. The railroad man was enormously fat, with a heavy, bulging neck and a face that one sometimes finds painted on children's balloons, a friendly, Buddha-like face. He said he had happened to see a little picture in town that the chief steward might like to see, ha, ha, ha, and he gave him a picture of Lincoln with the number '5' in every corner. The chief steward said that Lincoln was his favorite sujet d'art. He collected all the pictures of Lincoln he could get. There were two incidents — one when the corporation lawyer started singing 'Hail, Columbia' just as the second officer was going through the dining-room, the other when we were trying to get the railroad magnate down the narrow iron steps that led to C Deck, where our staterooms were. He almost broke his fat neck, and it took all four of us, the three other guests and me, to get him down successfully.

After dinner the first violinist from the *Ile de France* came over to say hello and good-bye. She was sailing at midnight. He looked at the happy citizens all over the place, many of them now singing, and at Maurice, carrying all that money in his bulging pockets.

'I wish I were here with you,' he said. 'Over there we can't do this sort of thing. Too many customs men and coppers hanging around Fourteenth Street. Mince alors, how I hate those big boats!'

I said, 'Well, at least you're near Times Square and in the heart of the big city. That's what you told me in Paris, remember?' He gave me a disgusted look and left.

One after another, the citizens drifted out. Before leaving, each had to rinse his mouth with a special mouthwash which Maurice prepared himself. Then Maurice sniffed at the breath of each one, and if there was a trace of liquor left he made the man eat a piece of apple and drink some milk. 'Milk always helps,' he said. 'Can't take a chance with the *types* standing outside the pier.'

The railroad magnate was fast asleep on Dimitrij's berth. We worked on him for ten minutes, but he kept sleeping.

'Those railroad men are the worst,' Maurice said. 'He's the director of a big railroad. It's an unbelievably big railroad and he's making more money while he sleeps than the four of us playing a whole month. I wonder if a director of the Paris–Lyon–Méditerranée Railroad would go to sleep in somebody else's stateroom.'

We carried the railroad magnate out and dragged him over into a cabin which was used as a storage room for old mattresses. We put him down on a pile of mattresses, closed the door, and went back to our staterooms to clean the glasses and the bathtub. Maurice counted the money, carefully writing down the total. All our business debts were to be paid tomorrow so that too much interest would not accumulate. The rest was equally divided among the four of us, eighty-three dollars apiece. It was almost three times as much as a musician's monthly salary aboard the *Ile de France*.

We went up to the dark sun deck. The night was stifling hot, and we sat down, watching the reddish glow over what we decided was Broadway. Fifty-Ninth Street was deserted and two cats were fighting on the roof of Pier 99. Maurice took a drink from the wine bottle he had brought along and Dimitrij lay down flat on his back and stared up at the stars.

'There's some stuff left for tomorrow,' Maurice said, 'and the day after tomorrow, too, unless they come for breakfast and lunch. Sometimes they can't even wait until afternoon. Each of you will have more money than those *types* make aboard the *Ile de France*, and the hell with Louis Quinze stuff and Impressionist paintings in the grand saloon. I think I'm going to buy my wife a fur coat. She wants a new one, and I guess they're cheaper now in summer.'

From downstream came the long, deep sound of a siren. It was midnight, and the *Île de France* was sailing from her crowded, noisy pier. There were undoubtedly men in dinner coats and ladies in evening gowns seeing her off, and 'The Star-Spangled Banner' and the 'Marseillaise' were being played. There were also sure to be customs men and coppers and a lot of fun all around. I wanted to talk to Maurice, but he was already snoring.

Chapter 2

THE SLEEPY PIANO-PLAYER

THE laziest man I have ever known was Sebastiano, a Spanish pianist from Algeciras, who joined our four-man orchestra aboard *La Bourdonnais* for one voyage. On sailing day, Dimitrij, our regular piano-player, explained in a laconic radiogram addressed to Maurice that 'for personal reasons' he was unable to leave Paris. The personal reasons were, as we found out later, a vendeuse from the Galeries La Fayette, fourth floor, caleçons, peignoirs, ladies' underwear. Fortunately, Maurice ran into Sebastiano at the Café des Quat'z' Arts three hours before the departure of our train for Bordeaux, and hired him at once.

Maurice had worked with Sebastiano at the Rendezvous des Américains, a tiny, permanently overcrowded boîte in a side street off the Boulevard Raspail on Montparnasse, where the customers literally sat on one another's laps and the lights were so dim that no one was able to read the bill. In the Rendezvous, Sebastiano sat behind an upright Pleyel piano in a corner, concealed from the rest of the boîte by a heavy velvet curtain, his job being to create what Monsieur Boniface, the proprietor, referred to as 'l'atmosphère — c'est tout.' He played soft, subdued, intimate piano music, en sourdine. On Saturdays, he would be joined by a violinist and a 'cellist, and it was on such an occasion that he met Maurice.

The atmosphere at the Rendezvous des Américains was anything but American, Monsieur Boniface having never seen more of America than the United States Treasury building on the back of a ten-dollar bill. The bartender was from Rouen and the headwaiter from Corsica, and Sebastiano, a pupil of Albéniz, played mostly Spanish music — Granados, de Falla, Albéniz. He was a short fellow with thin shoulders. He had beautiful dark hair, always uncombed and falling down over his forehead; prominent cheekbones, black eyes, and a colorless complexion.

Sebastiano was unbelievably lazy. He said he could sleep twenty-four hours a day for four days in a row, and I think he did not exaggerate. He liked to point out, however, that in Algeciras he was not known as an especially lazy type. 'You should see my father,' he once told me. 'Never gets out of bed. On Easter Sunday, Mother, my eleven brothers and sisters, and I have to work for an hour before we get him dressed and drag him all the way to church. There he falls asleep at once. C'est la vie.' Sebastiano shrugged and fell asleep himself.

Sebastiano had a tiny room at a little hotel near the Panthéon. The room was on the fourth floor and Sebastiano hated climbing up the narrow, winding stairway. Often he would sit down on the stairs between the second and third floors and fall asleep. Mademoiselle Renée, a pretty, dark-haired girl, who lived next to him, would go down and call the proprietor and his wife, and the three of them would drag Sebastiano up to his room. Renée was crazy about Sebastiano, but he was indifferent and resented her hanging up her washed panties and stockings on a string across her window. 'She's frivolous,' he used to say. 'Most girls are. C'est la vie.'

He got so tired of climbing the four flights that one day he decided that from then on he would stay at the Rendezvous and sleep under the piano. He took two plush seat covers and placed them on the floor in front of the piano. He hung his tuxedo across a chair and slipped into his pajamas, which he had brought from his room, and slept all day long The place was being cleaned, and Monsieur Boniface carried on noisy discussions with wine salesmen, and once the headwaiter from Corsica almost stabbed the cook to death with a fruit knife, but Sebastiano slept peacefully and undisturbed. Around eight-thirty that evening, the headwaiter, aided by the entire staff, started to wake up Sebastiano. By nine-thirty the pianist was ready to get up. He changed into his tuxedo, had a glass of dry sherry, and sat down at the piano. His fingers worked automatically, though his mind was still in a deep trance.

One day Sebastiano's tuxedo was stolen while he was sleeping under the piano. That night he had to play in his pajamas. He did not mind. He hated to dress and the place was always overheated, and he was safe, anyway, behind the velvet curtain. At two in the morning, two American tourists discovered him in his odd attire. They pushed him out onto the floor, where he was an instant success. Everybody agreed that wearing nothing but pajamas was a great idea. The two Americans jumped into a taxicab, went to their hotel, and came back in their pajamas. Everybody bought drinks for everybody else. The idea caught on, and three or four evenings later all habitués of the Rendezvous des Américains arrived at the place in their pajamas, over which they had put on their overcoats and furs. Monsieur Boniface, a man of sound business principles, increased the prices of liquor fifty per cent and put out more lights. The son of the Corsican headwaiter was posted as guard in front of the entrance, and a small sign, 'MEMBERS ONLY,' printed in English, was hung on the door. Only people dressed properly — that is, in pajamas — were allowed to come in.

Sebastiano, never given to loose talk, was particularly reticent about the weeks that followed. That epoch was, he indicated, characterized by cheerful abandon and wonderfully large tips. Then the cook, who was carrying on a vendetta with the Corsican headwaiter, got fired and went to the police. The agents raided the place, and that was the end. 'C'est la vie,' Sebastiano concluded gloomily.

The police tactfully suggested that Sebastiano find himself employment outside of France or they would have to ship him back to Algeciras. Sebastiano hopefully went to the Café des Quat'z' Arts and happened on the job aboard *La Bourdonnais*.

Sebastiano began his career as ship's musician promisingly by missing the 9 o'clock train which he had been ordered to take with the rest of us. He told us later that he took a taxi to the station and fell asleep. The cabdriver, unable to wake him up, took him to the nearest police station, where they managed to shake him out of his trance, but by that time our train had left. He took the midnight train and came aboard the following morning with the last group of first-class passengers. He had on his tuxedo, a yellow camel's-hair overcoat, and no hat. He had no baggage whatsoever and looked so bored and genuinely expensive that the maître d'hôtel, who took pride in his infallible judgment of his fellow men, made his de-luxe bow and asked him for the number of his stateroom on A Deck. Two smart, tall Vassar girls, returning from their European vacation, gave him a wistful look, and a vivacious divorcée from Boston, reclining in a deck chair, put down her Michael Arlen story and stared at him in fascination.

Sebastiano was much too sleepy to return her stare. I took him down to the two connecting staterooms where the orchestra slept. Maurice started a noisy tirade. Sebastiano, his eyes half-closed, dreamily inquired which of the four berths was his. He took off his overcoat, lay down in his tuxedo, and in four seconds was sound asleep. Baggage porters bumped into the door and uttered pungent oaths, women came into our stateroom looking for their husbands and husbands came

in looking for their wives, a steward swung his bell ('Visitors ashore, all visitors ashore'), the siren wailed, but Sebastiano slept peacefully through all the excitement that preceded the sailing and we had to pour half a glass of ice water into his open mouth to get him up on deck in time for the national anthems, which were always played as the ship was being towed away from the pier. After the last note of the 'Marseillaise,' he went back to bed again.

The eleven days that followed, en route to New York, were a nightmare. Sebastiano kept the three other musicians — Maurice, Lucien, who was our French first violinist, and myself, the second violin — in a perpetual state of nervous tension. We had fairly easy working hours aboard *La Bourdonnais.* There was an apéritif concert on deck, between eleven and noon; a concert in the tourist-class dining-saloon from three to four, which was merely a rehearsal for the afternoon concert in the first-class saloon from four to five; and a concert, after dinner, from eight-thirty to nine-thirty, either in the saloon or outside on deck, depending on the weather. From ten to eleven, we played dance music. All in all, it was only five hours' work a day.

From the very first day, Sebastiano never showed up in time for work. As long as he was asleep in our rooms, we did not mind so much. You could always go down, pour some ice water into his mouth, and drag him upstairs. But he got tired of drinking ice water and began to hide. Twenty minutes before concert time, someone would discover that Sebastiano had vanished and there would be a mad scramble for our piano-player. You can play without your second violinist or your 'cellist, but you have to have your pianist. The first few days, we found him in fairly accessible places: lifeboats, heaps of rope on deck, the benches on the sun deck, the hospital, the tourist-class saloon. As the days went on, however, Sebastiano became more ingenious. He vanished behind stacks of breakfast-food boxes in the kitchen, in a corner of the wireless room, in the engine-room. We had ingenious helpers in all departments of the ship and so we always found him, though sometimes rather late.

Things started to get really tough when Sebastiano began to vanish in the staterooms of the passengers. First he vanished under the bed of Mr. Wayne, a real-estate broker from New Jersey, who had Cabin Number 7 and spent all his days on deck playing shuffleboard. Fortunately, the cabin steward discovered him before Mr. Wayne, a tough character with a top kick's voice, could raise hell. Next, Sebastiano was found hiding in Cabin Number 4, which belonged to a Mr. Rhys Price, Mr. Wayne's English shuffleboard partner and an outdoor man too. One evening Sebastiano went into Cabin Number 35B, where the two Vassar girls lived. It was dinner-time for the first-class passengers and Sebastiano thought the young ladies were in the dining-saloon, but they were in their stateroom, and not by themselves either, and they had forgotten to lock the door. Sebastiano's face was still red as he tried to reconstruct the scene for us. 'I said I was sorry, but the two men looked at me as though they were thinking of murder.' He thought for a minute and then added, 'And they were, I'm sure. They had that look in their eyes. I was frightened to death. I turned around and ran. C'est la vie, mes amis. All you want is some sleep and what do you get? Murder.'

On the day before we reached Halifax, *La Bourdonnais* ran into bad weather and many passengers became seasick. Some stayed in their rooms, but the majority spent the day on deck, lying in their chairs, their faces the color of long-dead halibut. The deck stewards hustled back and forth, carrying trays with consommé and crackers, taking care to keep the door to the dining-saloon closed because the smell of food made some of the passengers wish they were dead. Mrs. Sloan, the divorcée from Boston, was the sickest of all. She remained on deck until midnight, and the following day she was carried up there again early in the morning. Sebastiano had his own intelligence system among the deck personnel. That afternoon he was gone. We looked for him everywhere but did not find him.

We knocked at all the cabin doors and stammered foolish excuses when the occupants opened up and we glanced over their shoulders, trying to discover Sebastiano under a bed or behind a curtain. Some passengers got very angry, and Mr. Wayne spoke his mind in unmistakable terms. We did not find Sebastiano. There was no tourist-class concert that afternoon and no concert in the first-class saloon. We were reported to the captain and he ordered a methodical search of the steamer.

They found Sebastiano at seven o'clock. He was sleeping peacefully in Mrs. Sloan's bed. He was in his underwear, his shoes were placed beside the bed, and his tuxedo was hung carefully over a chair. He explained that he did not want to get the bed dirty. The captain had us all summoned to the bridge. He was angry as never before, but Sebastiano was his old, dreamy self. 'It must be a sort of hypnosis, my captain,' he said. 'It overwhelms you. There's nothing you can do but lie down. It is stronger than you are.'

Maurice said: 'Maybe he has sleeping sickness without knowing it. Were you ever in the Belgian Congo, Sebastiano?' Maurice always tried to help us out when we got in a jam.

'What the hell has the Belgian Congo got to do with this?' the captain shouted. We fell silent and looked at Sebastiano, who was standing in front of the captain. The pianist's eyes were half-closed and he was swaying back and forth, like a tall pine in a wind. Soon, I knew, he would be asleep.

The captain stared at Sebastiano, opened his mouth, shut it again, and shrugged. 'Get out of here,' he said. 'All of you. . . . No, wait, you!' He called Sebastiano back and ordered him to apologize to Mrs. Sloan for using her bed. Sebastiano went down from the bridge to the windy, isolated place on deck where Mrs. Sloan was lying in her deck chair.

He kissed her hand with all his inborn Algeciras grand manner, pulled up another chair, and sat down next to her.

The following evening, Sebastiano did not take his customary nap before the concert. He came down to our cabins for a moment, put on his camel's-hair overcoat and pulled up the collar, and went out again. At eight-fifteen, I found him in the chair beside Mrs. Sloan. I said I was sorry, but it was time for the evening concert. He nodded and helped Mrs. Sloan out of her covers and gallantly escorted her to the music saloon. I walked behind them. They called one another 'Sebbie' and 'Kathie.' The lady from Boston was still pale and somewhat weak, but there was a light in her eyes as she sat down in the music saloon not far from the piano. She was a pretty woman, dark-haired and a little taller than Sebastiano. She seemed restless and excited. She watched Sebastiano. He played very well that evening. He asked Maurice to let him play a few solo numbers, and he played two Chopin études, a piece by Debussy, and a Brahms waltz. After every piece he turned around and smiled at Mrs. Sloan. It was the first time I had seen him make a movement that was not absolutely necessary. I looked at Maurice and Maurice looked at me, and we must have had the same thought because we both forgot to close our mouths.

After the concert, Mrs. Sloan invited the members of the orchestra to the bar for a drink. It was cool and she shivered, so Sebastiano volunteered to go for her mink coat. 'Sebbie is such a dear boy,' she said when he had gone. 'He sits next to me and I talk and he just listens.' She sighed and looked down at her fingernails. 'My husband never did that. He never listened to me. He wasn't interested in anything I said.'

There was a pause, then Maurice said, 'Sebastiano is a quiet man. Very quiet.'

Mrs. Sloan sighed again. 'He's so understanding,' she said. 'Doctor Wellman, my nerve specialist, always told me, "It's hard to find an understanding person. A man who will listen to you and ——" '

Sebastiano came back with her mink coat and she stopped in the middle of her sentence. That night, after the dance, Mrs. Sloan and Sebastiano sat in the bar. She talked all the time and Sebastiano listened, motionless and rigid, like a Brahmin on the shore of the Ganges who has vowed never to move.

Sebastiano did not make the return trip with us to Europe. Two days after our arrival in New York, he vanished again. We looked in all the staterooms, including the captain's, but there was no trace of our piano-player. The next morning, Maurice got a telegram from Sebastiano. Our pianist was not coming back. He was up in Boston and he had decided to stay there for good. There was one particular sentence in Sebastiano's telegram which I remember: 'Boston is a nice, quiet place,' he wired, 'colder than Algeciras, but a good place to sleep.'

Chapter 3

QUAT'Z' ARTS

THE Café des Quat'z' Arts was the rendezvous and exchange for all Parisian musicians, and it was there that I spent many afternoons. From five to seven-thirty the café was crowded with pianists, trumpeters, violinists, trombonists, and vocalists looking for employment. Here they met proprietors, headwaiters, managers, agents, orchestra leaders, and other important people who had jobs for artistes. Transactions at the Quat'z' Arts were beautifully informal. The parties met in front of the café and discussed the job and salary. If they reached an agreement, the musician was given a cachet, a slip of paper with the proper address, date, and hour. As a final gesture the employer took the artiste to the bar and bought him a Byrrh or a hot chocolate, depending on the season.

The Quat'z' Arts was conveniently located in the heart of Montmartre, three blocks west of Place Pigalle, almost next door to the Moulin Rouge Music-Hall. About a hundred boîtes de nuit, cinemas, Bals Musette, music-halls, cafés concerts were within easy walking distance. If a musician working in one of these places did not show up because he was drunk, had the measles, or been in a fight with his wife, the manager hurried to the Quat'z' Arts for a substitute. Judging from the café's volume of business, the turnover was large.

The Quat'z' Arts was spacious and bright, with plenty of mirrors, chromium, and concealed lights. As a café it had as much tradition as a Los Angeles drive-in. It completely lacked the refined atmosphere of the Dôme or Rotonde in Montparnasse, where painters, littérateurs, tourists, and fugitives from Greenwich Village sat around, wearing velvet coats and large-brimmed hats, and radiating substantial trust funds and bank accounts. There were no such phonies at the Quat'z' Arts. Many of its habitués were quietly starving because they wanted to be musicians and nothing else, but they showed none of the outward characteristics usually associated with Murger's *La Vie de Bohème*. They looked like haberdashery clerks. They were 'dance-band musicians,' snubbed by the highbrow artistes of the Concerts Colonna and Lamoureux, and the haughty members of the Conservatoire de Musique. Once Pablo Casals was said to have been seen at the café, drinking a café au laît; but the man turned out to be just another bald-headed fellow with a Beethoven profile who played the okarina.

There were little tables and wicker chairs under the awnings in front of the café. In winter small charcoal-burners, placed between the three rows of tables, spread the illusion of warmth, but the clients were either too unhappy or too jubilant to bother about rain or cold. There were performers of every conceivable musical instrument — viola, balalaika, zither, accordion, tymbal, English horn. I remember occasions when entire orchestras of thirty or forty men for a big hotel were recruited within less than half an hour. However, such lucky breaks were the exception, even during the boom around 1928, and there were always more musicians than jobs. Most artistes had become resigned to the nonexistence of steady employment and all they hoped for was a week-end engagement. In those days many cinemas hired orchestras only on Saturdays and Sundays — every combination from two on up was called an orchestra —

and the rest of the week the audiences had to be satisfied with a lonely piano-player. There were also Saturday night balls in the small suburban villages, private parties, banquets, and thés dansants.

The proprietor of the Quat'z' Arts was an ex-harpist who had no delusions about the financial standing of his former colleagues. He was a heavily built man with a Vandyke beard, and had done a little wrestling as a sideline when nobody wanted a harpist. His instinct for giving credit to the right people and refusing it to the wrong would have made him an asset to Dun and Bradstreet's. If you asked him about his career as a harpist, he launched into long reminiscences and at the end offered you a ham sandwich, or the Choucroute de la Maison (frankfurters, sauerkraut, boiled potatoes). Near mealtime, many people developed a sudden interest in the technique of playing the harp.

There were two waiters, Pierre and Raskolnikoff. Pierre was an old Frenchman from the Midi and looked like a deflated facsimile of President Doumergue, whom he loathed. He talked to everybody about his varicose veins, always mixed up messages, and knew so little about music that he was unable to distinguish the 'Marseillaise' from the 'toreador' song. The other waiter, a Russian called Raskolnikoff, probably because of his bushy eyebrows, black hair, and generally sinister appearance, was the café's leading petty racketeer. He always knew of a cachet if a musician was willing to pay him fifty per cent. The Frenchmen hated him; twice Raskolnikoff was bumped over the head with apéritif bottles by Les Clochards, a tough outfit of brass-players.

Until four in the afternoon the Quat'z' Arts looked as forlorn as a gasoline station in the Arizona desert. Besides the proprietor and the two waiters, there were only 'Les Misérables,' a group of eight or ten old-timers, whose musical education had not progressed beyond the waltz age. They spent their days on the bright-red, leather-covered benches in the rear of the café, playing dominoes, listening to the proprietor's

anecdotes and eating his choucroute, awaiting their early decay. Some of them were very old, unable to take a job, and nobody understood how they kept alive. Sometimes they were joined by Leduç and Barthélemy, two members of the Clochards, whose job it was to keep strangers and tourists away from the café. The Quat'z' Arts did not encourage visitors; the policy was contrary to that of the Café de la Paix or the Dôme. When a couple of American Express stragglers, tired from wandering around Sacré Coeur or the Cimetière Montmartre, came into the Quat'z' Arts and the ladies were about to take their shoes off and relax, Leduc and Barthélemy would put on an apache cap and red scarf, which were kept under the counter for such emergencies, and sit down next to the unfortunate tourists. Their routine, though varying in nuances, never failed. First there was tough talk and fists pounding the table, then a hot dispute with Raskólnikoff, and finally, unmistakable references to the gentlemen's wallets and the ladies' handbags. By this time even the more courageous tourists would call, 'L'addition, s'il vous plaît,' pay, and leave. Leduc told me that British spinsters were the first ones to flee; Americans had more tenacity and, due no doubt to native training, were less easily frightened; and Germans were the last ones to give up. 'They're always a little disappointed because their Baedeker does not mention the Quat'z' Arts,' Leduc said. He pronounced the word, Baedekér, putting into the one syllable his deep, inborn hate of the Boche.

By five in the afternoon the sidewalk and street in front of the café were crowded with men and women carrying violin, saxophone, and banjo cases. Musicians without connections and new arrivals always carried their instruments or at least the empty cases. This method of displaying one's instrument saved unpleasant, superfluous questions. If a man was seen carrying his instrument, it meant that he was available. It had its drawbacks for drummers, bass-players, bombardon-players, and all performers of outsize instruments. Drummers often carried sticks, contrafagotto-players stuck their reeds into their hatbands, and pianists carried briefcases which were accepted as their trade-mark.

On Thursdays and Fridays, the important days, the crowds would seriously impede traffic on the Boulevard de Clichy. Two good-natured policemen would tell the artistes to move on, but nobody did and after a while they gave up. There were some females at the café, though they were considered out of place by the bourgeois musicians. Everybody spoke French and felt bien Parisien. Actually, half of the clients were foreigners. The largest alien group were the Tziganes, oddly assorted Balkan characters with dirty fingernails, perfumed silk shirts, and weird accents. They talked a lot about their alleged careers as concertmasters of the Warsaw Philharmonic or the Moscow Opera. Most of them had no passports, but two or three cartes d'identité, each made out in a different name.

The Tziganes played in Russian, Hungarian, Yugoslav, Bosnian, Bulgarian, Rumanian boîtes and cafés, where they wandered from table to table, catering to the musical whims of the customers. Their répertoire included hundreds of sentimental folk-songs, melodies, mazurkas, polkas, lieders, rhapsodies, serenades. They played everything by heart and could go on for hours without ever repeating themselves. The Tziganes were the only ones in the business who made real money. They were very 'exclusive' and snubbed all 'Westerners.' Their geography was arbitrary; when the owner of the Troika, a Russian boîte, once offered me employment, the members of the Tzigane orchestra turned me down cold because I was Czechoslovak, 'ninety per cent Westerner,' as they said — a definition not always shared by the British and French diplomats at the League of Nations in Geneva.

Only by accident did I become a one-night Tzigane. On New Year's Eve of 1928, I came back from a trip to New York aboard *La Bourdonnais*. As usual, I went straight to the

Quat'z' Arts to meet my friends. It was only six o'clock, but the place was already deserted, everybody having left for work. The 'Misérables' were still in the rear, playing dominoes and eating ham sandwiches, and Raskolnikoff was telling poor old Benedetti how much he had made on commissions that evening. Christmas Eve and New Year's Eve were two nights when almost everybody worked. At a table in the front row sat Gigi, a supercilious, oily-haired Rumanian xylophone virtuoso. On any other day Gigi would hardly have looked at me, but because of the scarcity of available men I found myself addressed by the Rumanian. Would I be willing to take a cachet for the night?

'We're working at the Boeuf Stroganoff, upper Rue Pigalle,' Gigi said, thoughtfully winding his long black forelock around his finger. 'A real hot spot, just across from the Château Caucasien. The Sucker's Paradise, if you know what I mean, mon vieux. Table reservations ten days in advance.' He explained, in some haste and without going into detail, that the second violinist of their 'magnifique' Tzigane outfit had met with a slight accident. Gigi offered me a hundred and fifty francs, and the hours were to be from nine until the last guest left. Misinterpreting my hesitation, he went up to two hundred francs, then to two hundred and twenty. At two hundred and fifty I accepted.

The Boeuf Stroganoff was a somewhat obscure, crowded place which concealed its shabbiness under very dim red lights. There were about forty tables around a dance floor not larger than a small living-room. In the rear small booths were formed by partitions, each thoughtfully equipped with a curtain, plush sofa, a crucifix, and a sketch of Leningrad when it was still St. Petersburg. Near the entrance was a large picture of the Tsarist family with three old menu-cards shoved into the side of the frame. Gigi told me that the proprietor, Monsieur Borodine, was a former headwaiter at a famous St. Petersburg restaurant. The whole staff, two waiters, two cooks, the bartender, and the ladies' room attendant, were more or less close relatives of Monsieur Borodine, a friendly, fat, apoplectic fellow.

The orchestra — first and second violin, double-bass, piano, xylophone — occupied a small platform to the left of the entrance. We were desperately short of space. Every time I played somewhat rubato, my chair slipped off the edge of the platform and I fell down. Boris, the first violinist, was not up there with us. He was a swarthy, stocky Balkanese with a Cossack's mustache and jet-black eyes, who circulated between the tables, fiddle under his chin, smiling at the guests and bowing ceremoniously. Occasionally, he snatched up some caviar with his right hand, playing a stunning pizzicato sequence with his left. His vibrato was as thick as maple syrup and his style of bowing somewhat unorthodox, but he seemed to be immensely popular with the ladies. Most of the guests were Russian, and the ladies wore long evening gowns that might have been risqué three years before the Revolution, and their fur coats smelled of camphor. There were also three or four Anglo-Saxon tables.

Boris had the quick fingers of a magician. When he was given a tip, he seized the bill with his left thumb and forefinger and, playing all the time, quickly put it into his waistcoat pocket. Gigi and the other members of the orchestra watched him closely. He was supposed to share all tips with them. Every time Boris got one, Gigi made a note on a slip of paper which was lying on his xylophone.

Musically, the situation was confused. Boris would step to a table and start a heart-breaking melody, and the orchestra would fall in, producing lamentoso chords. The guests ate and drank and wept. When Boris bent toward one of the ladies, she would break into short sobs. Presently Boris himself would start weeping, the tears running down his cheeks onto his violin. We had no scores, and I was at a complete loss, my knowledge of Tzigane music being limited to 'Ochie Chernyie' and the 'Song of the Volga Boatmen,' both of which were little in demand. However, nobody bothered about me,

and Gigi told me to 'keep on going through the motion.' The main thing, as he explained, was to have a five-man orchestra in plain sight, as it said on the menu.

At midnight the Russians and Anglo-Saxons drank to each other. The Anglo-Saxons were singing and the Russians crying. The place was hot, and it smelled of fish and sour cream and sweet wine and cigar smoke. New guests came in and sat down on the dance floor, there being no other space. Apparently it was possible to get into the Boeuf Stroganoff even without advance reservations. Boris went from one booth to another, putting his violin through the slit in the curtain and playing until the enraged clients gave him a tip to get rid of him.

During the general fraternization, Gigi accused Boris of having secretly pocketed a five-dollar tip. They shouted and Boris hit Gigi with his bow. Gigi retorted by viciously kicking him in the shinbone. Both fell down from the platform, along with some stands, cases, and the double-bass, which made a terrific clatter. The bass-player picked up his instrument and went on playing with the pianist, while Monsieur Borodine and the waiters pushed Gigi and Boris into the ladies' room. Through the open door I saw them give a beautiful demonstration of catch-as-catch-can wrestling. After a while they got tired of kicking, slapping, and boxing, and fell weeping into each other's arms. Boris took his fiddle and played a wild Cossack dance, and Monsieur Borodine danced, his thighs almost touching the floor. Everybody got excited. One of the Anglo-Saxons tried to imitate Monsieur Borodine's routine, but lacking experience, he fell down and had to be brought to with wine. Two Russian ladies danced on a table, their skirts whirling. At seven in the morning, Monsieur Borodine said, 'Enough is enough,' and, with the help of his family staff, threw out all the guests. He took me to the kitchen and gave me one hundred and fifty francs instead of two hundred and fifty, as promised by Gigi. I pointed this out to Gigi, but the xylophone virtuoso had not the slightest recollection of having offered me more. The waiters came into the kitchen, with the bass-player and Boris, who was swinging his bow. Gigi told me to get out if I knew what was good for me.

I took the money and my instrument and went out into the cold, crisp, beautiful New Year's morning. Halfway across the street, I heard a voice and turned around. Monsieur Borodine was running after me. No hard feelings, he begged. The next time he would give me more money. Business had not been good. 'It was a quiet, disappointing New Year's Eve,' he said sadly.

Chapter 4

LOOKING FOR A BLUEBIRD

WHEN the 'Blackbirds,' famous American all-Negro revue, came to the Paris Moulin Rouge, I and five other white violinists were hired to form a string section in the orchestra. The 'Blackbirds' had their own fifty-man band, each musician a virtuoso on several instruments, but there were no strings, and on the afternoon preceding the opening night, somebody decided that the old-fashioned sound of six violins might help make the show a success. A fellow violinist, a Pole, whom I shall call Timanovich, called me up and offered me the job at a hundred and twenty-five francs a night. It was good money for four hours of work. In those days I made fifty francs for two cinema shows and eighty francs in a boîte de nuit, which was all-night drudgery, from eight to six in the morning.

I accepted at once and went to meet Timanovich at the Café des Quat'z' Arts. I gathered that our group was to consist of Murat, a Frenchman with a harassed look; Jean Carpentier, a Belgian with whom I had worked in two 'American' places; two ill-shaven Rumanians who specialized in 'gypsy' music and as a sideline sold cocaine; Timanovich, and myself, a Czechoslovak.

'There'll be no rehearsal,' Timanovich said. 'The conductor doesn't think it's necessary. He'll give us instructions before the show. You speak English, do you? Everybody at the Moulin Rouge must speak English, mon vieux.'

I pointed at the Paris edition of the *Herald Tribune* which I always carried with me. I could not read it, but it was a great help in getting better-paid engagements in night-clubs where the proprietors, because of their considerable American patronage, insisted on bilingual musicians. Sometimes I got fired when the proprietor found out about my English, but there were other places and the *Herald Tribune* always worked.

I wanted the job with the 'Blackbirds' and decided to take a chance. I thought of Calvin Coolidge. If a man could become President of the United States by keeping his mouth shut, the same strategy ought to work with the Americans at the Moulin Rouge. I bought a Pernod for Timanovich and a Byrrh for myself and the deal was closed.

Timanovich was a short, stooped, thin-shouldered fellow from Polish Galicia, with the face of a sad, sick owl. We had met in Madame Dubois's Boulevard-Cinema in Aubervilliers, a suburban workers' district, where we played every Friday and Saturday night and two shows, matinée and night, on Sunday. Madame Dubois, a buxom lady in tight silk prints, took a poor view of musicians, whom she considered immoral. The cinema was an overgrown barn, filled with old wooden chairs, many of them broken or minus one foot. The outstanding feature of the place was its crowded condition. Madame considered aisles a waste of space and the customers stumbled over one another on their way to and from the seats.

The orchestra (piano, two violins, trombone, and a drum-and-sound-effects man imitating shots, automobile crashes, and the cloppety-clop of Tom Mix's horse) was crammed into a chicken coop between the first row and the screen. The violin-players were warned against sweeping movements of the bow, which might endanger the near-by customers. Once a violinist, during an agitato sequence, stabbed a man in the stomach and was knocked cold on the spot. Most of the movie fans patronizing this house were husky characters from the abattoirs who appreciated American films, especially Westerns and gangster pictures. The boxes in the rear of the auditorium were equipped with bolts on the inside and curtains which could be lowered.

The Sunday matinées were attended by young couples in the boxes and by children in the first rows. During boring love scenes the kids amused themselves by spitting at the members of the orchestra or sticking pins into them. We violinists hit at them with our bows, and Grandin, the trombone player, a dignified patriarch, sometimes reached for the beer glass under his chair and poured stale beer on them.

Before the performance began, Lisette, the pianist, a frail, tubercular girl, sorted the music into three piles on the top of the battered Pleyel piano. On the left pile she wrote 'Mon amour' in her neat, gentle handwriting. This pile contained music for sentimental sequences, such things as Drdla's 'Souvenir,' the Berceuse from 'Jocelyn,' and Reynaldo Hahn's 'Si mes voeux avaient des ailes'; there were also such sad pieces as Smetana's 'Yearning,' 'Chant sans paroles,' Dvořák's 'Goin' Home,' and several funeral marches. Lisette knew about love and that it often meant suffering.

The pile in the middle was called 'Gangster,' an assortment of lively overtures, 'William Tell,' 'The Flying Dutchman,' 'Zampa,' the finale from Offenbach's 'Orpheus,' and the 'Ride of the Valkyries.'

The third pile, which had no name, contained music for all other purposes, from Mendelssohn's 'Festival March,' the 'Song of the Volga Boatmen,' all the way down to Oswald's 'Bébé s'endort' and Sousa's 'Washington Post.'

Since we were not paid for rehearsals, we did not have any. On Friday, Lisette would watch the picture on the screen and toss us music from one or another of the piles, depending on whether, to her, the scene seemed to be romantic, criminal, or indefinite. The numerous pauses between the selections were filled with what we called 'general tremolo.' Lisette's scheme did not always work. You would have thought that it would be easy to figure out what was going to happen next in an American film, but frequently we were caught flat-footed with the 'Ride of the Valkyries' when the hero had begun making love. At times Lisette was mistaken about a gangster's sinister intentions and let us play Offenbach's 'Barcarole' during what really was a blackmailing sequence. Such mistakes were corrected during the Saturday show. By Sunday afternoon we knew the score by heart and concentrated on watching the picture. Sitting right below the screen, we violinists had to keep our heads in a horizontal position, holding the violin between our left ear and collarbone. Some of the films were really wonderful, though, and we did not mind the physical discomfort.

It was a cheerful life, and would have lasted longer if it had not been for an American film called *Le Mystère de Madame M.*, if I am not mistaken. As usual, the whole orchestra was watching the picture during the Sunday matinée, playing in a perfunctory way. The situation on the screen became quite involved, what with three murders, a woman with a past, and a villain who was getting the upper hand. One by one we stopped playing and looked up at the screen in breathless excitement. We were not aware of the silence in the theater until from one of the boxes came a noise and a girl's voice saying, 'Mais non, chéri, pas ici!' There were more noises and then a man said irritably, 'Zut alors! Qu'est-ce que tu veux, le Ritz Hôtel?'

From the audience came laughter and bold encouragement and the man in the box shouted angrily, 'Où est l'orchestre?' and there was more laughter. After the show, Madame Dubois, shocked to the depth of her virtuous soul, fired the orchestra in a body.

Timanovich lived with his mother in a tiny, neat two-room apartment in the Rue de la Nation, within walking distance of the boîtes around the Place Pigalle. Mamma Timanovich was a little, white-haired, sad-eyed woman who liked to cry. She was very homesick for her Galician home town of Andrychów, which she had left when her son was awarded a scholarship in Paris. Back home you could go to the little cemetery where her husband, Aaron, God bless him, was buried, and cry on his grave, but on Montmartre everybody seemed so gay and there was no place to go. She did not like the smell of oil from the kitchens and was mortally afraid of cabs and the Métro.

Timanovich, a devoted son, suffered because of his mother's unhappiness. The apartment was expensive and he had to give violin lessons to the anemic children of neighborhood grocers so he could pay the bills. He had a chronic headache and during the lessons he usually lay on a couch, his head heavily bandaged, while the unhappy pupil labored on a Ševčík finger exercise. Timanovich looked depressed the night I came to the Moulin Rouge to play for the 'Blackbirds.' I met him at the entrance to the place, and we stopped and talked for a few moments.

'The doctor told me that Mamma needs fresh air,' he said, 'but she won't leave the house. She gets pale and sick and I'm worried.'

I said, 'Don't worry now. We have a show to do,' and we went in.

There were about forty Negro musicians in the big room, wandering around and practicing scales on saxophones and trumpets. They had on silver-gray tail-coats with dark-blue lapels, and we six violinists felt foolish and out of place in our tuxedos. The Negroes came over and shook hands with us and said something, presumably nice. They were a happy, friendly lot.

'No wonder they feel that way,' one of the Rumanians said. 'They get five hundred francs a night. We don't even get a hundred and fifty.'

'You do get a hundred and fifty,' Timanovich said. 'But twenty-five of it is my commission.'

The Negro conductor shook hands with us and grinned and pointed out different things in the score. He spoke very rapidly and I did not understand a word of what he said. He asked, 'Okay?' We all nodded and said, 'Yes, yes,' and Murat said, 'Sure!' The conductor slapped us on the shoulder and departed. The bell was ringing and the musicians were filing into the orchestra pit.

I stared at my colleagues. Their eyes were blank. It was clear that none of us had the faintest idea what it was all about.

'What was it he said about the Boccherini "Minuet"?' Murat asked nervously.

Timanovich was plucking his A string. 'Didn't you understand? You told me you speak English and ——'

'Berlitz School English,' Murat said. 'Six months, three times a week. I must have taken the wrong course. It sounded all different then.'

'C'est la barbe,' the taller of the Rumanians said. 'Come on, Timanovich, what did he say?'

Timanovich was busily colophaning his bow. The bell was ringing again and the drummer, who was near the entrance, motioned us to come in. We took our seats, Timanovich in front, as concertmaster. I sat behind him. Across the aisle a tall, dark-brown trumpeter with the physique of an athlete gave me an encouraging smile. Murat and Carpentier were behind us. The Rumanians had the third desk and immediately got acquainted with two ladies in mink coats in the first row.

'Nom de Dieu, what's going to happen?' Murat whispered nervously. 'If they find out about the English, we'll get blacklisted.'

The house lights dimmed and the conductor made his way through the orchestra pit. A short introductory harp arpeggio, and the whole band went into 'I Can't Give You Anything but Love, Baby.' Now I understood why the conductor had not insisted on a rehearsal. No one in the audience was ever going to learn about the existence of six violin players in the orchestra. Our feeble attempts were drowned by the ear-splitting racket of fifty saxophones, clarinets, trombones, trumpets, banjos, helicon horns, pianos, and drums. After the second chorus they went into a regular jam session, playing 'Diga Diga Do,' 'I Must Have That Man,' and 'Magnolia's Wedding Day.' They were having a wonderful time.

The curtain went up. There was a chorus number, and Adelaide Hall sang, and a tap-dancer did Bill Robinson's stunt of dancing up and down a set of steps. The curtain came down, and after another violent interlude it rose again on what looked like a Southern plantation scene. Girls in white crinolines were poised for action. The band stopped playing and the men put down their instruments and looked at us, in anticipation.

After the preceding din, the sudden silence was frightful. The conductor gave us the cue, but we did nothing, staring at him in a trance. Up on the stage the girls were shifting uncomfortably and from the audience came the sound of subdued laughter. The conductor looked aghast. The silence seemed to last for years. Suddenly the tall, athletic trumpeter next to me pointed at our score of the Boccherini 'Minuet.'

'Solo,' he whispered. '*Solo!*'

Timanovich started and we came in on the second bar, and the crinoline girls began dancing. After the second repetition the rest of the orchestra fell in and the minuet turned into a frenzied cancan, with the big trumpeter giving out with a formidable improvisation, while the rest of his colleagues were blowing, singing, whipping their feet, laughing and happy.

The applause was terrific. A pretty girl sang 'I'm a Little Blackbird Looking for a Bluebird,' in a small, birdlike, bubbling voice, and the audience went mad. There was no doubt that the revue was a success, set for months.

After the show, Timanovich said to me, 'Mamma wants you to come over for a bite. We've got to celebrate. Carpentier and Murat and George Washington are coming along too.'

'George Washington?'

'George Washington Hayes, the trumpeter who saved our jobs. He seemed sort of lonely, so I invited him too.'

In front of the Moulin Rouge, musicians and members of the cast were standing, discussing the evening, lighting cigarettes. Our two Rumanians came out and were met by the two ladies in mink coats from the first row. The four of them got into a taxi. We walked down the Boulevard de Clichy, Timanovich and George Washington, Carpentier, Murat, and I. George was wearing a yellow camel's-hair coat. He was about twice the size of Timanovich, who tried desperately to keep in step with him and kept bumping into doormen, rug-peddlers, cops, and sidewalk painters. The air was brisk and full of noises from the cafés, boîtes, bals, and cinemas.

Mamma Timanovich greeted us in her little hall. The smell of roast chicken filled the rooms. There was white bread on the table and two candles in massive old-silver candlesticks. It was Friday night. Mamma Timanovich hurried into the kitchen for another plate. 'It was good of you to bring him along,' she said to her son. 'I'm sure the poor man has no place to go in this awful town. Go ask him if he wants breast or leg and wings.'

The conversation was fragmentary, but somehow we understood George and he knew what we meant. We ate, drank pinard, and had fun remembering the Boccherini 'Minuet.' After dinner Murat played the Bach 'Chaconne' and George went to the piano and sang some of the most beautiful songs we had ever heard. He had a powerful, deep-throated voice, and the room became very small. Timanovich played 'Kol Nidre' for his mother, and George sang.

Mamma Timanovich wept happily. 'I haven't heard such singing since we left Andrychów,' she said, drying her tears. 'I wish George would come back tomorrow and sing again.'

The following night Timanovich seemed excited as he took

his seat beside me at the Moulin Rouge. 'George came for Mamma this afternoon,' he said. 'He took a cab and they went to the Cimetière de Montmartre. Mamma always wanted to see the grave of Heinrich Heine and George also likes cemeteries. Mamma came back crying and happy and she had a big dinner.'

Timanovich kept me well posted on Mamma's subsequent excursions. George took her to the Cimetière Montparnasse, the cemeteries of Saint-Bernard, Saint-Pierre, and Bonne Nouvelle. Every afternoon the two of them went to another cemetery, crying a little, each in his own lonely way, and having a chocolate at Dupont's (Chez Dupont Tout Est Bon), around the corner. George took Mamma Timanovich to the Cimetière de Picpus and the grave of Lafayette, telling her of General Pershing and how he may or may not have said, 'Lafayette, we are here.' They went to Père-Lachaise, but the big place frightened them, though Mamma was impressed by the Rothschild chapel. When they had seen all the cemeteries, they started going to churches and synagogues — Sainte-Chapelle, Saint-Etienne-du-Mont, Saint-Eustache. Mamma Timanovich liked the small ones best.

At Notre-Dame-des-Victoires she bought a candle for George's mother, whom, she told us, he had never known. Once I saw them get out of a cab in front of the flat, George in the long yellow overcoat which made him look even taller than he was, and the old woman shriveled and tiny. He led her across the street, gently holding her hand.

The six of us played for five months with the 'Blackbirds' at the Moulin Rouge and learned to speak a little English. George said he enjoyed going to the nice quiet places with Mamma Timanovich and Timanovich worried about his mother and how she would feel about George's departure.

The 'Blackbirds' finally went to London and I began going back to the Café des Quat'z' Arts for cachets. I was still carrying the *Herald Tribune*, but now I could read it. I asked Timanovich if Mamma kept going to the cemeteries.

'She says it isn't fun to go there alone,' he said. 'George writes every week. He says there are many beautiful cemeteries in London and he'd like Mamma to see them.'

I went to Nice for a season and returned late in spring. At the Quat'z' Arts the two Rumanians were still drinking Pernods, selling cocaine, and waiting for Tzigane cachets. Murat, the Prix de Conservatoire, looked more worried than ever, though business was not bad. Timanovich was not there any more. The boys said he had gone with his mother to New York, on the same boat that took the 'Blackbirds' back to America.

Chapter 5

AUDITION

PEOPLE have always asked me how I happened to become a ship's musician, as though the making of a seafaring fiddler were more mysterious than the making of, say, an embalmer or a B.-M. T. motorman. The simple fact is that in those days in Paris there was always an opening with the French Line for an experienced instrumentalist who could produce a certificate of good character from the police commissioner, pass the medical examination by the steamship line's doctor, and, above all, come successfully through the audition. Many a poised and self-confident musician was mortally terrified of the audition. Candidates for a job aboard a French Line vessel were given an audition before Monsieur Arnould, the musical director of the company, at his apartment, 36 Avenue Parmentier.

I went there one afternoon with Maurice, with whom I had worked at the Folies-Bergères and the Bal Chez Laboule, at Nogent-sur-Marne, a rustic establishment mainly frequented by somewhat battered lovelorn ladies from the capital. Maurice, an old hand at ocean crossings, told me not to worry about the audition, since he happened to be a great friend of Monsieur Arnould. They had worked together in the old days aboard the *Provence*, Monsieur Arnould as bass-player and orchestra leader, Maurice as first 'cellist. After twenty years of faithful musical service to the passengers of the French Line, Monsieur Arnould had been retired from sea duty and made musical director in charge of personnel.

A narrow, winding staircase led up to Monsieur Arnould's apartment, on the fourth floor. The waxed wooden stairs were as slippery as ice, quite a problem for Maurice, who was carrying his 'cello and had had a number of apéritifs and digestifs, with some demies, bocks, and glasses of wine for good measure. Twice he stumbled over his instrument and almost broke his neck. The staircase smelled of onion soup, and between the second and third floor we met a tall, cool blonde coming down. She gave Maurice an encouraging smile out of the corner of her almond-shaped eyes. He whirled around and would have followed her if I had not blocked his way. At last I got him up to the fourth floor. The bell beside the Arnould door did not work, and Maurice raised his fist and hammered a melody from Massenet's 'Manon' on the door. 'Watch the rhythm,' he said to me. 'Arnould is crazy about "Manon."' A fat, smiling, perfunctorily made-up lady in a silk dressing-gown opened the door and exclaimed with delight as she saw my friend. Maurice hugged her fondly, introduced her as Madame Arnould, and we went in. Madame said Monsieur Arnould would be in right away.

The music room was large and bright. There was an upright piano in one corner, next to a large window, and a harmonium in the opposite corner. Two of the four walls were covered with a peculiar collection of instruments — a violin with bow, a clarinet, a banjo, a tenor saxophone, a bombardon, a trumpet, an English horn, a viola d'amore, and an instrument identified by Maurice as a Japanese samisen. These instruments were traps for wise guys who didn't bring their instruments, hoping to get away without an audition — except, that is, for the viola d'amore and the samisen, which were purely ornamental.

The other two walls of the room had a distinctly nautical flavor. There were pictures of the great steamers aboard which Monsieur Arnould had worked in his earlier days: the *Leviathan*, *Majestic*, *Aquitania*, *Provence*, and the *France*, her four funnels proudly smoking, including the one that was a dummy. On the piano was a small model of the Capitol at Washington and an ebony elephant of the sort that was cynically displayed and sold on Victoria Street in Colombo as 'genuine Ceylonese' in spite of the imprint on the bottom — 'Made in Czechoslovakia.'

Monsieur Arnould made an impressive entrance through a side door. He was a formidable, huge, heavy man and as he moved through the room the instruments on the walls trembled softly. He had a carefully trimmed Vandyke beard, and wore striped trousers, a cutaway, and a mariner's cap. A thick gold chain, from which was suspended an enormous black stone, dangled over his stomach. He looked as though he had walked out of a Rembrandt painting. Had he been dressed in dirty dungarees, unshaven, and carrying a half-emptied bottle of gin, it would have been easy to visualize him as the skipper of a pirate schooner running his sinister craft between Hong Kong and Macao for the benefit of the old Vitaphone Company. He shook hands with us and gave me a broad grin. As musicians grow old, they often begin to resemble the instrument they play. Violinists look moody and wear their hair almost half as long as that of their bow; flautists are gaunt and nervous; bass-tuba players, full of beer, have shiny, pink, broad, tuba-like faces. Monsieur Arnould had something of the jovial, placid dignity of the bull fiddle. There was a photograph on one wall, hanging next to the smoking S.S. *France*, which showed him amidst a crowd of early-century lovelies with wasplike waists and enormous hats covered with zoos and flower gardens, and I remembered Maurice's saying that Monsieur Arnould had been a great success with les Américaines on their way to Europe without their husbands.

Monsieur Arnould asked me if I had traveled aboard ships and I said, according to Maurice's instructions, 'Through all the seven seas, Monsieur,' a stock phrase which reportedly never missed its effect on the musical director in charge of personnel. The statement was not entirely true. My only ocean experience had been a half-hour trip between Marseilles and the Château d'If, where I had gone to look at the gloomy cell of Edmond Dantès, the Count of Monte Cristo.

Monsieur Arnould nodded and casually took up a few sheets of music from a large, disorderly pile on the floor beside the piano. He handed me a crumpled, much-used one. 'On commence avec la "Manon" fantaisie,' he said. Monsieur Arnould always used the indefinite pronoun when referring to himself. This habit he had acquired as a result of frequent conversations with American passengers, who, as he put it, 'were driving you crazy talking all the time of themselves. Nothing but I's and I's. On en a assez.'

My audition was perfunctory, no doubt owing to Maurice's recommendation. Monsieur Arnould sat down at the piano, I unpacked my violin, and Maurice took out his 'cello. We played the first twenty bars from the 'Manon' fantasy, and Monsieur Arnould remarked that I sounded 'assez bien, un violoniste classique.' Apparently I confirmed this flattering judgment by my performance of Kreisler's 'Caprice Viennois,' for Monsieur Arnould nodded in satisfaction, saying, 'Bon, bon.' He wrote my name in a small, red-leather book and thus I became a full-fledged ship's musician.

From then on, whenever Maurice and I got back to Paris from a crossing, we would go to see Monsieur Arnould and report informally on our work. The world of the ship's musician is round and full of fun, and Monsieur Arnould was delighted with such bits of gossip as that the pianist aboard the *Berengaria* had been caught in a stateroom with a red-headed woman from Minneapolis; that aboard the Hapag Liner *Hamburg* there was an idiotic brass band of Musik-Kellner, who waited on tables and, between Sauerbraten, Klösse, and Rote Grütze, blew the 'Hohenfriedberger Marsch' and excerpts from 'Rheingold'; that a new purser aboard the *Statendam* made the musicians get up and rehearse at nine in the morning, an unheard-of brutality; and that the 'cellist aboard the *Majestic* was robbed in a Hoboken bar.

One day in Paris — I had just completed my fourth transatlantic round trip and been promoted to first violinist aboard *La Bourdonnais* — I encountered at my hotel a dear friend, Franzl, from back home, in Prague. Franzl was in Paris on a three-week vacation, for which he had slaved and saved all year long. He was an underpaid clerk at the Prague Petschek Bank, where he spent eight dull hours a day picking up the telephone and supplying the customers of the bank with the latest New York Stock Exchange quotations. Bank clerks in Prague, as everywhere, have a lot of holidays. These Franzl spent at his piano. He was an excellent amateur pianist and the principal attraction at many musical parties which worried Prague matrons gave for their unmarried daughters. His specialty was a musical trick which fascinated his listeners. His audience would give him three widely different themes, such as the 'Tannhäuser' Pilgerchor, 'Vilia, Oh, Vilia,' from 'The Merry Widow,' and 'Yes! We Have No Bananas,' and he would work them into a beautiful improvisation, complete with counterpoint and a fugue at the end.

There was only one subject that fascinated Franzl more than music, and that was Wall Street. Being on the receiving end of the New York quotations had filled him with the ardent desire to visit the sacred places where the market prices were being made. He searched the anterooms of all the dentists in Prague for old copies of American magazines and newspapers, and clipped out all pictures of and references to Wall, Broad, Pine, and Nassau Streets. He had read so much about the financial district of Manhattan that he knew it better than many people who worked there. His room was full of photographs of the Stock Exchange, the Morgan Bank, the Subtreasury, and the Irving Trust Building, and he owned, among other relics, a Manhattan telephone directory for spring, 1925, six inches of genuine New York ticker tape, envelopes of various brokerage firms, and two shares of United States Steel. He would have given his right hand to see Manhattan, and he told everyone of his desire to go there. His friends shrugged benevolently and his boss, the Herr Prokurist, said rather pointedly that Prague bank clerks do not travel to America — that is, not unless they rob the vaults or defraud their clients.

The day before I met Franzl, Maurice and I had been to see Monsieur Arnould, who had told us that there was an opening for a pianist aboard the *De Grasse*, leaving the following night from Le Havre for New York. I talked to Maurice and we decided to take Franzl to Monsieur Arnould for an audition.

At Monsieur Arnould's apartment Franzl stammered dutifully that he had been through all the seven seas and Maurice recommended him as an old friend and a 'pianiste classique.' Franzl was trembling with excitement — this was different from playing at the party of the Herr Prokurist's daughter; this was the great chance of his life to go to America and see Wall Street — and even to get paid for it — and when Monsieur Arnould suggested that we all play the beginning of the 'Manon' fantasy, he turned pale and lost his head. We had taken him to Arnould in a feverish hurry and I had forgotten to ask him if he knew 'Manon.' Unfortunately, it was one of the few pieces he had never played at the Prague matrons' parties. In the 'Manon' fantasy the pianist begins first, playing trioles, and, naturally, setting the tempo. Franzl did not know the tempo, and he did not take a good look at the score. His mind was in Lower Manhattan, not in 'Manon's' Paris. He hammered out the trioles twice as fast as prescribed. When Maurice and I joined him and tried to slow him down, he became completely lost and broke down. The rest was utter horror. Monsieur Arnould shook like a piece of jello and told us, to stop, nom de Dieu!

'C'est assez,' Monsieur Arnould said. 'On est dégouté. Dé-gou-té!'

It was very quiet in the room. Franzl, his forehead covered

with perspiration, looked out of the open window at one side of the piano. For a moment I had the silly notion that he might jump out. There was a faraway, broken look in his eyes. Good-bye, Wall Street, Pine, and Nassau. Gone the dream of a lifetime. Good-bye, America!

Monsieur Arnould cleared his throat, but Maurice spoke up first. 'I was telling the boys about the old days when we both played at the Cirque,' he said. 'About how every time Madame Desdemona, La Reine de Far-Ouest, made her spectacular leap across the backs of three white horses, the orchestra would stop and there was only a fast beating of the drums. Until that night when she turned you down, mon vieux. We were all silent, with the drums beating furiously, when you made a horrible glissando on the D string of your contrabass. The third horse got wild and ran away and Madame Desdemona fell down flat in the sand.'

I had heard this story half a dozen times and it had always had its effect on Monsieur, but this time he remained silent and hostile. He shrugged. 'On est très pressé,' he said coolly. 'Il faut s'en aller. Il faut chercher un pianiste.' It was three o'clock and the *De Grasse* was sailing at midnight.

Franzl got up, a prematurely aged man, from his seat and wiped his forehead, and Maurice and I packed our instruments. Nobody spoke a word. We went down with Monsieur Arnould, who had exchanged his mariner's cap for a black derby. He kept away from Franzl as though my friend were a leper. To Arnould, not to know 'Manon' was a crime worse than robbing the Banque de France. As we reached the street, hot and sleepy in the glaring afternoon sunlight, Maurice pointed at the Brasserie Parmentier, a shabby, little establishment across from Arnould's house. 'It's hot,' Maurice said, putting a finger under his collar. 'Let's go over there and have a bock.'

'Why don't we go to the Renaissance, instead?' I asked. The Café de la Renaissance, near the Porte Saint-Martin, was the musicians' favorite downtown café where they met friends, found jobs, and had unlimited credit.

Maurice gave me a furious look. 'Shut up,' he said, without his customary restraint. 'I'm thirsty.' He led us straight into the back room, where the temperature was even higher than outside. 'It's much cooler in here,' he said, and gave me a wink. I was completely mystified, but I did not say anything. There were no guests present at the early-afternoon hour. An old waiter dozed at a table in the rear. Standing a couple of feet out from the rear wall was an upright electric piano of a relatively modern type. Maurice shook the waiter and ordered beer for everybody, then more beer. For a while we kept the old waiter busy running for more bocks. After the fifth or sixth glass, Monsieur Arnould reminded Maurice of the circus lion that could not stand the sound of a flageolet and how Maurice produced a flageolet at the end of the lion act while the orchestra was playing Sousa's 'Washington Post.' The lion had grown fractious and refused to jump through a burning hoop, and the lion-tamer, a phony from the Argentine, had got frightened and made a sudden exit, walking backward out of the cage.

Maurice said, 'And what about la petite femme that we found in your double-bass case, mon vieux? She didn't wear four bass strings. She didn't even have on a single G string.'

Monsieur Arnould drank his beer and nodded moodily. 'She had a throaty voice,' he said. 'When she laughed, there were dimples in her cheek.' He sighed, and Maurice said gravely, 'Let's drink to her memory.' We ordered another round of bocks and drank to the memory of la petite femme in the double-bass case. Monsieur Arnould opened his stiff collar, stretched out his long legs, and leaned back comfortably. The derby fell down over his eyes. He hummed 'Ah! fuyez, douce image' from 'Manon,' and, using his cane as a baton, conducted an imaginary orchestra. Maurice beckoned to me, winked, and pointed to Franzl, who sat motionless at the other side of the table, pale and as unhappy as a seasick yogi. Maurice whistled softly through his teeth, a sure sign that he was up to something. I did not care. I felt too unhappy about Franzl's bad luck. It was unbearably hot, and I was sick and tired and wanted to get out of the place.

Maurice got up and tiptoed over to the electric piano. Beside the instrument was a small table with a heap of perforated rolls, the piano's entire répertoire. Maurice selected a roll and put it into the piano. I watched Monsieur Arnould, whose head was tilted sideward. He was asleep. Maurice pulled on a lever at the back of the piano, then came over to Franzl. 'Get over there and sit down at the piano,' Maurice said, in a whisper. 'I put in the "Manon" roll. It's a lousy reproduction, but the tempo is correct. Exactly the way Arnould wants it.'

Franzl raised his head and stared at Maurice with an empty, forlorn expression. Maurice became impatient.

'Sit at the piano, you fool, and act as though you were playing. Just try to go through the motions. Haven't you ever played on a dumb piano?'

I said, 'If Arnould finds out ——'

'Don't worry,' Maurice said. 'He's had six bocks. He'll be half asleep, anyway.'

Franzl staggered over to the piano and sat down, a study in bewilderment. Maurice tried to wake up Monsieur Arnould. 'Ecoute, mon vieux!' he shouted. 'We've got to get a man for the *De Grasse*. She can't sail without a pianist.'

The French Line's musical director grunted and rubbed his eyes, very disgusted with the world and himself. Maurice bent down and spoke in a soft, suggestive voice, trying the child-and-drunk approach. 'Why don't you give that man Franzl another chance? He got frightened up there. Let him try "Manon" once more, will you?'

Monsieur Arnould yawned and said, 'Mince alors. He didn't know the tempo, l'éspèce d'imbécile. On s'en fiche.'

'There's a piano right behind you,' Maurice said. 'Keep

your seat and listen. If I'm not right, I'll buy you ten bocks. You don't want to run around Paris on a hot afternoon looking for a pianist.'

Monsieur Arnould grunted again and wiped his mouth with the back of one hand. Maurice walked over to the piano and pushed another lever. I kept my eye on Monsieur Arnould. There was a noise like an empty barrel rolling down the cellar steps and the trioles of the 'Manon' fantasy came out, battered and metallic, but definitely in the correct tempo. Franzl was trying desperately to adjust the speed of his fingers to the sounds. It took him a while to get used to the *rubati* of the electric piano, but soon the illusion of his playing the instrument became convincing.

Monsieur Arnould tilted his derby to the back of his head and turned around heavily. He looked at Franzl with, it seemed, new interest. He shook his head and murmured, 'Pas mal, pas mal du tout.' By now Franzl was doing a job of synchronization that might have fooled even Toscanini if he had drunk six bocks on a hot summer afternoon. Monsieur Arnould nodded happily and raised his hand. 'C'est assez,' he said. 'Tiens — vous êtes un pianiste classique. Vous êtes engagé.'

Franzl took his hands off the keyboard, but the piano went on playing, so he quickly put his hands on the keyboard again. Arnould repeated, 'C'est assez,' waved his derby, and turned his back to the piano. Franzl, in despair, looked for the lever to stop it, his eyes wild, while the damned piano kept on grinding out more 'Manon.' Maurice jumped behind the piano and fumbled with the lever that was supposed to stop the piano. It seemed to be stuck. We are through, I thought. Franzl will never get his job and Maurice and I will lose ours. Maurice lost patience with the lever and viciously kicked the piano with his right foot. There was a crash and then silence.

Monsieur Arnould started and said, 'What's that?'

'The loose pedal always falls down,' Maurice called out.

He came over to Monsieur Arnould. 'Didn't I tell you the man is good?' he asked.

Monsieur Arnould nodded. He twisted his head around and addressed Franzl. 'How about Chopin?' he asked. 'Do you play Chopin? The études? And more beer. Four bocks!' he roared toward the front room.

Franzl's face had a broad, relaxed grin. Chopin was his oyster. He knew by heart many of the études, nocturnes, valses, mazurkas, and preludes. He got set to launch himself into the sweeping passages of the Opus 10, Number 12 étude, but as soon as his fingers touched the keyboard, he turned pale. The ivories were stuck and no sound came out of the piano. Apparently Maurice had done a thorough job of destruction. Franzl hammered down desperately on the keyboard, his lips thin and grim, but there was no sound, Chopin or otherwise. This time the arrival of the old waiter, carrying four bocks, saved the situation. Monsieur Arnould drank his and my glass. There followed the usual noble argument as to who should pay for the beer and Chopin got lost in the shuffle.

Franzl left for Le Havre on the seven o'clock boat train. Monsieur Arnould, Maurice, and I saw him off at the Gare Saint-Lazare. I shall never forget Franzl's face as he looked down at us from the window of his car, flushed with happiness. 'So long, mon vieux, give my regards to Wall Street!' Maurice cried as the train pulled out.

Monsieur Arnould decided to see Maurice and me off, so the three of us took a cab to the Gare d'Orléans, where the train for Bordeaux was to leave at nine. Roger, our new second violin, and Dimitrij, our piano-player, were already waiting. Monsieur Arnould had completely recovered from the afternoon's party and was his old self again. We marched through the station, led by Monsieur Arnould, who carried his derby aloft on top of his cane, like a banner, walking erect and with a powerful stride. Roger and I held our violin cases shoulder-arms fashion, and Dimitrij carried the big drums and beat them as we marched out to the platform. Maurice, with his 'cello, formed the rear end of the column, singing a horrible Arabian ditty, which I hope nobody understood. People stopped talking and stared after us in amazement. We took noisy possession of our first-class compartment, and Maurice sent the second violinist for the dining-car waiter.

Monsieur Arnould sat down in a corner, breathing heavily. He took out a cigar and thoughtfully bit off its end. 'Votre ami, François — he was very happy to go to America, was he?' he asked me.

I remained silent, nonplussed by the unexpected question.

Maurice came to my help. 'Sure he was. Who wouldn't be glad to leave Paris for a couple of weeks in this damned heat?'

'One likes to see people happy,' Monsieur Arnould said thoughtfully, and lighted his cigar. 'But that was not a very good one you tried to pull on me this afternoon, Maurice. Non. The electric piano wasn't half as good as the one about the lion and the flageolet. You are slipping, mon vieux.' He showed his broad, double-basslike smile. 'Enfin, on s'en fiche pas mal,' he said.

The second violinist appeared with the dining-room steward and Monsieur Arnould ordered cinq bocks.

Chapter 6

CAPTAIN'S DINNER

ABOARD the passenger liners of the Compagnie Générale Transatlantique, the Captain's Dinner was given on the evening before the ship's arrival in New York or Southampton. If we were due in New York early in the morning, the celebration was advanced twenty-four hours in order to give the passengers time to sober up and put away their evening clothes. Smart habitués of Atlantic crossings knew that you do not dress the night after the Captain's Dinner. Only greenhorns would put on their tuxedos a few hours before the arrival in New York.

The Captain's Dinner presumably was a courtesy on the part of the steamship company, a gala fancy-dress farewell party, which, it was hoped, the passengers would remember when they made next year's reservations. On the French liners, the fête began with a banquet, followed by a concert by the ship's orchestra, with additional free talent supplied by the passengers. Then came the collection for the Société Maritime des Veuves et Orphelins, or a similar charitable institution, and around midnight there was a late supper — Polish hams, cold turkey, lobster, pâté de foie gras, salad. By two o'clock, everybody was theoretically resolved to make his next crossing aboard a French Line ship.

Even on a comparatively small boat, such as our nine-thousand-ton *La Bourdonnais,* where the cuisine was modest compared to the Brillat-Savarinesque standard aboard the *Paris,* the *France,* and the *Ile de France,* the Captain's Dinner was a treat:

Le Caviar Astrakhan
La Bouillabaisse Marseillaise
Les Raviolis Niçoise
La Sole Meunière
La Poularde Rôtie Lafayette
Les Asperges à l'Huile
Les Pommes de Terre Marie
Marrons Glacés — Petits Fours — Pâtisserie
Les Fromages de Savoie
Le Café de Colombie

The pièce de résistance was a giant ice-cream bombe which had the contours of the Statue of Liberty, the Washington Capitol, or the Panthéon. Once the pastry cook tried to model the Eiffel Tower, but the melting ice did not keep its delicate shape and by the time the captain was cutting the first piece for the guest of honor, the Eiffel Tower was but a sad scrap-pile of vanilla and pistachio.

The stewards did not bother to show the wine card, simply asking the passengers if they preferred Mumm Cordon Rouge or the more expensive vintages of Charles Heidsieck, Reims, without mentioning the lesser brands. The diners were given paper hats of various exotic shapes and designs: Annamite coolies, bayadere, sheik, maharajah, maharani, Balinese dancer, Foreign Légionnaire. For some reason Wall Street men preferred maharajah or sheik hats, while matrons from the Middle West wanted to be Balinese dancers. The very young and rather old passengers dressed up in fancy style. Some had elaborate, expensive costumes, bought in Paris. Others borrowed ingenious disguises from the deck officers, firemen, cooks, sailors. A Yale man once appeared in the second officer's uniform which he embellished by putting on gold braid all the way up to the elbows, revealing his innermost ambition, Grand Admiral of the United Fleets of the World. Smart young men simply got a piece of burnt cork and painted black stripes and a serial number on their bare torso, impersonating convicts from Devil's Island. This was an inexpensive and practical costume, especially in the summer days when the overcrowded dining-room was stifling hot. Some elderly ladies pretended to be shocked — but they really did not mind as long as the convicts had broad shoulders and large, masculine chests.

The only ones who did not participate in the general spirit of joy and festivity were the kitchen and restaurant personnel and the members of the ship's orchestra. To the staff the Captain's Dinner meant a lot of extra work with nothing but trouble in return. The pastry cooks prepared large trays of mille-feuilles, tarts, napoléons, éclairs; the bartenders cut vast quantities of ice; the deck stewards, cursing under their breath, spent trying hours fixing garlands and paper decorations. The waiters set elaborate tables, putting small surprise packages under the napkins of the ladies. The packages contained, 'avec les compliments de la Compagnie,' small bottles of perfume, clips, handkerchiefs, très chic.

But it was the musicians who had the worst time of it. For several days preceding the Captain's Dinner, we were buttonholed by overzealous amateurs who wished to display their talents at the fête. Most of the gentlemen pretended to be excellent magicians, fortune-tellers, pianists, experts in card tricks, or simply raconteurs. White-haired, dignified executives, rejuvenated by a four-week stay in Paris under the auspices of Messrs. Thomas Cook and Sons, volunteered to join the orchestra as honorary drummers. A man who was always hanging around the bar wanted to be master of ceremonies. Once we had a lawyer from Boston who was an excellent whistler. He did trills with double-noting and uncanny staccato effects. We were sure he would be the sensation of the evening. Unfortunately, he burned his mouth badly with hot potage à la Reine at the Captain's Dinner and his performance of 'Liebesfreud' was a horrible fiasco. After that, we refused to have anything to do with whistlers, no matter how good they were.

The ladies were even worse because they were tenacious. You could not get rid of them. Practically every one of them seemed to have hidden talents as singer, pianist, dancer, or diseuse. The pianists always wanted to play Chopin, Rachmaninoff, or Gershwin. The singers never suggested anything less pretentious than 'Un bel dì vedremo' from 'Madame Butterfly' or the 'Hallenarie' from 'Tannhäuser,' and such comparatively untaxing numbers as Schubert's 'Erlkönig' and the songs from 'Rose-Marie' invariably ran far behind. We always had more Suzukis and Rose-Maries than pretty girls aboard — a continuous source of irritation to Lucien, the first violinist, who kept a diary of his affairs.

'C'est la barbe,' Maurice would say in disgust. 'When I was chef aboard the *France*, we didn't bother about those amateurs.' He gave the word the derogatory intonation usually attached to 'horse-thieves' or 'draft-dodgers.' 'We had Paderewski and Kreisler and Chevalier and Lily Pons. The amateurs wouldn't dare offer their lousy services.'

On one particular crossing, we had among the passengers a woman whom we called the High-Voltage Lady. She was the wife of a man whom I shall call Mr. Pringle, a utilities magnate from the West. We called her the High-Voltage Lady because Maurice had said he would rather sit in the electric chair than in her lap. The Pringles had Stateroom Number 1, which did not mean a thing because Number 1 was in no way more luxuriously furnished than Numbers 2 to 11. None of them had rare woods from the Orient, sculptured glass, chromium, pillars of light, or similar travel-folder features, *La Bourdonnais* being strictly a poor-man's *Normandie*.

Unfortunately, the Pringles had a letter of recommendation from a former member of the board of the Compagnie Générale Transatlantique. They had to be seated at the captain's table, and in no time Mrs. Pringle, a prominent clubwoman in her home town, was taking charge of all social activities on the ship. She was a tall, bony woman, with the hard, weather-beaten face that Hollywood casting directors call the 'pioneer type.'

Her energy was formidable. Every morning she made a round of the ship, starting in the kitchen, where she inspired thoughts of murder among the cooks, and winding up at the *télégraphie sans fil*, where she sent long, superfluous messages to friends on both sides of the ocean. Her husband, the utilities man, was of diminutive stature and a visibly depressed state of mind. He usually walked behind his wife, one step sideward, one behind, a permanent aide-de-camp, or errand boy. During the eleven-day crossing from Bordeaux to New York, he was never seen smiling. He took long walks on the sun deck, accompanied by Dimitrij, who had a weakness for the underdog, being one himself.

Soon after we left Bordeaux and entered the always stormy Bay of Biscay, the High-Voltage Lady became seasick and summoned the ship's doctor to her stateroom. She told him that she was going to die.

'You are not, madame,' the doctor said, with cold regret. 'In a few days we'll pass the Battery and you will be very much alive, thinking up ways and means of hiding your French perfumes from the United States customs.'

The doctor was a jovial, rotund Frenchman with a baby's face and very fine hands. His passion was playing chess, but, since he could not make a living at it, he chose the profession of ship's doctor, which gives a man more time to play chess than almost any other profession. The doctor never bothered with trivial cases of indigestion or la grippe. Instead of wasting his time with those hypochondriacs in the first class, he usually would send the cabin steward up with castor oil or aspirin, and go on studying the latest games played by Messrs. Capablanca, Lasker, and Bogoljubow. He was playing, by wireless, with his colleague, the doctor aboard the

De Grasse, four moves every twenty-four hours. The game was in its third week and the doctor was greatly worried. After a violent exchange of pieces, he had found himself a rook behind. He was about to improve his position by daringly sacrificing a knight when his consultation with the 'dying' High-Voltage Lady interrupted the flow of his thoughts. Later, he went to the radio cabin and wirelessed his next move. Thinking of the High-Voltage Lady, he made a bad mistake, aggravating his already precarious position.

'Because of that canaille, I'm going to lose my game,' the doctor said to us. 'She tells me of her delicate health. Her health is as delicate as that of a brewery horse.'

A few days before the Captain's Dinner, the High-Voltage Lady stopped Dimitrij on the stairway. 'She dragged me to the music saloon and made me accompany her the aria from "Madame Butterfly," ' Dimitrij told us afterward.

'Mon Dieu,' Maurice said. 'How was she?'

By way of reply, Dimitrij shrugged and closed his eyes.

'If she's set to sing "Butterfly," she's going to do it,' Maurice said gloomily. 'She also wants to sing the beautiful aria from "Tosca." ' He sighed and hummed the melody of 'Vissi d'arte.' 'She can hardly hit the B and the aria goes up to the high D,' he said. 'Now she wants me to transpose the piece a whole tone down.' He shuddered at the thought of this atrocity.

'Tomorrow I'm going to talk to Mr. Pringle,' Dimitrij said to us. 'Perhaps he will be able to convince his wife that she'd better not sing at the concert.'

Maurice laughed sourly. 'You might as well try to convince Mistinguett to tell her real age,' he said.

Sad and unhappy, Dimitrij went down with me to the ship's hospital to see his good friend, the doctor. Dimitrij spent a lot of time in the doctor's office, especially during his frequent spells of depression. Dimitrij said that the antiseptic smell had a calming effect on his nerves. He would lie down on the linoleum-covered couch in the outer office. If the door was closed, indicating that the doctor was busy with a patient, Dimitrij would walk around the corner into the small, white operating-room and go to sleep on the operating-table.

'One day you'll wake up and find yourself cut open by a scalpel,' Maurice said.

Dimitrij lay down on the doctor's couch and told the doctor of the High-Voltage Lady's horrible intention. 'Can't you give her something that would keep her in bed for three days, doctor?' Dimitrij asked, playing idly with a syringe. 'A mild poison, perhaps?'

'Nothing mild will work on her,' the doctor said grimly. 'She's one of those fascinating cases where the heart keeps beating for hours after the death.' The doctor went off to the sun deck to send a message to the *De Grasse* and we went down to our quarters.

In the following two days, nobody was allowed to enter the music saloon during the early afternoon. The High-Voltage Lady was rehearsing with Dimitrij. The doors were closed, the curtains lowered, and Mr. Pringle, reading an old copy of the *Saturday Evening Post*, was sitting on guard in front of the door. In spite of these precautions, the passers-by could not help hearing shrill, high sounds, like fingernails scratching on glass. By the time we got to the Captain's Dinner in the gaily decorated dining-saloon, Dimitrij could hardly touch the food. As a rule, we had our meals before the general service, but that night the maître d'hôtel made us wait and gave us the drafty table near the waiters' entrance, there being a shortage of stewards and no time for special service.

There was the traditional, colorful collection of Devil's Island convicts, bayaderes, pirates, maharajahs, admirals, dominos, and Balinese dancers. Doña María, a luscious brunette from San Juan, Puerto Rico, appeared in a stunning black, silver-embroidered costume that made Lucien swallow hard. However, he refrained from action, since Doña María was accompanied by her husband, a sinister individual who did not let his wife speak to anybody who was male and over six years of age.

The Pringles came in after everybody else was seated. Their entrance was sensational. The High-Voltage Lady was dressed as what seemed to be a Bedouin tribeswoman. She wore an indigo cotton tob reaching to her ankles, with seams of dark-blue silk, a cream-colored sleeveless aba, and sandals of red Morocco leather, with upturned toes and iron heels. She carried a few pounds of silver bracelets, rings, silver ornaments, and glass beads. As she walked through the dining-saloon, she jingled like a fully decorated Christmas tree in a breeze. Her head was tied up in a large, square black hatta of silk with a design of silver threads.

Dimitrij quickly reached for a glass of water. Across the aisle from us, the doctor watched the High-Voltage Lady with sharp, clinical interest, as though she were carrying a strange bacillus. Maurice almost fell from his chair, trying to hide his laughter.

'She's wearing a virgin's headgear,' he said. 'Nom de Dieu, how do you like that? I've lived in Morocco long enough to know. A maiden wears a square black hatta. A married woman folds the cloth into a band and ties it around her head.'

Behind his wife, Mr. Pringle straggled, trying to keep in step. He had on a Tyrolean costume, footless wool socks, bare knees, chamois-leather shorts, embroidered suspenders, and an Alpine hat with edelweiss.

Dinner was magnificent. Champagne corks were popping everywhere and a couple of bayaderes from Kansas City got tight. We left the dining-saloon before the coffee was served. By the time people began to enter the music saloon, we of the orchestra had set up our desks and were ready. Everybody was loud and happy, as always after a good dinner and good champagne. We opened the program with the American and French national anthems. Then Maurice played his solo number, Saint-Saëns' 'Le Cygne,' but his melodious efforts were frustrated by the High-Voltage Lady, who was sitting in the front row and jingling violently. Next, an insurance man from Buffalo tried a few card tricks which failed to come off. Twice he guessed the wrong card and once he dropped the cards altogether, but the audience thought he was funny and he got a big hand. Doña María danced a fandango, to the accompaniment of the orchestra with the exception of Lucien, who was too busy watching her. The man from Buffalo, who had been at the bar celebrating his success, came forward to take Doña María in his arms. He found himself grabbed by her husband. The Puerto-Rican seized the insurance man's coat-collar. For a second the situation looked critical, but the doctor stepped forward and took the Buffalo man for a walk outside. The maître des cérémonies announced that Madame Pringle was to sing 'Un bel dì vedremo' from 'Madame Butterfly.' Several passengers left the music saloon.

The High-Voltage Lady stepped on the platform. Her poise was amazing. She had the suave smile of a world-famous prima donna facing a Carnegie Hall audience. When she began to sing, her technique was not altogether bad and there was a certain feeling for phrasing and musical expression. The trouble was that she had no voice. There was no volume, no timbre; the high tones were thin and shrill and the deep notes sounded like a fat Dutchman snoring. There was a sprinkle of perfunctory applause after her song and Dimitrij quickly got up from the piano stool. But the High-Voltage Lady was not willing to give up easily.

'Thank you, thank you from the bottom of my heart,' she said to the audience. 'And now, as an encore, the aria from "Tosca." ' She gave Dimitrij a nod and he began to play 'Vissi d'arte.'

After a few seconds, I saw that something was wrong. Madame's poise and savoir-faire had vanished; she was looking in despair at her accompanist, but Dimitrij was working in deep concentration and did not seem to notice that anything was wrong. Maurice said to me, 'Dimitrij is playing the aria the way it's written.'

'Why shouldn't he?' I whispered back.

'Have you forgotten? He was supposed to transpose it down a whole tone. This way she'll never make the end.' There was a tender smile on Maurice's face. 'I'll buy him a drink,' he said. 'Dieu d'un Dieu, I'll buy him two drinks.'

The High-Voltage Lady was a lamentable sight as she sang the number. She was bent over like the Tower of Pisa. Her voice trembled and her breath came in fits. I saw beads of perspiration on her forehead. Some people in the audience began to whisper and cough. She made a brave but utterly futile effort to hit the high D at the end. There was a short, shrill cry, as though you had stepped on a little Pekinese dog's feet. Then her voice broke into a short, violent sob.

The audience stared at her in merciless silence. On the faces of the bayaderes, Balinese dancers, and maharanis, there was satisfaction. The High-Voltage Lady had no friends aboard. At long last, the captain, as if awakening from a bad dream, began to clap his hands, nodding sternly toward his junior officers. They started applauding, too, and the second engineer, an ambitious man, even cried 'Bravo!' but the High-Voltage Lady did not hear him. She had left the room right after her last, disastrous tone, followed by Mr. Pringle, by now a very sad Tyrolean.

There was an uneasy moment. Everybody looked sheepish. Dimitrij saved the situation by jumping to the piano and playing the Rachmaninoff Prelude. The audience relaxed and Lucien started looking at Doña María again.

After the collection for the widows and orphans, Doña María went around, making the customary collection for the musicians. She handed the money to Lucien and he kissed her hands, though not because of the money. The quête wasn't worth mentioning. There were only seventy or eighty passengers aboard and hardly anybody gave more than a dollar.

Later the doctor joined us. He handed Maurice an envelope.

'From Mr. Pringle,' the doctor said. 'Pour les musiciens.'

'And how is Madame?' Maurice asked, looking thoughtfully at Dimitrij, who combed his long hair.

'She's a little hysterical,' the doctor said. 'But she will survive.'

Maurice opened the envelope. There were three ten-dollar bills and an unsigned note saying simply, 'Thanks, boys.'

'I think I'll buy you three drinks, Dimitrij,' Maurice said. 'Will you join us, doctor?' The doctor took Dimitrij's arm and we all walked to the bar.

Chapter 7

A VISITOR FROM AMERICA

I WAS NOT GIVEN what one would call a warm welcome when I returned to my home town, Moravská-Ostrava in Moravia, Czechoslovakia, late in 1928 after three consecutive crossings aboard *La Bourdonnais*. My mother and my brother were at the Přivoz railroad station when I pulled in on the Prague–Warsaw express. My mother, weeping, kissed me and said she had been worried to death. My brother Max, then at the juvenile-delinquency age, glanced sharply at my two pieces of luggage, covered with hotel labels, and asked me why I had no label from Chicago and whether I had met Al Capone. When I said no, he looked disgusted.

As my mother had twelve brothers and sisters, there was usually a great deal of family traffic in our house, but I found it ominously quiet. Nobody came to see me. My mother cried a little more and told me that I had become the family's Number 1 disgrace. It was bad enough to interrupt one's law studies at Prague University and go off to America, that strange country populated exclusively by gangsters, cowboys, film stars, millionaires, and G-men, but to go there as a ship's musician, practically on a social level with pickpockets and gigolos, was a crime they could not forgive. Gradually I was told of what had happened during my absence. When my mother received word that I had left for New York, old friends of the family stopped her on the street and offered their condolences. My former mathematics teacher sadly predicted the end of my earthly career. 'He'll never come back alive from America!' the teacher said to my mother. 'Nobody does. He'll get a bullet or a tomahawk in his head.'

One week after my return our old family doctor asked me to come and see him at his office. He gave me a thorough checkup. I'll never forget his incredulous face when he discovered that I had not caught cholera, leprosy, or the bubonic plague.

It was not narrow provincialism that made many people in my home town suspicious of the New World. Ostrava — as it was called for short — was Czechoslovakia's third largest city and had what all the natives fondly called a fast, 'American' growth as the country's leading iron, steel, and coal-mining center. But the town was thirty hours away from the nearest seacoast and the natives had somewhat reluctant feelings toward ocean travel and overseas countries. If someone went to America, he had very definite reasons. Within the past three years only two men from Ostrava had gone there. One, a coal-mining executive, hurriedly departed for Panama City because of what his lawyer called 'lamentable miscalculations.' For weeks the case provided the shocked though delighted citizens with a most interesting topic of conversation. Everybody was sorry when the former executive was finally apprehended and jailed in Cristobal, Canal Zone. The other traveler was a waiter at a local night-club. He happened to serve a woman from Detroit who had come to Ostrava to visit her poor relations and had taken them out to celebrate. The woman from Detroit, on the mature side of life, returned to the night-club the following two nights, and on the fourth day eloped with the waiter.

There was a numerically small but noisy segment of the local population who did not entirely disapprove of my musical-nautical career. They were the town's younger generation who supported a highly inexact conception of America. Their ideas originated in newspapers that featured the 'terrific heat waves' or 'tremendous crime waves' in America, and pulp magazines starring the exploits of one Percy Stuart, 'Avenger of the Disinherited,' a twentieth-century Robin Hood. It was smart to adopt the 'American' expressions used by Percy Stuart, such as 'dammit,' 'well,' 'by Gad!' It was equally smart to drive around in American cars, no matter how old and dilapidated, to wear American-cut suits and to smoke American pipes.

Many of Ostrava's America-conscious young men, including myself, were former 'chachars,' the local brand of ruffians. A chachar played football on the street instead of going to his violin lesson. He found ways to get into circuses and movie-theaters without paying. He spit into gas street-lamps, thus blacking-out whole districts. The chachars were ingenious and displayed great ability in coping with the manifold problems of life. Several chachars became in due course noted bank presidents, surgeons, politicians, businessmen, lawyers, and writers. They are now spread all over the globe. I remember one, by the name of Filip, whom I once met deep in the jungles of Sumatra, where he drove an ancient Ford loaded with candies, which he sold to the natives. The candies, a dark-brown, sticky mass, were produced in Filip's garage in Batavia. Now and then the Ford got stuck in a tropical river, and the candies became a wet, tacky cake. Such minor catastrophes did not upset a former chachar. Filip simply pressed the stuff into small jars labeled 'Hot Plakt' (It sticks), and sold the product as 'glue for all purposes.' Another chachar was the manager of a place called 'Rainbow Club,' in Singapore, who catered to the diversified tastes of Singapore's multi-racial clientèle by having at his place Chinese hostesses on Mondays, Wednesdays, and Fridays, Malayan girls on Tuesdays, Thursdays, and Saturdays, and Russian émigrée personnel on Sunday nights.

The chachars hung out at the Palace Café, geographically

and socially the heart of the town. There they occupied the balcony running around the large coffee house. No member of the balcony crowd would be seen, dead or alive, in the Café's center or 'European' section, where the town's substantial citizens met to discuss the general decay of good manners in the balcony. The guests in this section spent their vacations at Karlsbad, read the conservative papers, and criticized the balcony crowd for introducing such 'American' customs as chromium chairs and telephones plugged in at the tables.

The third section of the Palace Café was called 'Little Asia,' and was frequented by professional cardplayers, traveling salesmen from 'the East,' Slovakia, Hungary, and assorted Balkan countries, and the 'Schiebers,' men of indistinct origin with frequent, if not always friendly, contacts with the police and customs authorities of many European countries. The Schiebers were a product of Ostrava's geographical location as 'crossroads between Western Europe and the Balkans.' They had excellent connections and were able to deliver at a moment's notice Polish passports, Bulgarian hides, original Persian rugs from Slovakia, Moravian potatoes (with a special discount if they turned out to be frozen), or Rumanian brandy.

Shortly after my return from New York some chachars ventured the opinion that I had probably never been in America. Their skepticism was pardonable. Two years ago a native returned from an alleged twelve-month trip to China. Only by accident it was discovered that the man had spent that year at the Cernauti (Rumanian) jail, for smuggling saccharine.

Since I had traveled aboard *La Bourdonnais* as a member of the ship's crew, I had neither ticket, passport, nor visa to 'prove' my journey. I had sent home postcards from New York, but the balconyites pointed out that two Schiebers in the Asiatic section specialized in procuring postcards from 'all civilized European countries and Poland.' The customer — say, an executive who took his secretary for two weeks to

Paris — wrote his message on a postcard showing the Kurgaeste at the Karlsbad colonnades, and in due time the executive's wife received the card, postmarked Karlsbad, 'Digestion improved, wish you were here.'

I offered, as a last resort, a genuine American five-dollar bill signed by Jimmy Walker, then Mayor of New York. This exhibit was rejected unanimously by the balconyites. Every Schieber at that time carried paper money of half a dozen different countries in his pocket — Polish zlotis, Rumanian lei, Hungarian pengös, Swiss francs, Yugoslavian dinars — which he needed for general trading and bribing purposes. Some men owned such exotic bills as Ecuadorian sucres, Japanese yens, Straits Settlements dollars, and Egyptian pounds. I had finally decided to give up and let the chachars spread their rumors, when I got unexpected help from a 'real' American. This man, whom I shall call Stephen, wrote me from Prague that he was coming to Ostrava for a couple of days.

Stephen was a casual acquaintance whom I had met on my third return trip aboard *La Bourdonnais*. I had talked to him on the promenade deck and during the intermissions of our evening concerts, but when I got his letter, I could not quite recall his face because he looked so much like the man next to you on a streetcar. He was a medium-sized, lean fellow with a plain, friendly face and a mass of red hair falling down over his forehead. He was a quiet man who seldom laughed except when he read the funnies. Because of a stomach ailment he was forbidden to drink hard liquor, and at the bar he could only gloomily ask for a glass of milk and a chess partner. He was unmarried and devoted to his mother who lived in Pennsylvania and ran what he called a 'respectable' autocourt. 'Only married couples admitted,' Stephen said. 'No hard drinking or movies on Sunday. I go home every other week to mow the lawn.'

Stephen worked as traveling salesman for a big printing-press manufacturer in Pittsburgh, Pennsylvania. He was not a bad speaker as long as he was with his customers, but when he talked before a crowd, he got nervous and began to stammer. This was his first European business trip. 'We've got an amazing, rather complicated new printing press,' he had told me. 'A few people in Europe are genuinely interested. I hope I can swing a couple of deals. If I could sell four or five, I might become assistant sales manager.'

Stephen arrived at Ostrava two days after his letter, wearing a havelock, a woolen, grayish, thick Alpine raincoat which he had bought in Innsbruck, Tyrol. The havelock was half a size too large because the storekeeper in Innsbruck had told Stephen that 'they always shrink half a size after the first rain.' It was a dry fall and Stephen was nervously waiting for the rain. He looked as American in his oversized havelock as a Tyrolean yokel after a county fair, and my heart sank. Here was my only proof that I had actually been in America, but the skeptical balconyites would never believe that Stephen was an American himself.

Stephen was in high spirits. He had already sold two printing presses, one in Zurich and one in Vienna, and he showed me his correspondence with Paul, the owner of Ostrava's largest printing firm. Paul, a former chachar who had won success and wealth, was still a faithful habitué of the balcony, much to the disappointment of the financially prominent citizens in the center section downstairs. He was a great admirer of things American. I suspected that his sympathies were partly based on the financial success of the magazines running the adventures of Percy Stuart, which were printed by Paul's firm.

'The deal's practically closed,' Stephen said, 'just a few details to be discussed. He's going to meet me tomorrow afternoon at five at the Palace Café. Don't those guys discuss business at their offices?'

I explained to Stephen that a great many enterprising businessmen in Ostrava preferred to carry on their transactions at the coffeehouse because of the stimulating atmosphere there. That night I was invited to give a short lecture at the English Club. I asked Stephen to join me. The English Club consisted of thirty or forty Berlitz-School addicts who suffered from the illusion that they knew English. They were forbidden to speak anything but English, and were fined one crown for every non-English word. This harsh rule led to bizarre conversations on such topics as 'The Bridges of London,' 'Mandalay and the Burmese Empire,' 'The Age of Wordsworth and Byron.' The club's president was Madame Sickl, professor at the local lycée for girls, a somewhat withered spinster in her third youth who joined a great many local organizations hoping she might yet find a husband. The first vice-president was the wife of a socially (though not judicially) prominent judge, and most members were either teachers or lawyers whose wives, for some reason or other, wanted to be in the good graces of Madame Sickl and the judge's wife. I introduced Stephen and the club members shook hands with him, saying, 'How do you do? Thank you, I am very well.' Stephen looked startled. Tea was being served. Madame Sickl asked Stephen, 'Do you prefer your tea with sugar, or lemon, or milk, or rum, or plain?' in her mechanical voice. Stephen's face turned as red as his hair and I quickly got up to begin my lecture, 'One Week in New York.'

There was little applause when I ended and the president asked Stephen to say something. Stephen got up and cleared his throat and was silent. Madame Sickl smiled encouragingly. Stephen coughed and said, 'I'm sorry, folks, I'm really not much of a speaker, except when it comes to printing presses.' A fat, apoplectic lawyer, who was considered an authority on America because seven years ago he had attended an international Rotary convention, said, 'Is that so?' At that Stephen turned toward the lawyer and started giving him his Grade-A sales-talk on printing presses.

The club members looked blank, the enterprising ones taking out their pocket dictionaries, trying to look up difficult words. The vice-president became bored altogether and began to eat chocolate. A girl behind me whispered, in Czech, 'He doesn't look like an American,' and another girl answered, also in Czech, 'He doesn't talk like one either.' Madame Sickl interrupted Stephen's talk to fine each of the two girls four crowns for speaking Czech. Stephen got nervous and the fat lawyer declared that Stephen was probably a phony and should be investigated. Some members protested and there was a lot of bilingual confusion. I took Stephen home.

Stephen was gloomy. 'They think I'm a phony,' he said. 'Suppose the owner of the printing firm here feels the same way? He won't buy my press and I won't be a sales manager.' He paced the floor. 'They keep asking me if I know Al Capone. Hell, what do they think I am? A Chicago triggerman?' Suddenly Stephen stopped pacing and stared at me, and I stared back. It was a great, decisive moment. I said slowly, 'Maybe you should look like one. Sharp and tough like the people's idea here of an American gangster.'

Stephen shrugged. 'How can I look sharp in a havelock half a size too large? Doesn't it ever rain in this damn place?' I explained to him that a havelock, irrespective of size, was out of place and so was Stephen's inconspicuous gray suit. Unfortunately, Stephen had nothing else to wear. Early next morning I called up a friend whose father owned the town's largest men's store. We made a special appointment during the noon hour when the store was closed to the public. We took my brother along as an expert and went in through the store's back door so no one would know of Stephen's metamorphosis. Assisted by my brother, a frequent moviegoer and up-to-the-minute on what the well-dressed gangster in America was wearing, Stephen chose a sharply tailored, broad-shouldered, double-breasted suit of wine-red woolen, a light-blue shirt, a yellow necktie, patent-leather shoes, and a snap-brim hat. My brother said that Stephen should look 'silent and grim' and smoke a big cigar. Stephen, after a strong protest, accepted the cigar, but he definitely rejected my brother's suggestion that he should carry a 'bulging object' in his pocket.

Stephen made an instantaneous hit with the habitués of the Palace Café balcony. None of them was a member of the rather conservative English Club and last night's incident had not become known around the balcony. Stephen played his part well. He kept his hat on, held his right hand inside his pocket, stretched out his legs, and munched his cigar. There was prolonged silence on the balcony, everybody deeply impressed. Oskar, the arrogant headwaiter, a nauseating character with a cynical smile, approached us meekly and asked for our order. Stephen, momentarily falling out of his rôle, wanted a glass of milk. I hastily ordered 'Two double Scotches, straight,' explaining to the perplexed headwaiter that in certain circles of the Chicago underworld 'milk' was the name for Scotch. Oskar retired and told everybody that Stephen was the real thing, dammit — what a guy! There was a critical moment when he returned with the drinks. Stephen made a brave effort and swallowed down the Scotch, putting the glass down hard on the table. He had become a legendary figure, tougher than Al Capone himself, and I was completely rehabilitated. Several prominent balconyites came to our table. A well-known criminal lawyer declared that he had never believed the rumors about me in the first place, by George, and how about dinner tonight?

Paul, the printer, arrived at five o'clock. He was a businessman of what people in Ostrava called 'the American school,' hard-hitting and fast, but he, too, was so stumped by Stephen's tough appearance that he hardly interrupted Stephen's sales talk. Only when it came to terms did Paul try to raise a few objections. Stephen pulled back his hat, gave me a short glance, and said, out of the corner of his mouth, 'Let's go.' Paul hastily pulled Stephen back to his

chair, took out his pen, and signed a contract for one printing press.

We had dinner at the Palace Restaurant and later went to the town's fanciest night-club. Paul ordered champagne and Stephen emptied three glasses in a row and confessed that he had never been near a gun except in Coney Island. I hastily proposed a toast to America, another to the Chicago underworld, and a third one to the continued success of Paul's firm. I think Stephen kept talking about his mother's autocourt in Pennsylvania and mowing the lawn there, but after three more glasses of champagne there was nothing to worry about.

Chapter 8

MY LIFE IN THE CLAQUE

A GREAT MANY people whom I have talked to during intermissions at the Metropolitan Opera House seem opposed to the idea of a permanent claque, some going so far as to call it a cheap, disgraceful racket. There was, of course, a permanent claque at the Metropolitan when Gatti-Casazza was director, and there were permanent claques at La Scala, Milan, the Paris Opéra, the Prague National Theater, and the Warsaw Opera, where at one time a fellow by the name of Artur Rodzinski acted as claque chef. And there was nothing disgraceful about the claque at the Vienna Staatsoper, which I had the honor of belonging to in the middle twenties.

The claque was far more exclusive than the aristocratic Jockey Club. Anybody with a good family tree and who had not been caught stealing silver spoons could get into the Jockey Club. To become a member of the claque you had to know by heart the scores of popular operas — all arias, recitatives, solo numbers. In addition, some courage and diplomacy were essential.

The claque chef's name was Schostal. He had become a claqueur under Gustav Mahler and at one time or another he had worked for Scotti, Hesch, Titta Ruffo, Chaliapin, Galli-Curci, Farrar, and Caruso. The claque consisted of thirty to forty regulars, youthful lovers of good opera, most of whom, like myself, were somewhat insolvent students at the Vienna Conservatory or the Akademie für Musik und Darstellende Kunst. If we had two schilling, we would rather spend them for an opera ticket than for a dinner. However, we had to eat now and then, so we all tried to get into the claque. The 'work' was fun and we were given a free admission to the standing room. Schostal was a citizen of the world and liked foreigners, so at one time there were two Frenchmen, a Czech, a Chinese, an Ethiopian prince, and Childs, an American pianist from Cleveland, among his employees.

I met Schostal one night after the opera. Pachtinger, a fellow violinist at the Conservatory and a member of the claque, took me to the Peterskeller, a noisy, smoke-filled cellar across from the Staatsoper and frequented by night chauffeurs and bums, where Schostal was sitting at a table in the rear, near a battered piano. He was a powerfully built man with a black mustache and sideburns and an immense bald head. His family owned large textile mills in Moravia. When Schostal, a passionate opera fan, discarded the flourishing textile business in favor of the claque, the disgraced family broke off relations, except that every year they sent him a Christmas parcel containing material for a new suit — always the same material, blue serge. This accounted for Schostal's wardrobe of nineteen more or less worn blue-serge suits.

Schostal listened while Pachtinger introduced me, and then moved over to the piano and hammered out a few bars from 'Salome,' 'Fledermaus,' 'Lucia di Lammermoor,' 'Walküre,' and 'The Queen of Sheba.' After each piece I had to tell the act and the scene from which it came. The air was heavy with the smell of goulash and cigars, and the guests were noisily discussing politics. Schostal held his beer mug in his left hand and played the 'Liebestod' with his right. 'All right,' he said to Pachtinger. 'We'll try him out at "Tristan" next Sunday. There is little to do.'

A claqueur's operatic perspective is really upside down. 'Tristan und Isolde,' 'Walküre,' 'Götterdämmerung,' 'Pelléas et Mélisande,' and 'Elektra' are extremely 'light' operas. The claque works only at the end of each act; there is no other applause. On the other hand, Rossini, Massenet, Verdi, Puccini, and Bizet operas are very 'difficult.' Take, for instance, the second act of 'Carmen,' a claqueur's nightmare. You start working right after Carmen's gypsy song, 'Les tringles des sistres tintaient,' and you applaud after her dance with the castanets. Then Escamillo enters (applause), sings his famous 'Couplets' (applause), and leaves (more applause). By that time the public is likely to applaud spontaneously after each number — the quintet (Carmen, Mercédès, Frasquita, and the smugglers), Don José's offstage 'a capella' song, Carmen's dance for Don José, and the tenor's famous 'La fleur que tu m'avais jetée.' The trouble is that the enthusiastic listeners are apt to break into 'wild' applause in the wrong places, such as in the middle of an aria, after an effective high C. In Vienna, where opera was a way of life and even the small boys discussed opera as they discuss baseball in this country, 'wild' applause was considered heresy and one of the claque's functions was to influence public acclaim into orderly channels.

Our claque's base of operations was high up in the fourth balcony, where the acoustics were best. At the extreme left, Schostal occupied a Säulensitz. This was one of the two seats behind each massive marble pillar, from which you could not see the stage. They were sold at half price, mostly to music-lovers who did not care or to out-of-town people who did not know, and who therefore had the tantalizing experience of hearing Jeritza as Tosca and not seeing her. From his headquarters, overlooking the balcony, Schostal directed the claque, which was scattered around in inconspicuous groups of two or three.

Schostal had a perfect sense of timing and he had a showman's instinct for the mood of the public. He could feel whether an aria was going over or not. A claqueur's most unpardonable crime is to start applause which is not taken up by the public and perhaps is even drowned out by enraged hisses. Schostal seldom made a mistake. He himself never applauded during a performance — generals do not shoot rifles — but at the end of an exceptionally good one he would step down to the breastwork and benevolently clap his hands for the stars. They never failed to look up and give him a smile. During an ordinary, more or less routine performance, Schostal would get up from his seat shortly before he had to give a cue, and the claqueurs, throughout the balcony, could see his bald skull shining under the pillar lamp. There would be from ten to thirty of us, depending on how many clients we had in the cast. At the critical moment he would give the cue, a short nod to three lieutenants standing behind him, and they would start applauding in a cautious, subdued manner; the rest of us would fall in, and within three seconds a wave of applause would sweep the house.

Schostal detested high-pressure methods and preached subtlety. 'The best claque works in secrecy,' he said. 'We must not impose applause upon the audience. We stimulate them and give them the cue at the right time and they take care of the rest.'

The business of giving the cue demanded perfect timing. Many operatic arias end with a high, sustained note and the artists deliberately build toward that ultimate bravura effect. You have to start applauding at the instant the last note ends, while the public is still under the singer's magic spell. To start too early, as do all amateurs, spoils the carefully calculated effect. If you wait too long, the conductor leads the orchestra right into the next piece and the opportunity for a spontaneous ovation is gone. Conductors hate it if the singers get too much applause during the acts, because they want to get home and take off their dress suits and stiff collars.

There was not any special training. Newcomers to the claque would be assigned to a group of claqueurs operating during the less 'difficult' operas. I worked during 'Tristan,' 'Siegfried,' and 'Salome' before I was given my first independent assignment, just before a performance of 'Rigoletto,' with Selma Kurz as Gilda, Piccaver as the Duke, and Bohnen as Rigoletto. At a brief conference in the foyer preceding the opera, Schostal gave me orders to start a 'short salvo' after Rigoletto's monologue in the second scene of the first act. It was a difficult job; baritones are always a little hard to handle when co-starred with famous divas and tenors, and Rigoletto's recitative, short and not especially impressive, is followed immediately by Gilda's appearance.

I was standing with two fellow claqueurs at the extreme right of the balcony. On special occasions, when there was a great deal of work to be done, Schostal always appointed extra lieutenants who were stationed at various points in the balcony. They would individually start the applause on their own initiative, which gave a better impression of spontaneity than if Schostal started it all himself. People get suspicious if they hear applause always emanating from the same spot.

Bohnen began his soliloquy, 'Pari siamo!' My heart was beating wildly and I am sure that I was far more excited than Bohnen himself. I stared down into the vast, dark auditorium, with two thousand people silently listening, and I thought I would never have the courage to clap my hands. I had the absurd feeling that everybody would turn around and look at me. My cue came and I sent a prayer to heaven, hoping that somebody else would applaud first, but nothing happened. I took a deep breath, closed my eyes, and boldly clapped my hands. Then there came response from other spots in the balcony, from the boxes and the orchestra stalls, and suddenly a cataract of applause was sweeping the house. It was the sweetest sound I've ever heard. During intermission, Schostal called me to the buffet in the foyer and bought me a Dehmel chocolate cooky for twenty groschen and a glass of water for ten groschen, which was his way of promoting a novice to a full-fledged senior member of the claque. This meant I could come any night I wanted to and get my free ticket.

Members of the claque never got anything except the ticket. We had nothing to do with business details, which were attended to by Schostal. Of course, everybody knew that he was given money by the singers and that he bought the tickets and kept part of the money for himself, but this seemed fair enough. There was no set fee. The artists gave him as much as they thought applause in a particular rôle was worth. They all knew that Schostal was incorruptible and never took money from singers who were not good enough for special applause. Once the ambitious wife of a Viennese big-shot manufacturer, who reputedly had influence in the Unterrichts-Ministerium and with the management of the Opera, was to sing 'Tosca.' The tycoon called Schostal to his office and offered him a thousand schilling for tickets and another thousand for himself. Schostal said, 'Sorry, but Madame is not good enough for the Staatsoper,' and left. The furious husband bought up hundreds of seats, which he distributed among his acquaintances, but the result was disastrous. They applauded at the wrong moments and the enraged public started hissing. From his seat, his hands folded in his lap, Schostal watched the tragedy with grim satisfaction. Madame was through forever.

If Schostal really liked a great singer, he did not mind working without any compensation. When Kirsten Flagstad sang for the first time in Vienna, Schostal went to see her and offered his services, as he always did in the case of famous singers who had not appeared in Vienna before. Madame Flagstad refused, unaware of the local practice. After the first act of 'Tristan,' Schostal said, 'She's great. Get going, boys.' The next day Flagstad sent for him and became a steady client.

Puccini's 'Turandot' had a double première in Vienna. The first night, Lotte Lehmann and Leo Slezak were starred as Turandot and Calaf; the following evening the parts were sung by two younger stars, Maria Nemeth and Jan Kiepura. Having studied the score of 'Turandot,' Schostal knew that Kiepura's young, brilliant tenor would be better for the high part of Calaf than the aging Slezak's, and gave orders to 'build up' Kiepura. A few months later, Slezak stopped singing the part and Kiepura had the field to himself.

The claque was frequently denounced by the critics, who were reluctant to share with us their right to influence the public, but it was nevertheless tolerated by the directors of the Opera. Some of them, like Felix von Weingartner and Franz Schalk, preferred regulated applause to the enthusiastic outbursts of amateurs. Bruno Walter always had some kind word for us. (Schostal never took money from any conductor.) Richard Strauss considered the claque a necessary evil, like the ladies of the chorus, the ticket-jobbers outside the Opera, and the cockroaches under the plush seats of the Kaiserloge. When Clemens Krauss became the director of the Opera, he publicly threatened to 'rub out the claque.' Schostal took up the challenge. The following evening Krauss conducted 'Don Giovanni.' Schostal bought thirty expensive orchestra seats, which he distributed among those of us who owned tuxedos. When Krauss entered, we started a terrific ovation. During the intermission Schostal asked Krauss how he liked our work.

'Don't be ridiculous,' Krauss said. 'The applause was made by my followers in the orchestra pit. Since when do your boys sit in orchestra seats?'

During the second act, we applauded too early after Don Giovanni's 'Deh vieni alla finestra' and after Don Ottavio's beautiful 'Il mio tesoro intanto' and started several 'wild' salvos. After the cemetery scene several of our boys shouted 'Bravo, Walter!' and when told by kindly neighbors that Krauss, not Bruno Walter, was conducting, they looked dumbfounded and unhappy. The midday papers played up the story and for weeks thereafter Krauss was greeted by malicious friends with 'Bravo, Walter!' After that, Krauss did not object to the claque any more.

Many performances were saved by the claque — the dull nights when an uninspired conductor, a lukewarm orchestra, and singers walking through their parts might have made the audience wish they had stayed at home and saved their money. The apathetic atmosphere presented a challenge to Schostal. Giving orders right and left, directing carefully timed outbursts, he would wake up the house. Suddenly the singers would snap out of their lethargy, the orchestra would play beautifully, and the conductor would get worked up. Schostal derived great professional satisfaction from these blood transfusions and was always happy when he heard people saying, 'A bad first act, but the rest was wonderful.'

Schostal got depressed by the long scenes of Wagner's 'Ring des Nibelungen.' During 'Siegfried' and 'Walküre' he would walk over to the Peterskeller, preferring the political arguments of the night chauffeurs to those of Wotan and Fricka. He was always back in time for the curtain applause. He knew that the first act of 'Tristan' under the passionate leadership of Richard Strauss was eleven minutes shorter than under fish-blooded Robert Heger. Schostal never walked out during Puccini or Verdi operas, when the claque was facing difficult problems. At a performance of 'La Bohème' a famous coloratura wanted to have stronger applause in the first act than the tenor. Unfortunately, that night the tenor was in great voice and the diva was not. Sensing that the public might let us down, Schostal rescinded his orders to the effect that no special attention was to be given after her aria. Rodolpho got a terrific ovation after 'Che gelida manina' and the coloratura was let off with a sprinkle of applause after 'Mi chiamano Mini.' She was very angry — coloraturas often are — until Schostal told her that she had not been good enough.

The stars respected his judgment. Some singers took him

along on short trips to small houses in the provinces where Schostal arranged for suitable ovations. His secret ambition was to organize a world-wide claque trust with 'branches' at London's Covent Garden, the Metropolitan Opera House, San Carlo at Naples. He figured on becoming the president, making numerous trips of inspection. Schostal was very sad when he had to fire Childs, the pianist from Cleveland whom he had groomed as his apostle in the New World. 'Scheeltz' twice broke down when given independent assignments. He got frightened by his task and failed to applaud.

'Imagine if he does such a thing at the Metropolitan,' Schostal said. 'They'd call us gangsters.'

Schostal spent his summers in Salzburg, where he went simply as a 'private citizen.' He lived at the Hotel Oesterreichischer Hof, drank beer at the Peterskeller — there is a Peterskeller practically in every Austrian town — and bought expensive tickets to all opera performances. He returned to his job at the Vienna Opera House on September 1 and appeared there every night until July 15. His only holidays were the four or five performances of 'Parsifal,' a Stage Dedication Festival Play which, according to sacred Bayreuth tradition, must not be profaned by clapping hands.

Paid applause at the Staatsoper was not limited to the claque. There was a second group, numerically and, we always insisted, musically inferior, who had their headquarters down in the parterre standing room. They were known as the clique, which must have been confusing to the layman, and their leader was a man named Stieglitz who carried a heavy cane, was not given to subtle treatment of applause, and was frequently mentioned in Viennese newspapers in connection with alleged attempts at blackmail. The undeclared war between the claque and the clique exploded into a showdown one night, when 'Rosenkavalier' was being given with Lotte Lehmann as the Feldmarschallin and Maria Jeritza as Octavian. Madame Jeritza was a client of the clique, Madame Lehmann was our favorite client.

After a special conference with his lieutenants at the Peterskeller, Schostal decided to send one of his men, by the name of Loew, down among the clique in the parterre. This Loew was a husky fellow, and, like Siegfried, he had not learned what fear was. Loew's orders were to watch for possible flaws in Jeritza's performance and subtly to influence the bystanders in favor of Lehmann.

Loew played his part well. He closed his eyes in deep enchantment while Lehmann sang her aria in the first act. When Jeritza missed one cue by an eighth of a bar, he seemed surprised and whispered, 'I'm afraid she's through.' Soon the whole standing-room section was under the impression that Lehmann was wonderful and Jeritza should go home and practice.

Afraid that this defeatist sentiment might spread into the auditorium, the clique characteristically decided to solve the problem by brute force. Stieglitz ordered two of his boys to push Loew out of the standing-room section. Loew stood firm. The three were shoving back and forth, like boxers in a clinch. All through the beautiful 'Presentation of the Rose,' a silent, grim battle was raging between Loew and his opponents, but they were so careful not to make a noise that only the nearest bystanders were aware of what was going on. After the performance, Loew looked beaten up and the pockets were torn out of his coat, but he did not mind. He was happy at seeing Lehmann called before the curtain more often than Jeritza. At the Kärntnerstrasse stage door, we gave Madame Lehmann a tremendous ovation. This was the high point of our activities and of course one for which we made no charge. All was fine until the clique tried to break it up.

I do not remember who started the ensuing free-for-all. We were all arrested, claque and clique, and were brought to the nearest police station. Schostal, looking dignified even without the tie and hat he had lost in battle, explained to the inspector in charge that the clique had deliberately torpedoed a celebration for Lehmann after her great performance.

Stieglitz tried to protest, but the inspector told him to shut up. 'I was at the Opera myself,' he said. 'Lehmann was great. Jeritza overplayed in the third act, as usual. That woman's getting older.' He ordered the clique boys locked up for the night. We were told to leave.

Schostal said, 'Thank you, sir,' his voice betraying satisfaction that Viennese justice still prevailed. We said good night to one another and went home.

Chapter 9

THE CLAQUE CHEF GETS AN OVATION

LIFE was never dull for the members of the claque. Schostal often said that when he wrote his memoirs, they would make more exciting reading than the dry reminiscences of Hötzendorff or Ludendorff. None of us thought this an overstatement.

Schostal, an Austrian lieutenant in the last war, displayed presence of mind, self-control, and resoluteness in critical moments. During a performance of 'La Forza del Destino' in 1926, Vienna was hit by an earthquake just as the tenor, Koloman von Pataky, a client of the claque, sang Don Alvaro's aria 'O tu che in seno agli' Angeli.' The big crystal chandelier began to sway alarmingly and the listeners high up in the fourth balcony, being less accustomed to violent shocks than the citizens of Los Angeles or Tokio, had a funny feeling in the pits of their stomachs. A few women squealed and two or three nervous claqueurs tried to rush toward the exit, but Schostal's soft but firm voice stopped them. 'Nobody leaves until the end of Pataky's aria,' he said. 'Soldiers don't leave their post before the attack!' Pataky got his ovation and the audience regained its composure, assuming, apparently, that the situation could not be so bad since the claque was functioning normally.

The members of the claque met every day at noon, informally, under the Staatsoper arcades on the Kärntnerstrasse, where Schostal gave out the order of the evening and chatted with the singers who came there to rehearse. He would sit on the bench near the janitor's box with Richard Mayr or Erik Schmedes, the once-famous Wagnerian tenor, then an impoverished, sick old man who nostalgically came back to the place of his past triumphs.

In the afternoon, Schostal rested at his apartment, like a great prima donna, and was not to be disturbed except in an emergency. 'A claque chef needs more strength than a Heldentenor,' he would say. Once I was at his place, before a performance of 'Rigoletto' with Jan Kiepura as the Duke. We were discussing the order of the evening — 'a spontaneous ovation after "La donna è mobile" forcing Kiepura to repeat' — when Marcel, Kiepura's secretary and also one of the claque's regular members, rushed in, breathless with excitement. 'The order has been changed,' he said, quoting Scarpia's words from the second act of 'La Tosca.' 'I have altered my purpose. Cavaradossi will be shot . . . pay attention . . . Come facemmo del conte Palmiere.' Marcel was always talking in opera quotations. He explained that Kiepura was in fine form and wanted a special ovation which would 'force' him to repeat not only 'La donna è mobile,' but also his great aria 'Questa o quella' in the first act.

There had never been a repetition of 'Questa o quella' in the annals of the claque, and Schostal refused. Marcel added that there would be a special bonus of two hundred schilling, but money meant little to Schostal, so Marcel dropped that angle, merely observing with diplomatic finesse that it would make claque history to force a repetition of 'Questa o quella,' and that the chances were never better, Kiepura being splendid. This remark turned the trick. Schostal called up Professor Karl Alwin, the conductor of the evening, and cautiously disclosed his intentions. Alwin said, 'I'm only the orchestra conductor, and I bow to no one but my audience.' That was all Schostal wanted to know. Even the best claque is powerless against a hostile conductor who can kill the most powerful 'salvo' with an imperceptible movement of his baton, leading the orchestra into the next piece.

By this time it was almost six, an hour and a half before the beginning of the performance. We alerted, by telephone, all regular members, about forty men, for immediate emergency duty, took a cab and raced to the Staatsoper. All seats were sold out as always when Kiepura sang and about six hundred people were standing in line, waiting for the standing-room box offices to open. Right up in front were the 'Kiepura girls,' forty or fifty teen-age girls more or less crazy about the tenor. They would not miss a Kiepura performance and did not mind standing in line all afternoon to get the best places in the parterre standing room. Strictly amateur claqueurs, the Kiepura girls had an intense dislike for the claque because we did not refrain from applauding for Alfred Piccaver, Leo Slezak, and other tenor competitors of their beloved Kiepura.

Schostal approached the girls subtly. He happened to know that Kiepura was better than ever. How would they like to hear him repeat 'Questa o quella'? Would they help with a few enthusiastic outcries and sustained applause. The girls smelled a rat and remained aloof. Schostal hastily added that this was Kiepura's birthday (which was a lie), and what more beautiful gift could a tenor wish for than a spontaneous ovation? The collaboration of the Kiepura girls practically assured, Schostal hired fifty 'special' men, finding their names on a waiting list which he always carried. Each man was given a free ticket and promised a Mailänder — Dehmel chocolate cooky — to be distributed after the first act, 'in case of success.' Regulars and reinforcements were strategically posted in small groups of three or four all over the fourth balcony, and two trusted lieutenants were sent down into the parterre standing room to give the Kiepura girls a 'lead.'

Schostal, usually not given to defeatism, later confessed

that he did not dare hope the repetition would come off. But after Kiepura made a triumphant entrance and sang his first high notes, stirring the audience, the claque chef turned around to three of us, the bright smile of victory all over his face. At the exact fraction of a second following Kiepura's last note, Schostal boomed a deep, powerful 'Bravo!' into the house. This famous battle-cry was, we knew, reserved for rare, truly great occasions. The claque burst into a thunderous ovation, the reserve corps fell in, and from downstairs came the high-pitched, ecstatic cries of the Kiepura girls. After that, pandemonium broke loose. Most listeners got up from their chairs and cheered. Professor Alwin, the conductor, gave a flawless performance of utter surprise. Twice he raised his baton to continue and put it down again, seemingly overpowered by 'the will of the audience.' At last he turned back the pages of his score and motioned the orchestra to repeat.

We did not hear Kiepura as he sang 'Questa o quella' again. We gathered around Schostal, shaking hands with him and congratulating one another. In the intermission Schostal took us to Frau Piebitz, the Wasserfrau in the foyer, and bought two Mailänders and one glass of water for everybody whose name was on his list.

Schostal was discovered as a master-claqueur by the famous tenor, Carl Aagard Oestvig, one night in 1918, when Schostal, then a mere fourth-balcony enthusiast, started single-handed a terrific ovation after Oestvig's 'Salut demeure' in 'Faust.' At that time the claque, under the leadership of one Herr Freudenberger, an incompetent patriarch, was in a sorry state. Schostal belonged to a small group of stout opera enthusiasts who, rain, cold, and storm notwithstanding, after every performance went to the stage door to pay their personal tribute to the singers. One night Oestvig, at the stage door, asked Schostal to take over on an experimental basis. Two evenings later, Schostal made his professional début at a performance of 'Pagliacci,' with Oestvig as Canio.

After 'Vesti la giubba' the audience, inspired by Schostal, kept on applauding through the entire intermission.

Shortly thereafter, Oestvig's wife, the soprano Maria Raidl, became Schostal's second client. Lotte Lehmann, Alfred Piccaver, and Maria Jeritza soon followed.

For several years Maria Jeritza was one of our star customers. When Jeritza sang, you did not merely applaud or cry 'Bravo!' Her ovations were strategically planned and masterfully executed. At a Jeritza performance of, say, 'Tosca,' 'Salome,' 'Die Tote Stadt,' or 'The Girl of the Golden West,' Schostal divided his forces into two groups. After the last act one group would wait under the Operngasse arcades and give a terrific ovation as Madame Jeritza came out through the stage door and got into her car. The second group, commanded by Schostal in person, would run over to Stallburggasse Number 2, where she lived, and take up battle formation in front of her house. There would be roll-call and Schostal would give out various assignments, such as jumping on the running-board of Jeritza's car and opening the door of her house. Then he would hurry into the Bar Sanssouci, across the street, and from a telephone booth overlooking the front of Jeritza's house, call up Gretl, the singer's trusted secretary, and report the exact number of men present. Jeritza's car would arrive, there would be a powerful ovation, she would hurry upstairs, and a few moments later appear at the window and throw down little flower bouquets, 'one for every person,' while Schostal from his observation post issued orders, 'One more bow, please,' or 'Seventeen bouquets, please.' There was, somehow, always a large number of these bouquets available.

Flower bouquets played an important part at the première of Hermann Goetz' 'The Taming of the Shrew,' in 1931, which Schostal considered a high-light in the history of the claque. At that performance the title rôle was sung by our favorite, Lotte Lehmann. Schostal was informed by his spies, whom he had everywhere, that Madame Lehmann was promised a new, splendid contract if she would make a success out of her part, and that Herr Schneiderhan, the General-Intendant himself, would be in his box. At a meeting in Schostal's apartment it was agreed that 'special actions' had to be taken to impress the General-Intendant. We went to an expensive Ringstrasse flower shop, and Schostal ordered a magnificent laurel wreath and forty Wurfsträusschen, little bunches of lilies-of-the-valley and other sturdy plants that would safely survive being thrown across the orchestra pit. At the Staatsoper there was an unwritten law against the use of flowers. The Wurfsträusschen were concealed by our commandos in the parterre standing room and the wreath was smuggled in through a side door and hidden in the fourth balcony ladies' room, the attendant of which was one of Schostal's faithful followers. As usual, nothing was left to chance. After Madame Lehmann's great aria a claqueur by the name of Fischer, a famous athlete and obstacle runner, was to race down with the laurel wreath. There was another short scene after the aria, which would give Fischer time to arrive at the orchestra pit exactly at the end of the act. Schostal made a thorough study of the score and the action was meticulously timed.

Unfortunately, the conductor decided at the very last minute before the performance to cut the short scene following Lehmann's aria. For some reason or other Schostal was not notified of this change. We were still applauding after Lehmann's aria when, to our utter horror, the curtain came down. Schostal did not lose his presence of mind. He grabbed Fischer's sleeve and thundered, 'Down!' Fischer ran into the vestibule of the ladies' room, grabbed the wreath and began his historic descent. There are about two hundred stairs from the fourth balcony to the parterre floor. According to Inspector Samek, the policeman in charge, Fischer jumped four or five stairs at a time. As a matter of fact, he arrived inside the orchestra pit sixteen seconds after leaving the fourth balcony — a world record. We saw him run down to the orchestra pit and hand the wreath to the second violinist who put it at Madame Lehmann's feet as she appeared for her second bow. Simultaneously our shock troops from the parterre standing room broke through, took the Wurfsträusschen out of their pockets and threw them at the diva. Madame Lehmann, who had known nothing about the planned demonstration, stood dumbfounded, and the Viennese audience, a folk partial to pleasant surprises, broke into a terrific ovation. The General-Intendant, as much impressed as everybody else, went to see Madame Lehmann in her dressing-room and offered her the new contract on the spot.

There were other evenings when we did not deliver the goods and Schostal refunded money that had been paid him in advance. One such disaster was the début of Joseph Rogatchewsky of the Opéra-Comique, who sang des Grieux in 'Manon,' which in Vienna had for years been monopolized by Alfred Piccaver. Piccaver always sang a shortened version of 'Ah! fuyez, douce image,' and when Rogatchewsky started the famous aria, it occurred to none of us that he might sing it uncut. After the first part Schostal gave the usual cue, nodding his bald head to the claqueurs standing behind him, and a thunder of applause went down on poor M. Rogatchewsky who kept right on singing, his beautiful pianissimi murdered by our brutal handclapping. The next morning Schostal, heart-broken, made his pilgrimage to the Imperial Hotel. (Schostal always knew which hotel famous guest artists went to, though such information was supposed to be highly secret, and five minutes after Lauritz Melchior arrived at Meisel and Schadn or Gigli or Rogatchewsky at the Imperial, he would be there.) Rogatchewsky was a good sport. 'Ne vous en faites pas,' he said to Schostal. 'Deux fois applause est mieux que rien de tout.'

Schostal's other great passion was the ballet. He never missed a performance of 'Josephslegende,' 'Scheherazade,' 'Geschichten aus dem Wiener Wald,' or 'Puppenfee,' even if we had no clients in the cast. He was very devoted to Madame Gusti Pichler, the blind, graceful, toe-dancing prima ballerina and after every appearance accompanied her home to her house at the Prinz Eugen Strasse. Madame Pichler sent Schostal little, pencil-written notes, full of exact instructions, Viennese charm, and orthographical mistakes, 'Net warten, nach der letzten Pirouette,' 'net warten' (do not wait) three times underscored. Her bitterest enemy was Madame Krausenecker, the assistant prima ballerina, whom Pichler hated with all her excitable little heart. The prima ballerina was a client of the claque and Krausenecker was not, but Schostal never concealed his enthusiasm even if it did not run parallel with his business interests and after a 'Josephslegende' with Krausenecker as Potiphar, called out his famous 'Bravo!' Worse, he repeated this crime a few days later at a performance of 'Die Nixe von Schönbrunn.' For several weeks Madame Pichler ignored Schostal's presence at the stage door and walked home alone, tears in her beautiful Blue-Danube eyes. 'If a man cries Bravo for that creature, he's dead for me,' she said.

Another Schostal favorite was Madame Wiesenthal, the great dancer and ballet teacher. After the dress rehearsal of the ballet 'Die Taenzerin von Wien,' with rather modern music by the Austrian composer, Franz Salmhofer, Grete Wiesenthal called Schostal into her dressing-room and asked him if he could manage a salvo after her Glockentanz, an extremely delicate piece. Schostal studied the score, breathlessly watched by Madame Wiesenthal, Professor Alwin, the conductor, and Salmhofer, the composer. 'He would have rewritten the score especially for me,' Schostal later said. 'But I told them I thought it could be done.'

That night we watched Schostal closely as he followed Madame Wiesenthal's Glockentanz, the score in his hand. At the prescribed moment he gave us the cue, a slight nod, and we went to work. The ovation came off in great style. After the performance, which was a terrific personal success for Madame Wiesenthal, we all waited at the stage door for the usual final ovation. Somewhat in the background were a group of fifty slim boys and girls, students of Madame Wiesenthal's famous Balletschule. As Madame Wiesenthal came out and stepped into her car, there was the usual ovation, 'Hoch Wiesenthal!' flawlessly executed by the claque. The car drove on slowly and Wiesenthal, a smile on her face, turned around and through the rear window beckoned to her pupils. It was, as we soon learned, a cue. The boys and girls took a deep breath and a thundering, warlike cry, 'Hoch Schostal! Bravo Schostal!' went up into the Viennese night, shaking the waiters of the Opernrestaurant out of their customary lethargy. They came running out, and Herr Bauer, the headwaiter, said to his piccolo, 'JesusMariaundJosef! Now, they're giving an ovation to Schostal himself! I always say nothing's impossible in this town.'

Chapter 10

CONCOURS D'ÉLÉGANCE

I CAUSED a family scandal when my relatives found out that I had become a member of the claque; one aunt, an elderly, high-principled dowager went so far as to call me a 'mauvais sujet.' Actually the claque was no sinister gang, but a rather innocent body. Nevertheless, the police were our permanent nightmare. There were four police inspectors in mufti attending every performance, two in the fourth balcony, one in the third, one in the parterre standing room. Most officers were gemütlich and never tangled with Schostal because of an atavistic belief that 'nothing good would come of it'; but some inspectors, toughened in many fist-fights with Pülchers, the local brand of bums, were what American soldiers would call strictly G.I. Inside the opera house small signs read: 'All Disturbing Manifestations of Approval and Disapproval are Prohibited.' The interpretation of what was 'disturbing' was left to the arbitrary judgment of the inspector on duty. I remember a performance of 'Samson and Delilah,' with the famous contralto Rosette Anday and George Thill, when Schostal instructed all members of the claque to be careful because Inspector Kramer was on duty. This Kramer, a tough, punctilious man, hated music and the claque, and after five seidels of Schwechater beer publicly declared that most operas were 'full of noise.' He sat near the middle aisle and we all scattered in small groups of two or three along the left balcony side. Schostal directed the claque from his headquarters behind the pillar. After the duet of Delilah and the High Priest of Dagon in the second act, we broke into 'spontaneous' applause which did not quite come off and caused a lot of raised eyebrows among the innocent fourth balcony patrons. Kramer got up and came to warn Schostal that if there should be one more 'disturbing' ovation, we would all meet at police headquarters.

The situation was critical. 'Piroshka' Anday was one of our best clients and a Schostal favorite. He had promised her an overwhelming ovation after her great aria, 'Mon coeur s'ouvre à ta voix,' and he had never broken a promise yet. We had to work fast; Kramer, suspicious and grim, watched us from near-by. Schostal gave out the order, 'Fall out inconspicuously through the middle toward the right side!' Because of an old tradition the claque always operated on the left side and Schostal hoped that 'spontaneous' applause from the right would fool Kramer. As the first groups began to take up their new positions, Schostal was joined by Professor Grünauer, prominent Viennese and the husband of Maria Nemeth, the famous Staatsoper soprano. Schostal was often visited in his headquarters by luminaries of music, literature, and politics who did not mind making the strenuous ascent to the fourth balcony to discuss opera with the claque chef. When told of Kramer's sinister intentions, Professor Grünauer called upon Schostal to be a man and fight it out with Kramer once and for all. The Professor promised his active support. Messengers went out around the balcony and all claqueurs were ordered back to their original positions. Schostal left his seat, which he did when 'special operations' demanded his presence among the claque men, and went with Professor Grünauer up to the so-called 'Einserplatz,' the extreme end of the balustrade which by unwritten law was reserved exclusively for Schostal and his guests of honor.

Madame Anday sang her aria splendidly, and Schostal nodded his bald head. The claque broke out into a thunderous ovation and the house cheered. Kramer muttered a malediction, took out the feared notebook, wet the pencil with his tongue, and asked Schostal the officially prescribed questions, 'Name? Birthday? Residence? Occupation?' Kramer knew all the answers, this being not his first brush with the claque chef, but the formalities had to be fulfilled. He then proceeded to write down Professor Grünauer's data. The Professor and Madame Nemeth lived at the Hofburg, parts of the Kaiser's former residence being rented to selected opera stars and other public dignitaries, but Kramer did not know that. When Professor Grünauer, asked for his residence, truthfully answered, 'The Hofburg,' Kramer got very angry and told him to shut up. 'Such bad jokes won't help you. On the contrary,' Kramer added darkly. A few enraged opera patrons began to hiss 'Quiet! Sh!' but Kramer, with typical disrespect for Camille Saint-Saëns, noisily took down my name and those of four other 'lieutenants.' We were ordered to appear the next morning at the Polizeipräsidium at Schottenring Number 11.

After the performance we waited for Madame Anday at the stage door and Schostal informed her about the incident. The diva was furious and called up Vice-President Pamer of the Polizeipräsidium, an opera-lover, and a great admirer of Madame Anday, who had also attended the performance. 'You were wonderful, Gnädigste,' the Herr Vice-President said. 'My hands are still swollen from applauding.' 'Unfortunately,' Madame Anday retorted acidly, 'your flattering sentiments are not shared by all members of the force, Herr Präsident,' and she went on to complain about Kramer.

The next morning, Schostal, Professor Grünauer, and we five claque members met at the office of Hofrat Ritzberger, chef of the Strafsektion. Somebody had notified the press and the room was full of reporters. They greeted Schostal fondly.

In Vienna, where opera gossip was prominently featured in all papers, the claque chef was always good copy.

Schostal did not disappoint them. He boomed 'Guilty!' to the charges raised by Kramer, who stood there, arrogant and tough. Then Schostal made an impressive speech about the immortal merits of the claque. 'If our men had operated in 1875 at the première of Bizet's "Carmen" at the Opéra-Comique, poor Bizet wouldn't have died so soon,' Schostal thundered. 'Beethoven, after "Fidelio," and Wagner, after "Tristan," would have been saved much grief. Caruso and others have declared that we are an essential part of the opera house, like the stage lights, the orchestra, the cashier. Who is a man named Kramer to dispute these axioms?' The reporters wrote with delight and the typist was so amazed that she messed up the testimony record.

Hofrat Ritzberger quickly penalized each of us ten schilling (two dollars), the minimum fine, and the clerk gave Schostal an Erlagschein — a sort of blank check — to use when sending in the money. Thereupon the press and the bystanders were thrown out of the room, and Schostal, Professor Grünauer, and we five 'lieutenants' remained alone with the Hofrat. He got up, shook hands with us, and apologized to each of us. The whole thing was 'sehr peinlich,' a misunderstanding, and the Herr Präsident Pamer was distressed. That night, when Schostal entered the Staatsoper foyer, the four inspectors on duty took off their hats and bowed deeply. Kramer was not among them. He had been transferred to the Brigittenau, a tough outlying district, considered the Siberia of Vienna's policemen.

As time went on, Schostal and Hofrat Ritzberger became good friends. Whenever Schostal was ordered to appear before the Hofrat because of some 'disturbing ovation,' they shook hands, wished one another a very good morning, and after a pleasant chat the Hofrat would say, 'I see there was another little matter last night. Well, here's an Erlagschein,

Herr Schostal. It's nice dealing with a cultured man. I wish my customers were all like you.' One day the Hofrat said, 'I don't want you to get up early and come here all the way from your apartment, Herr Schostal. Take a dozen of Erlagschein blanks with you and send in your ten schilling every time they mark you down. Or you can make them out on the first of the month, with the rest of your bills.'

The Hofrat's sympathies did not include our rivals, Stieglitz's clique or 'Stehparterre Club.' Stieglitz was in frequent trouble with everybody, including the management of the opera, which at various occasions barred him from the house. He went around in taxis, an unheard-of luxury, and tried to steal Schostal's clients. One of our good customers was the Rumanian tenor, Trajan Grosavescu. Schostal frequently dined at the Grosavescus' and at the stage door, after a Grosavescu performance, yelled 'Setrajaska Grosavescu!' the Rumanian equivalent for 'Bravo!' Stieglitz unsuccessfully attempted to 'get' Grosavescu. When the tenor turned him down cold, Stieglitz was out for revenge.

Fortunately, Schostal's intelligence system reached out into the circles around Stieglitz. One morning preceding a 'Carmen' performance with Grosavescu as Don José, Schostal was informed that Stieglitz was planning an anti-Grosavescu putsch that night. Schostal called up Grosavescu and told him that there might be trouble, but the tenor answered coolly and typically, 'I don't know why. I'm really in fine form.' Tenors seldom think of other troubles than those caused by their own larynxes. Schostal called up his friends at the Polizeipräsidium and asked them to send a few men in mufti into the parterre standing room—just in case. All regular members of the claque were called out and warned to be on the alert.

We did not know when Stieglitz would strike his blow, there being many opportunities for foul play in 'Carmen.' Looking down from the fourth balcony into the parterre standing room, we saw that Stieglitz had divided his forces into two groups, one on the right and one on the left side. This was unusual, as the Stehparterre Club habitually assembled on the left. The first act ended peacefully and Grosavescu sent up a message to Schostal which read, 'Ha! Ha!' The second act began and Grosavescu sang beautifully 'La fleur que tu m'avais jetée.' When he came to the high B after 'Et j'étais une chose à toi,' a terrific salvo of applause was started by the right-side Stieglitz group. Experienced opera goers know that the high B is not the end of the aria, but is followed by 'Carmen, je t'aime' — and no one knew this better than the Stieglitz men. The Stieglitz group on the left side pretended to be indignant at their colleagues' untimely outburst. They started hissing and cried, 'Quiet, over there!' ruining Grosavescu's love-making in high B. By that time Schostal gave his cue, and we of the claque came in with legitimate applause, which only heightened the confusion; people from the boxes and the galleries calling out 'Skandal!' and 'kusch!' Grosavescu's aria was killed and so was the following scene because the policemen at the standing room were taking down the names of the Stieglitz men. Some tried to escape, and there was a hell of a racket before the police got them all.

It was a Pyrrhic victory for the claque. The newspapers and the public were tired of the constant war between us and the Stieglitz men. One day in 1924 the soloists of the Staatsoper, after a secret meeting, published a proclamation which each singer was pledged to support. Henceforth no artist was allowed to get in touch 'with any member of the applauding bodies,' either directly or indirectly. Those breaking their word of honor would be instantly thrown out of the Staatsoper. The noon papers carried headlines, 'The Claque Is Dead!' It was the blackest day in Schostal's career, but he did not lose his nerve. Late in the afternoon, before the evening performance of 'Cavalleria Rusticana' and 'Pagliacci,' with Vera Schwarz as Nedda and Alfred Piccaver as Canio, Schostal had word to call U–88–5–94. This was the secret telephone number of Alfred Piccaver, known only to his intimates. Schostal took a cab and went to the tenor's apartment on Brahmsplatz. Madame Piccaver looked grave as she said, 'Go into the bathroom. Alfi is waiting for you.' This was serious. When faced with problems of real magnitude, Piccaver always retired to the bathroom.

According to Schostal, Piccaver was sitting on the edge of the bathtub, wearing blue slacks and a soiled sweater. He shook hands with Schostal and sighed deeply, the justly famous sigh of Rhadames in the sad last act of 'Aïda.' Piccaver said he was so sorry for Schostal, but there was, of course, nothing he could do, word of honor and so on. As Schostal was about to leave, still wondering why Piccaver had made him come over in such a hurry, the tenor pointed down to the floor, saying, 'You've lost something.' Schostal bent down and picked up two twenty-schilling bills from under the washbasin. 'I said "Thanks" and took the money,' the claque chef said years later when the story could be told. 'I always carried lots of loose bills in my pockets and for a moment I thought I had really lost the money. Only after I left, I remembered that forty schilling was exactly what Piccaver used to pay me for one evening.'

There was much tension in the fourth balcony that night when the claque, led by Schostal, made an impressive entrance. 'We are not quite dead yet,' Schostal said to the reporters who were up there with us. 'You can quote me on that.' We did not lift a finger after the 'prologue' in 'Pagliacci,' or after Vera Schwarz's aria. The reporters began to look bored. After Piccaver's 'Vesti la giubba' we gave the tenor a dramatic ovation that shook the house. The morning papers reported that Schostal had apparently decided to continue the claque on his own. The next evening they gave 'Faust.' None of the singers dared to get in touch with Schostal, 'directly or indirectly.' 'We won't work for any of them,' Schostal said. 'But after the ballet give all you have. That will stump them.'

The performance was dull and uninspired, and there was

scarcely any applause for any of the singers, but the ovation for the ballet was deafening. The following morning two divas sent their husbands to renew their agreements with Schostal. The rest of the singers followed, one by one, and to hell with their word of honor. Schostal was a happy man. 'The artists can't work without us,' he would say. 'Once and for all, we have proved that we have a definite place in opera history. Everybody come over to the Opernrestaurant for a seidel beer.'

On a Friday night in 1926, after a dull performance of Strauss's 'Die Aegyptische Helena,' two gray-haired, well-groomed gentlemen stepped toward Schostal in the Opera foyer and invited him for a cup of coffee at the Café Heinrichshof, across the Ringstrasse. They introduced themselves as the sole Austrian representatives of the automobile firms Lancia, Fiat, and Auburn-Cort.

The following day, the Concours d'Élégance, the annual automobile show, was to take place in the Schönbrunn Schlosshof. The show was sponsored by the aristocratic Autoklub, and was the outstanding social event of the season. The three winning cars would get gold ribbons and a great deal of free publicity, all of which would be dandy for their manufacturers. Having heard of Schostal's uncanny success in matters of promotion, the gentlemen wondered if he would be able to do something for their cars by subtly influencing the judges and the audience at the Schlosshof in favor of Lancia, Fiat, and Auburn-Cort.

'Suppose you would bring with you a hundred of your men, well-dressed and as aristocratic-looking as possible,' the younger Captain of Industry suggested. 'A little applause in favor of our cars, as they go past the judges, might work wonders.' The older man said that money made no difference; they would be glad to pay Schostal one thousand schilling and the cost of the men, adding that subtlety had to be the keynote of the operation. It would be disastrous if anybody found out the truth. It was agreed that each of the hundred men would get two schilling and one sandwich as 'Wegzehrung' plus free admission and transportation.

Time being short, the two gentlemen placed their own limousine and chauffeur at Schostal's disposal. All night long Schostal rode through the sleeping streets of Vienna, hiring men for the Concours d'Élégance. Most members of the claque were still drinking beer at the Opernrestaurant, passionately discussing the slim chances of immortality of 'Die Aegyptische Helena.' They were ordered to be under the Opera arcades the next afternoon at two. A few men grumbled, having made dates for the week-end, but Schostal threatened to take their names off the list for 'Meistersinger,' on Sunday night, unless they would ditch their girls and come out to Schönbrunn. At that all promised to be there, no girl on earth being worth missing a great 'Meistersinger' performance. Schostal rode to Piowatti, where some of the claque's regular members were having a late snack; at the Café Lustbader he hired eighteen men, at the moment playing billiards and not looking too aristocratic in rolled-up shirt-sleeves; at the Café Central nine men were aroused from their chess game and ordered to duty. The next morning Schostal was taken to the autodealers' showrooms in the Liechtensteinstrasse, where the two gentlemen showed him the three automobiles selected for the Concours: a sleek, light-blue Fiat, a stunning, black Lancia coupé, and a cream-colored Auburn-Cort. Not being much of an automobile expert, Schostal had the dealers turn on the engines of the cars so that he could recognize them accoustically.

At two o'clock two autobuses drove up under the arcades. After roll-call, Schostal held formal inspection of his men. Some of us were not up to the high standards of the occasion and had to be sent back for shoes shined and more discreet ties. The buses stopped at a hidden corner of the Schönbrunn Park and Schostal gave us last-minute instructions. 'No rough stuff today,' he said. 'This isn't a matter of encores and the Stieglitz men aren't here anyway. Provide incon spicuous but moderately strong applause. Don't forget, you are supposed to be part of the upper classes.'

Each of us received a ticket and we went into the Schlosshof in small groups, looking blasé, eyebrows slightly raised, the way (we thought) young men of nobility should look. We sat right down among the élite of Austria's high aristocracy, Schostal sitting behind a decrepit old duchess, not far from the tophatted gentlemen of the jury. The claque chef was nervous. It is one thing to applaud for Jeritza or Lehmann and another to work for automobiles that sing no high C and would race past before one could say 'Götterdämmerung.' A few of our men immediately tried to date handsome countesses, and Immerglück, an old member of the claque and an outspoken Sozialdemokrat, got into a vehement argument with a Baron.

The first cars drove by and from the bored audience came a trickle of applause. They had an amateurish way of clapping their hands, the gentlemen being afraid of dropping their monocles. The ladies wore long gloves and lorgnettes and applauded by clapping the back of their hands, a spectacle which drove Schostal almost crazy. At the sight of an old-fashioned Rolls-Royce, the old duchess in front of him burst into her idea of thundering applause, slightly tapping her umbrella across her handbag. Schostal was horrified. 'That's blasphemy,' he said. 'I could kill her for that.'

Schostal sat up straight at the high-pitched sound of an engine. 'That rhythm,' he said. 'Like the beginning of the Walküre Prelude. That must be the Lancia.' A black coupé drove on in front of the jury. Schostal got up from his seat and nodded his head, and suddenly a terrific salvo of applause overwhelmed the doddering aristocrats. Two members of the jury woke up from their stupor and the old duchess dropped her umbrella. A cream-colored car was next. Schostal nodded again, and there was another thunderous ovation. People in the audience looked at each other as if they would say, 'Really?' and began to applaud themselves, nothing being so contagious as well-staged applause. Graf Ulrich Kinsky, the President of the Autoklub, turned toward the audience in utter amazement and the jurors were visibly taken aback by the unexpected enthusiasm. By now our men were really warmed up and, when the light-blue Fiat appeared, there was the sort of ovation we usually gave when we wanted Slezak or Lehmann to repeat an aria. Schostal tried in vain to keep his men from giving too healthy, noisy, and proletarian an ovation; some men cried 'Bravo!' producing a mad, relentless machine-gun fire with their hands, and old Immerglück jumped on his seat and cried, 'Hoch Slezak!' which, he said later, was meant to be 'Hoch Fiat!' The applause died down only after two other cars, a Steyr and a Tatra, had passed the judges' stand and Schostal began to swing his handkerchief in a desperate effort to stop the torrent.

In the face of such unheard-of public acclamation, the judges could only award the three gold ribbons to the Lancia, Fiat, and Auburn-Cort automobiles, with additional prizes going to the Steyr and Tatra. After the Concours there was a final Vergatterung in a hidden corner of the Park. The Captains of Industry, beaming with joy, carried large rolls of silver schilling, and Schostal passed the row of men, giving each man two schilling and a large sandwich from a laundry-basket. Only eighty-eight men out of one hundred and two were present, the rest evidently having established promising contacts with the young ladies of the aristocracy. Schostal, in a benevolent mood, said they would get their money that night after the opera performance. We unwrapped our sandwiches and went home through the Schlosspark, eating the Salamibrote, throwing away the paper, while the bewildered barons and countesses stared.

Chapter 11

THE DEPUTY'S SPEECH

IN THE SUMMER of 1935, I was involved for five months in the minor intrigues of Central-European power-politics in the capacity of parliamentary secretary to a member of the Czechoslovak Chamber of Deputies at Prague. My friends, puzzled by this vague-sounding title, sometimes asked me for a detailed definition of my duties. I shrugged. I did not know my duties. Like many people in politics I was not quite sure what I was doing. My job gave me independence and a great deal of free time, and I was well paid. Best of all, I met a lot of interesting people: politicians, headwaiters, racketeers; people who wanted jobs, visas, licenses, citizenship papers, passports; saccharine smugglers and liquor salesmen, and many personalities who attained a sorry prominence in later years, among them the Slovak leaders, Tiso and Mach, and Czech small-time quislings.

I learned a great deal about politics from Voska, an old usher at Parliament, who collected the deputies' identification cards at the rear entrance to the Chamber. Voska had been 'in the business' for forty-five years, formerly at the Parliament of the Austro-Hungarian Monarchy in Vienna. He was a kindly man who had come to put politicians in the same class as drunks and children. 'Too bad that the average person can't see the House in session,' Voska would say. 'Pro Boha, if all the voters could watch those screwballs, most deputies would never get re-elected.'

The deputy for whom I worked was one of the town's best-known lawyers. He devoted most of his time to his law business. He was an honest man who had gone into politics because he never got tired of listening to the sound of his own voice, and there was a faint hope that he might become a member of the Cabinet, which greatly intrigued his wife. I saw him only twice a week for a couple of hours. My main job was to keep his constituents away from him, a task which the deputy loosely described as 'important liaison work.'

'There are only two kinds of people,' the deputy would say. 'Those who want something from us and those from whom we want something. Your job is to handle the first group; I'll take care of the second.' The deputy was proud of his infallible judgment in handling people. 'Always listen carefully, never promise anything. They must leave with the impression that they'll get what they want,' he said. When the deputy spoke, his eyes wandered around the room as though he were addressing a large audience. He was a stocky, dark, intense man, with a carefully trimmed mustache and powerful, sweeping gestures. He was able to make the most commonplace statement sound like a proclamation of paramount significance. He would say, 'Gentlemen, I cannot but emphasize certain obligations imposed upon us by our great historical traditions,' as though he were disclosing a state secret of utmost gravity. When he spoke in the House, I had to distribute in advance typewritten copies of his speech to all Prague newspapers and to make sure that every paper got one copy. The following day the deputy would study the number of lines that each paper had given to his speech, counting them with a blue pencil. Once, after the papers had referred to his latest speech at great length, the deputy called me in and gave me a raise.

Officialdom pretended not to know of the existence of the parliamentary secretaries. We were haughtily ignored by the political editors of the big papers, who never quoted us on taxes, the Sudeten-Germans, social security, or The Red Menace. Actually, there existed something one might call the invisible power of the parliamentary secretaries. When the Parliament was not in session and most deputies were out of town, the secretaries all but lived at the Parliament building on Riegrovo Nábřeží. We resided at the offices of our bosses, used their letterheads for our private correspondence and their telephones for our calls, and took their newspapers home. We intervened at the Ministries in their name; we wined and dined the officials at our bosses' expense and frequently got important advance information on the political situation.

My office — the deputy's office — was at the rear wing of the House, at the end of a long, dark corridor, next to the gents' room, no doubt because the deputy, one of the younger members of the Social-Democrat Party, was a novice in politics. When I complained about the location of the room, the Parliament's budget director said to me, 'Why don't you get a job with Beran or Machnik? That would assure you of a beautiful office, with heavy satin curtains and large front windows.' Beran and Machnik were the leaders of the powerful Agrarian Party. I felt very bitter about the Agrarians, their anti-social politics and appeasement tendencies, and their beautiful offices on the first floor. In my shabby, narrow little room, there were no rugs, curtains, pictures. There was hardly enough space for three people, which is a grave handicap in politics, where you may want to influence large groups of men over tables loaded with drinks and cigars. My boss refused to give me an office helper, so I put a sign on the door, under the deputy's name. The sign read, 'Private — By Appointment Only,' and succeeded in discouraging people, since it wisely omitted to say where you could make an appointment. I was not sure that the deputy would like the sign and always took it down before he returned.

During the off-season I went to the Chamber at eleven in the morning. Except for a few window-cleaners, charwomen, and ushers, only the parliamentary secretaries were there, walking gravely up and down the long corridors, or sitting in their bosses' chairs in the House Library. We tried our best to imitate the grave, important look displayed by our bosses. There were only a few callers during the day, people who had urgent tax trouble and wanted the deputy to intervene at the Finance Ministry in their behalf, people trying for a government job, and people who were just plain nuisances.

Most secretaries had lunch at the House restaurant, where they occupied the tables reserved for their bosses. Some men invited for lunch out-of-town visitors on whom, for one reason or another, they wanted to make an impression. For such occasions there existed an elaborate ritual, to which the secretaries of all parties, from the extreme left-wing Communists to the extreme right-wing Stříbrný-Fascists, adhered religiously. The man with luncheon guests at his table was greeted respectfully, even if you were not on friendly terms with him. If he was a pal of yours, you would say, 'Just a moment, pane kolego,' and call him aside. Then, while the out-of-towners were so impressed that they were unable to eat their srnčí hřbet na Madeiře (fillet of deer with Madeira), you would whisper, 'Going to the Sparta football game Sunday?' or, 'There's a swell movie at the Adria tonight. How about it?' The other man would nod gravely, shake hands with you, and go back to his table, explaining to his guests in a solemn voice, 'I'm sorry. A matter of utmost importance. You'll read about it on the front pages any day now. The gentleman I was talking to is the secretary of Deputy So-and-So.' The awed out-of-towners almost dropped their forks and knives. They went home and told everybody that the man to see, if you *really* wanted to get places, was not the deputy, but his secretary. They said they would not be surprised if that bright young man someday would become deputy or even Minister.

One of my fellow secretaries was a man whom I shall call Honza. We had been friends since our days at the Officers' Candidate School at Opava, where in 1930 and 1931 we spent ten excruciating months, walking endless kilometers, cleaning rifles, crawling through mud and snow, and wondering dully what it was all about. Honza was the model of a parliamentary secretary. He spent endless hours at the Ministries because one of his boss's constituents wanted a job as brakeman on the state railroads, or another needed his citizenship papers. He wrote excellent reports on the political sentiments in the voting district of his boss, who was a prominent member of the Czech National-Socialist Party. How he had attained that prominence, no one was able to explain. The deputy was a dull, colorless career politician who never expressed himself in favor of or against anything. He was just guessing the 'trend,' but somehow he often guessed right. People said that his position had something to do with his wife's father, an old-time party horse. The deputy was chairman of the board of several banks and insurance companies and frequently gave hunting and drinking parties on his wife's estate. His excellent speeches were written by Honza, who also kept up friendly contacts with newspaper editors, received deputations from home, made vague promises to farmers and grain merchants, and succeeded in keeping everybody happy.

Honza's only weakness was the girls. He was tall and broad-shouldered, and the women said that he had a soft, magic voice. They were all crazy about him. There were so many girls that Honza was afraid of mixing up their first names and telephone numbers. Things got so bad that he began to use his boss's 'Calendar for the Working Politician' to keep his dates straight and avoid confusion.

Honza's line was perfectly obvious. I never understood how so many seemingly smart girls could fall for it. He was a smooth dresser, spending most of his money for neckties, hats, shoes, silk shirts, and suits made from imported English woolens. The Czech National-Socialists were the party of unsophisticated government employees, teachers, small businessmen. The deputy told Honza that he should 'look the part' while he was in his office, but Honza disregarded this bit of advice. He was undoubtedly the best-dressed man at the Parliament. At five o'clock he left and took his darling-of-the-day to the Barrandow Café, the Adria-Bio, or the beer garden 'U Fleků,' depending on the girl's preference for soft music, moving pictures, or cold beer.

When the Parliament was in session and Honza was unable to invite his girls for lunch because 'the boss occupies my table,' he had a different routine. Each deputy was allotted two seats in the visitors' balcony. The secretary's job was to distribute the tickets diplomatically among the deputy's influential friends and voters and his wife's relatives, wherever they would do the most good. Honza's boss was too busy with his board meetings and hunting parties to care about the seats in the visitors' balcony. Honza took the tickets and presented them to his girl friends, which gave him a chance of putting on a beautiful act. We secretaries were permitted to remain inside the Chamber, 'during the performance of our secretarial duties,' in the room reserved for the deputies. The rule was interpreted rather liberally. We would stay inside the Chamber even if there was no work to be done. We stood near the walls, listening to the speeches or watching the deputies insult one another. It gave us the feeling of being part of the whole setup.

Honza rushed in and out, carrying papers and files containing nothing but advertisements or printed matter; he brought letters to be signed by the deputy, always one at a time. In between, he stepped over to the Ministers' bench and paid his respects to the Post Minister or the School Minister, who were party friends of his boss. Most girls, having only a limited knowledge of the inner workings of the

Chamber of Deputies, believed Honza when he told them he was 'a sort of second-class deputy.' During crowded sessions, when Doctor Beneš spoke, Honza would stand in front of the deputies' benches, nodding his head, approving of certain passages in the Foreign Minister's speech. The girls were deeply impressed by Honza's obvious importance in the Political Life of the Nation. When Honza suggested that they spend the next week-end with him in his beautiful cabin on the Vitava River near the vineyards of Mělnîk, the girls raised only a weak, conventional protest which was easily overcome.

Honza did not give up his girls even in the hectic spring of 1935, when the country was running a pre-election fever and we secretaries were the busiest people on earth. Honza's deputy and my boss campaigned for re-election in the same district, a rural-industrial area where about fifty per cent of the voters were farmers, the rest workers and small business people. In Czechoslovakia the people voted for party lists, not for individual names; the candidates were declared elected (for a six-year tenure) according to their position on the list, beginning with the name at the top. Our district sent three deputies to the Chamber. Honza's boss, heading the National-Socialist list, solemnly professed to be sure of 'his people.' My boss, the district's Social-Democrat candidate Number 1 just as solemnly declared his unabashed confidence in the 'sound political judgment of the voters.' Our bosses had long ceased to be on speaking terms. This did not keep Honza and me from getting together in inconspicuous spots to map out our own election strategy. We agreed that it did not matter which one of our bosses got re-elected as long as the Sudeten-German (Henlein) Party did not get three Chamber seats. The Nazis had become alarmingly active in the past six months. They had strong slogans, the support of many disgruntled elements, and unlimited campaign funds. The Sudeten-German candidates were strange, rugged characters, smelling of beer, with scars all over their faces. Some of them wore chamois leather trousers, edelweiss suspenders, and white woolen knee stockings, like members of an Alpine Singing-and-Wrestling Society. They thought the general elections were a Turn-Fest. They marched in formations from and to their meetings, goose-stepping, shouting at the top of their lungs.

The newspapers predicted that the strength of the parties would become apparent on the eve of the election, when the district's three major parties, the Czech National-Socialists, the Czech Social-Democrats, and the Sudeten-Germans had their last-minute public meetings in neighboring places. In order to avoid collisions the police set the hour for the German meeting at seven o'clock. The two Czech meetings were to begin an hour later.

At half-past seven I passed by the large beer-garden, meeting-place of the Sudeten-German fascists. The place was protected by a dense cordon of stolid Czech policemen, but apparently it was the Czech people who needed protection. Sturdy young Nordic men, with a fanatic, bloodthirsty look in their eyes, were patrolling all entrances. Girls in dirndl dresses distributed leaflets and bachelor's-buttons, the unofficial 'party-badges,' the swastika being forbidden. From the garden came sharp, staccato sounds, 'Sieg-Heil! Sieg-Heil!' twenty or thirty times in a row. I saw a sea of flags and giant pictures of the Nazi party leaders.

At the concert hall where the Czech Social-Democrats had their meetings, the mood was sober, businesslike. People in small groups were discussing the elections, reading newspapers, or just waiting. A large Czechoslovak flag covered the rear of the platform. Backstage, my boss, surrounded by party men, was studying his speech, on which he and I had worked for the past two days. Local party functionaries came in and the deputy shook hands with them and said that the ultimate victory of the Social-Democrats was assured, but from the way he twirled his mustache, I knew that he was worried. He told me to take a copy of his speech to the near-by Social-Democrat newspaper. 'They must not cut a single line,' my boss said, pointedly. I left, passing the National-Socialist Party building, where Honza's people had their meeting. Honza was not there. His boss, the leading candidate, was pacing the corridor in excitement. Somebody told me that he was waiting for Honza and the manuscript of his speech.

I met Honza in front of the newspaper building. He was perspiring and out of breath. 'Something terrible has happened,' he said. 'I lost the manuscript of the deputy's speech. I wrote it last night and had to make certain changes this afternoon and now . . .' He shrugged helplessly. Two Social-Democrat Party officers passed by. They looked shocked when they saw me talking to Honza. We stepped into the telephone booth near the entrance of the newspaper building and Honza told me his story. It was the girls, as usual. This last one was a red-head, and terrific. She had called him up and asked him to take her out for a ride in his open car. 'I couldn't say No,' Honza said. 'No one could, to her. I got the car and we rode through the Park. I had my briefcase with the manuscript of the speech on the front seat between us. Later she moved over to me. I shoved the briefcase to the edge of her seat.' Honza sighed deeply and his face became clouded with gloom. 'When we came back, an hour ago, the briefcase was gone. Fell out of the car, I guess. I looked everywhere, under the seats, inside the car. I drove all the way back. We didn't find it. Bože můj, what am I going to do? The deputy can't improvise. There is no time to write a new speech. The people are waiting. By now the chairman will be introducing the deputy.' Honza dejectedly slumped into a corner of the telephone booth. He looked up at me and saw the script in my hand. I explained that I was about to carry it over to the newspaper office.

Honza grabbed my shoulder. 'You *must* lend me the script,' he said. 'We can leave out the lead paragraphs, change certain expressions, and reshuffle the whole thing. Our parties belong to the government coalition. They have the same political aims. All our speeches are patterned after the same model. No one will notice the similarity.'

I refused. Even a political secretary has a minimum standard of ethics. We looked up. A man carrying in his buttonhole a party badge of the National-Socialists came running toward Honza, gesticulating. The deputy was yelling for his speech, he said. Honza swallowed and said, all right he'd be there in a minute.

From the Nazi beer-garden came shouts and martial music. The meeting was over and the audience formed a column of three and came marching down the street. They carried banners 'Ein Volk, Ein Reich, Ein Führer!' and wildly shouted 'Sieg-Heil!' 'Sieg-Heil!'

A number of tough hombres kept a watchful eye on those who did not show the necessary degree of enthusiasm. The Czech passers-by on the street stopped, their faces blank with bewilderment. Honza pointed at the weird procession. 'I don't care what happens to the deputy or to me, for that matter,' he said. 'I can always get another job. But look at them. Unless we stick together, they are going to get the three seats in the Chamber.'

I motioned Honza to follow me. We entered the newspaper building. To the left was a small empty library. We sat down and went over my manuscript. It was what we secretaries called the 'standard election speech,' promises of steady employment and opportunities for all, fruitful co-operation between country and city folk, lower income taxes for the working class; broad, indefinite pledges of social betterment, higher standard of living; mild criticism of the Agrarian, National-Socialist, and other government-coalition parties; violent attacks against the Sudeten-German fascists. We left out the first two paragraphs which contained specific local references and started with the fifth paragraph, Honza writing a new lead sentence. I reshuffled the paragraphs that followed and Honza crossed out such passages as 'future of Social-Democrat Party,' and 'interest of the exploited working class,' and put in 'future of the National-Socialist Party,' and 'interests of the underpaid government employees.' All high-sounding phrases such as 'Let's face the magnitude of our task,' 'improved economic adjustment for all,' were left in. We glued the pieces together, working hard and fast. It was almost eight o'clock. Honza grabbed the script and hurried away.

Honza's boss and my deputy were re-elected the next day, with the third Parliament seat going to a Sudeten-German. The newspapers said that the 'powerful speeches of the Czech candidates on the eve of the election' prevented the Sudeten-Germans from getting control of the district.

Chapter 12

ASSISTANT CROUPIER

THE SUN never shines for a night-club musician. When I worked in the boîtes de nuit and music-halls of Paris, in the cold, damp winter of 1929, I did not see the sun for three months. I came back from work in the dismal darkness before dawn when no one but the sullen old street-cleaners were around and the gaiety of another Parisian night was being swept into the gutter. I slept all day long and left my hotel at suppertime. The street lights were already reflected by the pools on the sidewalk, and I still felt tired. Possibly there was some life going on in Montmartre during the day, but all I knew were the night-shift people — the waiters at Dupont's coming to work at seven, the magnificently clad doormen of the Pigalle restaurants, the night policemen and the busy little girls, their high heels clicking a staccato d'amore on the asphalt of the Boulevard de Clichy.

One morning toward spring I had to get up at eleven o'clock to have my carte d'identité renewed at the Préfecture de Police. Montmartre seemed a strangely alien place. The bartender at Dupont's put sugar into my coffee, which none of the night men would have done; the women on the Boulevard de Clichy were dull little housewives, carrying yards of white bread and fresh vegetables in their market baskets; the

micky strobel

cafés, boîtes, shooting galleries, theaters seemed to have vanished overnight, and in their stead there were grocers' stores, wineshops, a second-hand furniture store, a haberdasher, and a bureau de poste. A fine thin rain soaked my overcoat and dripped from my hatbrim, and of a sudden I became terribly sick for the sun. I went to the Préfecture and from there to the Café des Quat'z' Arts where I had an interview with Monsieur Delacorte, a slick-faced, prosperous man from the Midi who was reportedly hiring musicians for the orchestra of the Casino de la Jetée in Nice. The next day, after a short audition at Monsieur Delacorte's office, I was hired as a first violinist, at two thousand francs a month. My salary was to start upon arrival in Nice, but Delacorte wanted his ten per cent commission at once. I convinced him, after an unpleasant quarter-hour, that I needed money for my traveling expenses and he agreed to accept a down payment of fifty francs, instead of the whole two hundred.

The skies over Nice looked even more azure than in the travel folders and little high-lights were dancing on top of the Mediterranean, for the benefit of the promenade photographers. The Promenade des Anglais was bathed in glaring, white sunlight. At the Casino de la Jetée I was informed by Monsieur Michel, a swarthy, choleric, flat-footed man, that I would not get the promised job. There had been a change of conductors in the past few days and Monsieur Delacorte had acted without authority. Monsieur Michel casually introduced himself as the new conductor and said that he had already filled all vacancies with his own men.

I threatened to bring this story to the attention of the Syndicat des Musiciens. At that Monsieur Michel shifted into friendly gear and invited me to give an audition, which turned out so well that he asked me to appear as soloist with the Jetée orchestra at the next concert symphonique. We agreed on the Mendelssohn violin concerto. The remuneration would be 'nominal,' Monsieur Michel said apologetically, a mere five hundred francs, but think of the prestige! As an afterthought he assured me that my picture would be printed on all the bills. I spent the next few days practicing the concerto, rehearsing at the Jetée, and wandering through the sunny streets of Nice, looking at my bills, 'CONCERT SYMPHONIQUE, Soloiste: M. JOSEPH WECHSBERG (Prix de Prague).' The notices also carried my picture, but it could not have been very good, since no one recognized me, though I spent a good deal of time standing casually juxtaposed to it. The 'Prix de Prague' was an invention by Monsieur Michel, who was not in the least apologetic. 'You've got to have a Prix,' he said. 'Absolument!'

I lived in a little room at the apartment of a Mr. Zapletal, in the old Riquier district. Zapletal was a croupier at the Casino Municipal, on Place Masséna; I had met him through a croupier at the Jetée. He was Czechoslovak — as I was myself in those days — an anemic, sickly man in his fifties, thin as a tailor in a Wilhelm Busch drawing, and he always wore clothes two sizes too large, so you were constantly worried lest he fall out of his suit at the slightest provocation. His face was pale and all bones, and his eyes were deep-set. He lived at the Côte on account of his lungs; at night he was often shaken by a soft, dry cough. He ate his meals in a little restaurant near the Place Garibaldi, where a Czech cook made him his favorite Czech dishes, thick potato soup, heavy with parsley and laurel leaves, or roast pork with dumplings and zelí (sauerkraut). After déjeuner he ordered four koláče, the famous Czech raised-dough cakes, filled with cottage cheese or with povidle (plum marmalade), which he took home and ate at night when he came back from work at the Casino. My room was small and very cold, since it had a stone floor and no heat whatsoever, but my landlord made up for these shortcomings by sharing with me the strong, thick coffee which he brewed every night, and his koláče.

Zapletal hated being a croupier. His true avocation was interpreting his and other people's dreams. He spent hours studying the '*Old Egyptian Dream Book*, edited and translated by Jar. Voženílek,' a bulky, dusty, worm-eaten, volume which interpreted the most unaccountable dreams and night visions. He was in constant demand among his fellow-croupiers' wives, whose dreams of dirty water meant babies; fire (bright flames) and smoke he interpreted as meaning, respectively, trouble, malicious gossip, joy, and sickness. On the night before my concert at the Jetée, Zapletal dreamed of a blond girl sitting on the beach and woke me up in the middle of the night to tell me that, according to the dream book, a blond in a bathing-suit meant 'hope for successful achievement.'

Zapletal made far-reaching arrangements, which involved changing practically all the croupiers' schedules at the Casino Municipal, so he could get the evening of my concert off and hear me. He accompanied me to the Jetée and went down to his front-row seat, which he had bought a few days before. The Casino de la Jetée, a hideous parvenu structure, was built out over the sea on steel piles. It had a large music-hall, with a stage for theatrical and concert performances, and a number of dining-rooms, terraces, balconies, and gaming-rooms. The audience consisted of hard-of-hearing old ladies, Niçoises who came there to play boule because the admission fee was only three francs, and bewildered tourists who did not know a better place to go. On the afternoon of the concert symphonique there had been a ballet performance of 'Scheherazade' by a group of exiles from the St. Petersburg Opera. Toward the end of the ballet, the antediluvian backstage machinery and footlights switchboard had broken down and 'Scheherazade' had wound up in mystic Arabian darkness. By eight-thirty, when the symphony concert was to begin, the stage lights still were not fixed. The electrician had not returned from his dinner, which, all Frenchmen present agreed, was more important than a few silly stage lights. Monsieur Michel decided that the orchestra would remain in the pit, where the lights were functioning, and I would play standing on the edge of the stage, my feet almost touching his head. The solo flautist and one of the viola-players, who were amateur electricians, set up three powerful lamps in the orchestra pit, tilted so that their beams were thrown up at me. When I came out on the stage, there was a frightened hush and two ladies with young children made a hasty exit. Later, the members of the orchestra told me that the powerful lights shining upon me from below had made my face appear contorted into a ghastly grimace. One of them said that with deep shadows under my eyes, my teeth eerily illuminated, and a violin under my chin, I looked like a perfect facsimile of the Phantom of the Opera. As I played, my super-dimensional shadow danced in grotesque leaps on the backdrops.

Nobody had bothered to put away the 'Scheherazade' scenery, so I played the Mendelssohn concerto standing in a sultry, exotic harem, amidst Oriental pillows, Persian rugs, and large, voluptuous divans. I had a tough time keeping up with the orchestra, which I could hardly hear, it being far below, but Monsieur Michel did an excellent job of holding us all together, and the impression on the audience seemed to be satisfactory. There was warm applause at the end and the violinists in the pit tapped the backs of their instruments with their bows. Monsieur Michel smiled and beckoned me to play Sarasate's 'Romance Andalouse,' which I had optimistically been working on as an encore.

Backstage, after the performance, Monsieur Michel embraced me and took me to his room, where he made me sit down on a chair which, he said, had been occupied by Rachmaninoff, Kreisler, and Casals. A number of people were already there and a few members of the orchestra dropped in to shake hands with me. Zapletal also came in, very happy and excited. Being a croupier, he knew everybody on the Côte, and he presented me to the music critic of the Eclaireur de Nice et du Sud-Ouest, a compact, bald, intense man chewing a dead cigarette. The critic coolly ignored Monsieur Michel and said to me, 'C'était excellent. Vous avez un beau violon.' He asked me whether it was insured by Lloyds' and seemed disappointed when I said it was not insured at all. He inquired whether Prague was the capital of Jugoslavia and made notes on a grease-stained menu. At the end of the interview, the music critic said, 'Any quotation?' I said I thought that the orchestra under Monsieur Michel had done a fine job. The music critic shrugged indifferently and walked out without saying goodbye, and Michel said, 'Espèce de salaud.'

A little later, there was a commotion at the door, and a girl and a man came in. The girl, blond, cool, and bored to death, looked as though she had just walked out of the latest copy of *Harper's Bazaar*. Her first name was Diana and she was from New York. Michel introduced her to me as 'our ice-cream queen.' 'Every day thirty million Americans eat her father's ice cream,' he said. The girl smiled and said, 'Thirty-three million, my dear Michel,' and went over to shake hands with Zapletal, who looked flustered. The girl's companion was a tall, urbane fellow, with oily black hair, bushy eyebrows, and long hands, which he threw around like a tenor singing a Verdi aria. He had the face of a handsome seal, and in his right eye carried a monocle which he dropped casually into his hand every time he started to speak. He wore the resplendent uniform of a captain of the Hungarian hussars — red trousers, blue dolman, and shining black boots. He said, 'Magnificent, Meister! Zee second movement was magnificent, zank you very moch.' He had a thick, singing Hungarian accent and showed the condescending smile of a country squire addressing his chief forester. 'It seems to me zat I heard you a few months ago at zee Grosser Konzerthaussaal in Vienna, or was it in Paris?' Without waiting for me to answer, he bowed deeply over the girl's hand and kissed her fingertips with an old-world grandezza. 'You look great tonight, drágám [darling],' he said. He was Baron Kallay Lászlo. Somewhere I had read that he was the only Hungarian on the Côte d'Azur who hated paprika schnitzel, paprika chicken, stuffed paprika, and paprika in any other form.

The Baron stepped to the door, put the second and third fingers of his left hand into his mouth, and produced a shrill whistle. A small man with the face of a rejuvenated Disney dwarf came in. He wore a light-gray chauffeur's uniform and carried a silver bucket containing a bottle of champagne in one hand and a tray with glasses in the other. 'A little celebration, my friends,' the Baron said. 'From my own winery in beautiful Hungary. Zank you very moch.' He filled the glasses and gallantly kissed the girl's hand again. 'To your continued success, Meister,' he said to me. 'Prosit! Let's drink pertu and be brothers!' We linked arms and drained our glasses, which meant that from then on we would address each other by the brotherly 'thou.' The Baron said 'Szervusz!' and I said 'Szervusz,' faute de mieux. Zapletal did not drink. He smiled at the girl, bowed stiffly, and walked out of the room.

Later that night, when I came home after the 'little celebration,' Zapletal explained his brusque attitude. He disapproved of the Baron. Through his private intelligence system of fellow croupiers, waiters, chauffeurs, policemen, and washroom attendants, Zapletal knew that the Baron was in debt and persona non grata at the Cercle Privé of the Casino in Monte Carlo; that he had moved into a suite at the Ruhl, on the same floor as the ice-cream queen; that he had brought with him seven uniforms, some no longer in use by the Hungarian army; that he changed his clothes three to four times a day; and that he dyed his hair. He was always accompanied by the dwarf-like man, his combination valet-chauffeur-nursemaid, who was called Hercules by the Ruhl people after they discovered that he carried the Baron's two hundred and thirty pounds upstairs, on his shoulders, whenever the Baron was drunk and unable to proceed under his own power. After putting his master to bed, Hercules would take some bills out of the Baron's pockets and go out and get drunk himself, whereupon he would get into a fight with Larrabée, the Ruhl's

night watchman, a husky, macabre fellow who always beat him up and threatened to kill the 'small, half-crunched bed-bug.'

It was no secret to Zapletal or anybody else that the Baron was trying hard to sweep the ice-cream queen off her feet. Every evening he came to the Casino Municipal with Diana. Three steps to the rear and one to the left walked Hercules, carrying Diana's sable coat and his master's magnificent tóga. The couple sat down at Zapletal's table and the Baron played his five-franc stakes with the casual grandeur of a man who has his yacht waiting in the harbor of Monaco and can afford to lose half a million francs in a single night. He never dropped a tip in the croupier's slot. 'He's a fake,' said Zapletal, who was usually reserved in his judgment of people. 'He's after her money. As soon as he gets his future father-in-law to give him a down payment on the dower, he'll beat up his wife and spend his evenings out with a second-rate chorus girl. Diana's too good for him.' He shrugged. 'I tried to warn her. I met her on the Promenade des Anglais this morning, and she told me that last night she dreamed she was being married to the Hungarian. I told her that a wedding ceremony means bad luck in love. But she just kept sighing and saying, "He's so sweet."' Zapletal sighed, and abruptly uttered a Czech curse. I could not help suspecting that he himself was in love with the ice-cream queen. He sighed again and resumed reading the 'Old Egyptian Dream Book.'

At that time the salles de jeux of the Casino Municipal had ten or twelve boule tables and several roulette tables. Unlike the casino at Monte Carlo, where there was a croupier on each side of the wheel and one at each end of the table, and a head croupier on a high chair behind the wheel croupiers, at the Casino Municipal each table had only one croupier, who spun the wheel and paid out the winnings, and an assistant croupier at the other end of the table. The tables were supervised by a chef croupier. The minimum stake of one franc (then four cents) and the small admission fee made the Municipal a poor man's Monte Carlo.

One afternoon shortly after my concert performance, Zapletal called me up at home and asked me to join him at the croupiers' room at the Casino, telling me that a wave of influenza had severely cut down the Casino's operating staff and offering me a temporary job as assistant croupier. He said that my 'character' had already been investigated secretly by the Casino's agents and that a few minutes' instruction in psychology was all I needed. I would, of course, get a smaller salary than the French croupiers, but that was nothing unusual.

I needed a job, since the concert had not brought any offer from a local impresario, so I went over to the Casino and met Zapletal. 'Don't worry about your duties,' he said. 'We'll tell you everything in a few words. You have the solid, serious look that is all-important, you own a double-breasted blue suit, and the directeur s'en fiche, and, besides, the controlleurs have the grippe, too.' I said that my arithmetic began and ended with the multiplication table, but Zapletal shrugged impatiently and took me to the head croupier, a fish-eyed man with a large skull and a black Lenin beard, who X-rayed me with his eyes and proceeded to give me a blitz course in how to be a croupier. 'Never observe the players' hands; always observe their faces,' the head croupier said. 'Try to look polite, yet forbidding. The assistant croupier is there merely to frighten people.' Finally, he taught me some of the finger signals between croupier and assistant croupier. Right-hand thumb touching the forefinger meant 'O.K.' Left forefinger pointed down, 'Caution.' Small finger of left hand pointed toward a player, 'Watch this person.' And so on. The signs were changed every month because it took the players only that long to catch on.

For over a week I worked at Zapletal's roulette table as assistant croupier, helping the players make their bets, discouraging them from trying to claim other people's money, and, in general, looking 'polite, yet forbidding.' Two frequent guests at our table were the Hungarian Baron and the ice-cream queen. The Baron never bothered to recognize me, though we had drunk pertu and were supposed to be brothers. He played a cautious game, staking five-franc jetons, intermittently kissing the girl's hands and murmuring 'Drágám.' I could hear Zapletal sigh as he said, 'Messieurs, faites vos jeux.'

My own private damnation was a fat, muscular woman of forty-five, who appeared every night at eight and for two hours did a tightrope walk on my nerves. She looked like the yelling ladies who flutter across the stage in the third act of 'Die Walküre.' She had enormous arms, rough, pointed elbows, and, from the side, resembled a lobster. She carried a heavy black parasol, which she used to shove her stakes all over the table. She always occupied the chair next to where I stood and before every stake pinched my arm or pushed her elbow between my ribs in order to get my undivided attention for her bets. Once, in Monte Carlo, she had been cheated out of a winning by a croupier's oversight and she was determined that no such thing would ever happen again. She played in a confusing fashion on quatre premiers, 0, 1, 2, 3, milieu, the second dozen, en plein, and single numbers.

All, however, went well until one evening when the Baron and the ice-cream queen sat down next to the lobster woman. The Baron smelled of brandy and kissed the girl's bare shoulder from time to time. He was in a splendid mood and made a few caustic remarks about the lobster woman. The ice-cream queen giggled and the lobster woman became red with anger. She seized her parasol and put it menacingly between herself and the Baron. Two English ladies of the rural tea-room variety looked frightened and got up. Zapletal pointed his left forefinger toward the table, meaning, 'Be on your guard!'

The lobster woman staked five francs à cheval, on the line

between 16 and 17. The Baron took a five-franc jeton and placed it on the same line, next to the lobster woman's, ignoring her venomous glance. They lost, and the lobster woman made another bet à cheval, this time on the 11–12 line, followed again by the Baron. They lost again. It is a common superstition among roulette players that being aped brings bad luck. 'Some people here need a nursemaid to make up their minds,' the lobster woman said to me in a loud voice. The ice-cream queen giggled and the Baron deftly dropped his monocle into his hand. I caught another warning signal from Zapletal and began to get nervous.

The lobster woman now began to play an elaborate, bewildering game, making simultaneous bets on passe, impair, rouge, en carré (four numbers), and en plein, apparently trying hard to confuse the Baron and shake him off, but he was on the alert, staking his jetons right and left next to hers. Other people stopped playing and crowded behind the lobster woman's chair. In a last-ditch attempt to outsmart the Baron, she finally resorted to illegal tactics. She placed her stakes and then, when the croupier said, 'Rien ne va plus,' she shoved her jetons to a near-by number. The Baron was just a split second behind her in moving his jetons. The ice-cream queen's face had the catlike, intense expression which you sometimes find on women watching the last round of a prizefight. I was seized by a panicky feeling of approaching doom.

On the next spin of the wheel the lobster woman staked five francs on the line between 8 and 9, followed, as usual, by the Baron. As Zapletal said 'Rien ne va plus,' the lobster woman, with an almost imperceptible movement of her right elbow, shoved her jeton over to the 11–12 line. The Baron's stake remained on the line between 8 and 9. A few seconds later, the ball stopped rolling and fell down into the Number 9 compartment. Zapletal raked in all losses, murmuring, 'Neuf, rouge, impair, et manque.' He counted out eighty-five francs, seventeen times the stake, and shoved the money over to the lobster woman. Before I could say that it was the

Baron's, not the woman's, jeton that had been on Number 9, she seized the money. The Baron jumped up. 'Zat money belongs to me,' he said. 'Zat was my bet on 9.'

A hush fell over the table. Two petites Niçoises exclaimed in delight, sensing a scandal. The lobster woman took her parasol and brought it down hard on the Baron's fingers when he reached for the money. 'Don't you dare!' she yelled. 'He gave it to me.'

The veins began to show on the Baron's forehead. The ice-cream queen, a frightened expression on her face, tried to tug his sleeve, but he was in no chivalrous mood and brusquely pushed her away. 'I'll take zis money, kérem szépen,' he said, with cold determination. 'I'll take it if it's zee last thing I do. Zank you very moch.'

The ice-cream queen said, 'Lászlo, *please!*' but he gave an impatient shrug without bothering to look at her.

There was a strange gleam in Zapletal's eyes as he said, 'Remove your hands, Monsieur. Madame's bet was correct.'

The Baron uttered what sounded like the descendant of a long and lurid line of Hungarian curses and his face took on the color of salmon. The American girl leaned over and whispered something to him, and he turned to her violently and said, 'Shut up!' The hot fighting blood of the fast-riding, paprika-loving Kings of the Magyar steppe was racing through his veins. The ice-cream queen said, 'Lászlo, stop that nonsense!' and when he did not bother to answer, she got up, took her sable coat, and departed. He did not look after her. He was staring like a madman at the lobster woman's hand covering the jetons. Zapletal's voice sounded triumphant as he said to me, 'Please verify Madame's winning, Monsieur.' He held the middle finger of his right hand down, the sign for 'Back me up.' I suddenly felt a lump blocking my throat which prevented me from speaking. I hated myself, but all I could do was nod toward the Baron, indicating my belief that he was the winner.

The lobster woman uttered a short, catlike, high-pitched

snarl. The Baron reached out for the money. The rest was what the Casino would shrug off as 'regrettable incidents of no consequence' and no newspaper along the whole Côte would ever mention, not excluding the always well-informed Eclaireur de Nice et du Sud-Ouest. In the ensuing scramble, the lobster woman's parasol was broken, the Baron lost his monocle, and Hercules had to be knocked down by the Casino guards. Zapletal was shifted to another table, and I was dismissed by the head croupier, before I had a chance to hand in my resignation, and ordered to leave the salles de jeux.

Zapletal came home late that night. He looked tired but very happy. He whistled as he put on the water for the coffee and took out the koláče. 'I spoke to Diana in the lobby of the Ruhl,' he said. 'She leaves tomorrow. *Alone.* She was a little heart-broken, but she will forget. The sooner she learns the facts of life, the better for her.' When the coffee was ready, he cautiously poured two cups and smiled. His thumb touched the forefinger of his right hand, the sign for 'Tout va bien,' or 'O.K.'

Chapter 13

THE JAPANESE EXPERTS

THE S.S. *Porthos*, on which I was once orchestra leader, belonged to the Messageries Maritimes, a government-subsidized, bureaucratically managed steamship line connecting France with her colonial empire in Africa and Asia.

The *Porthos* used to stay eight days in Yokohama, unloading cargo, refueling, taking on food and water for the thirty-eight-day return trip to Marseilles. According to our contract we musicians were supposed to work even in port like the rest of the crew, but the captain, who was musical and our great friend, never invoked the dreaded 'harbor clause.' As soon as the last passengers had got off, we would leave. We returned only at sailing time to play 'Kimi-ga-yo' (Reign of My Sovereign), the Jap national anthem, and the 'Marseillaise.'

One day in September, 1929, we were about to go ashore for our Japanese holiday, when the purser sent for us. It sounded like bad news. Relations between the orchestra and the purser, our immediate superior, had been strained ever since the red-headed art student from Dallas, traveling alone in stateroom Number 7, declined the purser's attentions in favor of Artie, our Yonkers-born pianist.

The purser had opened hostilities by making us play overtime in the crushing heat of the Red Sea, when nobody felt like listening to music, much less dancing. In Colombo he forbade us to go ashore because he knew that the red-head was waiting for Artie at the Galle Face Hotel. In Singapore he refused to give us the customary twenty per cent advance on our salaries. Regulations provided for payment only after our return to Marseilles and we had to borrow from the maître d'hôtel. Sometimes we borrowed from the bartender in First Class or the head cook. All maîtres d'hôtel, stewards, cooks, cabin boys hated the purser for his rigid, un-French attitude. They were on our side.

When the purser barred us from the swimming pool and the First Class bar, we retorted by abruptly changing from waltz to fox-trot and back to waltz time while he danced with our casus belli. A man without a sense of rhythm, he stumbled and stepped on the girl's feet. After this had gone on for some time, she left him in the middle of the dance floor and went back to her seat. The purser ran up to the bridge and informed the captain of our newest crime. The skipper's reprimand, though necessarily firm, was rather perfunctory. The purser came of a French-Colonial family in Saigon, French Indo-China, and the ship's officers, solid bourgeois from the Midi, resented his being too friendly with the Japanese passengers. He had three gents from Mitsubishi Company, Limited, at his table and made it a point never to join the ship's officers at apéritif time. He was a thin-faced, morose man with the anemic complexion and the prematurely aged features of white people in the tropics.

That trip our orchestra consisted of Artie, an easy-going American pianist, myself as orchestra leader and violinist, and Etienne-Marcel, aged sixty-two, a lovable bass-player from Brussels whom I had first met at the Quat'z' Arts Café. Even among the broke-but-cheerful habitués of the Café, Etienne-Marcel was an outstanding character. He carried a bass-bow under his arm, sporting it like a riding-whip. With his mag-

nificent white beard he looked like a reasonably well-done copy of Johannes Brahms. He had visiting cards, 'Etienne-Marcel Brahms, neveu,' which he distributed among unsophisticated audiences. He was a widower, living alone in a small house in one of the steep streets leading up to Sacré Coeur. Once a year he went to Japan to visit his only son, a civil engineer in Tokio, solving the financial problem of ocean travel by taking a job as ship's musician. When the passengers registered surprise at a bass-player instead of a 'cellist working with a three-man-orchestra, Etienne-Marcel would say, 'I have a friend at the hiring bureau. Any bass-player having a friend there is as good as a 'cellist.'

He was immensely popular with the passengers, especially those under seven years of age, for whom he produced eerie *sul ponticello* effects and imitations of the Roaring Lion, the Growling Leopard, and the Howling Tiger on his bass fiddle. But he was a serious-minded fellow when it came to making good music. He played difficult parts at sight from 'cello scores. His great idol was Serge Koussevitsky, a former fellow bass-player. 'I once heard him do Zigeunerweisen on the bull fiddle,' Etienne-Marcel said. 'I was so excited I couldn't sleep for two nights and had to get drunk.'

Etienne-Marcel was the purser's arch-enemy. He had his private fights with him. The climax was reached that day in Yokohama when we were called to the purser's office. He informed us that we were to stay aboard and give a concert of modern music for a party of Japs whom he had invited. Etienne-Marcel was furious. His son had wired that he was to leave for Hokkaido the next day; could father come to Tokio at once? As for Artie, he had a dinner date with the red-headed artist at Tokio's Imperial Hotel. I told the purser that the orchestra never worked in port. If necessary, I added, we'd take the matter to the captain.

'That's too bad,' the purser said, dryly. 'The captain went ashore. He won't be back until tomorrow.' He glanced over our contract which was on his desk. 'Harbor clause, hein?

Unless you are at the music salon at eight-thirty, I'll have you put off for breach of contract. That's all.'

We tried to slip away, but the purser had special sentries posted at all gangways. Artie spent the rest of the afternoon vainly trying to get a long-distance call through to the red-head. Etienne-Marcel was mad and silent.

There were about twenty Japs at the music salon. From every angle they looked like good material for a cartoonist. We saw tuxedos, morning coats, loud tweed suits. A three-hundred-pound specimen with the physique of a Sumo wrestler had on tails. There was the slightly nauseating odor of fish that always hovers over a Jap crowd. An old man in a ceremonial kimono with protruding underdrawers and bare feet in wooden getas was talking to a naval officer who picked his faulty teeth. The little Annamite cabin-boys from Tourist Class were serving trays with Scotch whiskey, Cognac brandy, French wine, Jap Kirin beer.

Etienne-Marcel skillfully held up an Annamite and stored a tray behind his bass. The purser came over for a briefing.

'This is an audience of musical experts,' he said. 'The old gentleman in kimono is Mr. Oshima, editor of *Ongaku-Sekai*, musical monthly. Next to him is Captain Takata, of the Musical Section of the Imperial Household Department. Over there is Professor Ikeda, secretary of Dai-Nippon Composers' Association, talking to Mr. Aoki, of Ryuginsha Publishers. And there are two men from the Osaka Broadcasting Association. I hope you won't disappoint them.'

'What is he up to?' Artie said when the purser had gone back to his guests. 'Does he want to become director of the Tokio School of Music?'

We had two rounds of Cognac behind the bass fiddle and went to work, playing Darius Milhaud's 'Three Rag Caprices' and Debussy's 'Voiles' and 'La Fille aux cheveux de lin,' arranged for small orchestra. The listeners showed the half-bored, impatient attitude of boxing fans during the preliminaries. The applause was lukewarm; a subdued restlessness was about the place. We went out on deck to get some fresh air. Artie lighted a cigarette, gazing across the piers and hangars toward where he thought was the Imperial Hotel and a red-head. Nobody spoke a word. Presently we were joined by the purser. He carried a hand-written score.

'I want you to play this next,' he said airily, trying to sound amiable. 'A simple thing, composed by a friend in Saigon. You won't have any difficulty playing the composition at sight. The audience will be very interested.'

He thrust the music into my hands, leaving me in silent rage. Drawing up the program is the orchestra leader's sacred prerogative. Now a man who scarcely knew the difference between a doorkey and a viola-key was giving orders!

The composition was titled 'Interlude Indochinoise, Arrangement for Small Orchestra,' by Kanji Ueno. Artie whistled softly. Etienne-Marcel said, 'So, we are plugging this piece for his honorable Jap friend, Ueno. Tiens! If that isn't the Bolero!'

We looked at the score. Kanji Ueno had done a good-enough job of camouflage, but the source of his 'Interlude Indochinoise' unmistakably was Ravel's 'Bolero.' The same repetition of a single theme, in unvarying rhythm, becoming a gradual crescendo. Kanji Ueno even used a similar theme.

'Imitating American fountain pens, French vermouth, and Belgian paintings,' Etienne-Marcel said with disgust. 'And now stealing Ravel!' He took the score, tore up the sheets and threw them over the railing.

'Good!' Artie nodded approval. 'And now what?' From the salon the purser beckoned.

We took up our places on the platform. The purser stepped in front of the piano and bowed deeply. 'Gentlemen! I have the honor of bringing to your attention the work of Mr. Kanji Ueno, the young, promising composer living in Saigon. This is the first performance of his new composition "Interlude Indochinoise," arranged for small orchestra.'

There was loud applause. The listeners leaned forward

in their chairs in anticipation of a musical and, above all, patriotic treat. Mr. Oshima, the old man in kimono, slipped off his sandals and pulled up his bare feet under his kimono, playing with his toes in utter concentration.

Etienne-Marcel helped himself to another glass of Cognac and stepped forward. 'Monsieur will permit me to add a few words of admiration,' he said. 'The piece we are going to play, a musical painting of great suggestive force, will give you the thrills of Indo-China's jungles. This discriminating audience will recognize the ultra-modern harmonies and rhythms of this daring creation of the Japanese genius who only recently emerged from obscurity into the light of the appreciation of connoisseurs. I dedicate this first performance to the memory of my immortal uncle, Johannes Brahms.'

There was a moment of stunned silence. Captain Tanaka, of the Imperial Household Department, stopped picking his teeth and said, 'Brahms? Brahms?' Etienne-Marcel stepped down and ceremoniously handed the captain a visiting card. Both men bowed deeply. Mr. Aoki, the music publisher, started writing in a notebook. The purser seemed flabbergasted. Etienne-Marcel, deadpan, came back to the platform. I had a cold, burning feeling inside as though I'd swallowed the sword of Admiral Togo.

'We are playing in C flat, 2/4 time,' Etienne-Marcel whispered. 'Let me do a few solo tricks. I'll give you a sign when to come in. From then on everybody's on his own.'

'But what are we going to play?' Artie asked.

'Just improvise. Ultra-modern, and strictly jungle.'

Artie nodded in delight. Before I could say a word, Etienne-Marcel launched into a sensational glissando, winding up with the Roaring Lion and the Howling Tiger, and throwing in a brand-new sound effect that may have been the Snoring Rhinoceros.

The listeners were transfixed. Etienne-Marcel gave us an imperceptible nod. I took a deep breath, like a parachutist on his first leap, and attacked the key of C flat, with Artie producing a series of rhythmical, discordant clashes that would have made the young Stravinsky turn green with envy. It was unmistakable genius, with perhaps a dash of 'Alexander's Ragtime Band.' We were careful to emphasize a strong rhythm and made frequent changes.

After five minutes of this, I put down my violin and stole a glance at the audience. Mr. Oshima's toes were wriggling, keeping time with the accentuated rhythms of Artie's bass chords. Captain Tanaka absent-mindedly used his toothpick in his wide-open mouth. The music publisher wrote feverishly in his notebook, and the three-hundred-pounder in tail coat slid down from his uncomfortable western chair and crossed his legs in reverse to his thighs.

Some lesser experts in the rear registered complete bewilderment. This music was not to be taken lightly. It was different, ultra-modern, and written by a compatriot. To all appearances our weird improvisation, aided by a little mass suggestion, had caught on.

Then I saw the purser. His wide-open eyes popped out of a bloodless face and his Adam's apple was moving up and down convulsively. He seemed on the verge of collapse. For a moment I was almost sorry for him.

Artie was showing signs of exhaustion, so I adjusted my instrument and took over. Somehow an old Czechoslovak folk-song, 'Téče voda Téče' went through my head — perhaps I had been thinking of home. Idly improvising on the beautiful melody, I was roused by Artie's whispering, 'Are you crazy? Get off that melody!' I changed to the cacophonous sounds of the Indo-Chinese jungle, and just in time, for some listeners seemed to be getting suspicious. Joined by Artie and Etienne-Marcel, I went into a fortissimo climax. We ended with an impressive C major whole-tone scale, in unison.

The audience burst into wild applause, Captain Tanaka crying, 'Banzai!' The fat man on the floor pounded on his chair. I bowed, modestly, and Etienne-Marcel and Artie bowed with me. It was too bad that Kanji Ueno from Saigon was not here to enjoy the greatest triumph of his career.

The purser seized my wrist. 'I'll put you into the brig,' he muttered. His hands were wet. He seemed to have aged in the past quarter hour. 'I'll blacklist you from the entire French Merchant Marine and ——'

'Pardon me,' Mr. Aoki, the music publisher interrupted. 'Congratulations, Monsieur le Commissaire for bringing to our attention a most gifted Japanese composer. And to you, gentlemen, for excellent rendition of most difficult composition. Altogether from memory. Truly astounding! May I see score, please?'

'Sorry, we don't have it,' Etienne-Marcel said, wiping his forehead. 'We studied the piece in manuscript with Mr. Ueno.'

'Monsieur le commissaire will undoubtedly be able to get you the score from Mr. Ueno,' Artie added politely.

'I shall be deeply obliged,' the publisher said to the purser, who snapped for air and nodded, unable to say a word.

The old fellow in kimono showered me with a torrent of Japanese words, fanning himself with his derby.

'Mr. Oshima requests humbly you repeat second part,' the publisher translated. 'Most beautiful melody, he thinks.'

'Yes,' several voices cried. 'Please repeat. Encore, encore.'

I explained, regretfully and truthfully, that we were completely exhausted. Mr. Oshima's parchment-colored face was twisted in an ugly grimace of disappointment. Two young men pushed forward, hissing through their teeth as they asked Etienne-Marcel for his autograph. He signed Etienne-Marcel Brahms, neveu. At last we were able to dodge further enthusiasm and left.

The purser was waiting outside. 'You are confined to your quarters until the captain returns,' he said, hoarsely.

I had my answer ready. 'Certainly. We'll just go in there for a moment and Etienne-Marcel will make another speech.'

He swallowed hard and ran his trembling fingers through

his hair. 'Get off the ship,' he finally said. 'Perhaps you'll get run over in Tokio.'

The following day the music-conscious *Jiji Shimpo* carried a two-column story of the 'sensational première.' Reporters called me up at the Imperial asking details about Kanji Ueno. I sent them to the purser. Mr. Aoki announced that his publishing firm was honored to bring out 'Interlude Indochinoise.' The Central Symphony Orchestra was reported interested in the score and the Osaka Broadcasting Association cabled to Kanji Ueno, offering him the job of music director. Captain Tanaka told the *Jiji Shimpo* a Japanese order was to be awarded to the purser.

On the trip back the purser never called us into his office. In Marseilles he requested to be transferred to another liner. We never saw him again.

A few months later, I met Etienne-Marcel at the Quat'z' Arts in Paris. He showed me the newly published score of 'Interlude Indochinoise' by Kanji Ueno which he had just received from his son in Tokio. There was no trace of Ravel's 'Bolero.' This time the Honorable Ueno's inspiration could clearly be traced back to Claude Debussy's 'Afternoon of a Faun.'

Chapter 14

ANYBODY SEE A VIOLIN IN DJIBOUTI?

PERHAPS the most engaging character aboard the *Porthos* was the printer, the man who printed the menu cards, music programs, and the ship's newspaper, and in addition was an honorary orderly to the musicians. He carried our cymbals, and other percussion instruments, set up the music stands and chairs, and shoved the piano across the promenade deck from port to starboard or vice versa, depending on the direction of the wind. His first name was Jean-Jacques. He was a thin-shouldered fellow with hungry eyes and an open, eager face covered with pimples. He tried hard to make us believe that he was almost nineteen, but everybody in the crew knew that he was certainly no older than seventeen. He had run away from his bourgeois home in Marseilles, in best Jack London fashion, to become a member of the merchant marine and lead a glorious, if at times dull, life on the high seas.

Jean-Jacques' burning ambition was to play the drums during the dancing every night from nine to eleven. Occasionally our second-violin player, who also acted as drummer, took time off for a smoke, letting Jean-Jacques work on the percussion instruments. The printer performed his assignment with more zeal than rhythm. His offbeat was elastic, to say the least. Anything more complicated than two-eight time was beyond him and his syncopation sounded like the trot of a limping dromedary.

On one voyage that summer, our orchestra consisted of four men instead of the usual three. Besides myself, there were Dimitrij, the highly unstable pianist I had known on *La Bourdonnais;* Gaston, a hot-tempered, walrus-mustached little Frenchman from Toulon, who played second violin; and Herr Müllenhoff, an elderly 'cello-player from Magdeburg, a sharp-featured, thin-lipped man with cropped hair the color of moldy straw, a pince-nez hanging on a black cord, and a vehement Teutonic inferiority-and-persecution complex. Herr Müllenhoff, who called himself 'staatlich geprüfter Professor für 'Cello und andere Streichinstrumente,' complained bitterly about the Berliner Philharmoniker, which he would have joined if he had not been the victim of a nerve-racking plot, the details of which he did not reveal. He was equally vague about how he had come to Marseilles and about why he had been fired by the Grand Hôtel Noailles et Métropole, on the Cannebière, before the steamship line's impresario had hired him.

Herr Müllenhoff caused trouble from the very beginning. No sooner had he set foot aboard than he told everybody that the *Porthos*, prior to the infamy of Versailles, had been a proud German liner and that the French were playing havoc with her. A seaman retorted with an upper cut which did not keep Herr Müllenhoff quiet long. Underneath the metal nameplate of the French firm which had outfitted the *Porthos*, he wrote in Gothic letters, 'Made in Germany.' On the second day Müllenhoff and Gaston, our little French violin-player, got into a terrible argument which started over the innocent question of whether Eugène Ysaye's or Joseph Joachim's style of bowing was superior and wound up with the pair beating each other up on the cabin floor. (Herr Müllenhoff was a Kriegsfreiwilliger, a volunteer, of 1914; in the same year Gaston's father, a poilu, had fallen at Ypres.) Dimitrij, a sensitive personality, had departed as soon as the fighting started, and I was wondering just how to stop the mêlée when, fortunately, Jean-Jacques arrived with the proofs of the next day's program. He dived into the arena with an adolescent's disregard for personal safety and separated the fighters.

At the evening concert Gaston refused to sit next to Müllenhoff and the 'Professor' made it a point not to join in while we were playing Bizet's 'L'Arlésienne,' which is almost a national anthem to music-loving Frenchmen. Next morning Müllenhoff put soap on the pegs of Gaston's violin and during the apéritif concert Gaston had a terrible time with his strings going down all the time. Dimitrij, who showed keen appreciation of Anglo-Saxon customs such as poker, Scotch whiskey, and turkey dinners, began to take bets on who would be killed first, Gaston or Müllenhoff. Then, to my great relief, Gaston deserted in Port Said, the first stop. Musicians who jump ship are an orchestra leader's worst headache, there being no possibility of picking up replacements in the tropical latitudes, but anything was better than a continual fist-fight.

I waited until we had left Suez, and then reported Gaston's desertion to the captain. He wanted to turn back and pick him up, but I told him that the second violinist was not essential at the apéritif and afternoon concert, and that at night, when we played dance music, Jean-Jacques could take over the drums. It was decided that he would get two hundred francs a month extra for his musical labors. Jean-Jacques was overjoyed. He had to get up at four o'clock to print his menu cards, and never went to bed before midnight, but at seventeen you don't worry about too little sleep.

It was July and we were in the Red Sea, working five hours a day, which is something Dante never thought of. Veteran ship's musicians, unperturbed by spells of fog on the North Atlantic or typhoons in the South Seas, shun the Far Eastern routes and break into a sweat at the mere mention of the Red Sea in summer. There was a dire need of breathable air. Drops of water formed on our instruments. The finger-board

of my violin became a slide on which my left hand performed cacophonous glissandi; the hairs of my bow were soaked and oily in spite of heavy colophaning. Everybody but Müllenhoff complained bitterly about cette sale chaleur. The 'Professor' played on doggedly with a masochistic complacency, while the sweat ran down under his stiff collar.

I had been warned by fellow violinists to take special care of my instrument in the Red Sea, the humidity being disastrous to the glue that holds a violin together. After each performance I wrapped it in heavy oilcloth and put it in its wooden case, and every night Jean-Jacques carried the case down to the vegetable refrigeration chamber, where he placed it between heads of lettuce and spinach, the most appropriate spot we had found after a number of experiments.

The passengers were a dull assortment of dried-out French colonial officials, bearded missionaries, and three or four matrons from Saigon and the French Settlement in Shanghai who were in desperate search of a good time. The ship's leading beauty was a charming, vivacious brunette called Yvonne. She had slim legs, sensual lips, and plenty of that certain something in her eyes. Even the Saigon matrons could have found nothing wrong with Yvonne — except that she dressed a bit daringly, wore too-high heels and stockings a shade too dark — if she had not talked. Yvonne, very Parisienne and as reticent as a barroom juke box, went around spreading contes drolatiques about her past which admittedly began at the toilet-goods counter of Le Bon Marché. After a number of shocking interludes, she landed at the Folies-Bergères, where she worked first as chorus girl and later in the galerie, the horseshoe-shaped promenade, in the rear of the fauteuils, where enterprising gentlemen of taste had no difficulty in finding charming company. In the galerie Yvonne made the acquaintance of Monsieur Jérôme, a high-ranking councillor at the court of the Emperor of Abyssinia. In due course, the gentleman proposed to her. 'He's good-looking, in a patriarchal way,' Yvonne said. 'He has a wonderful gray beard and is very smooth. He'll meet me in Djibouti and we'll go to Addis Ababa where the wedding will be. A couple of princes and lots of native sheiks will attend. I've bought the most gorgeous sky-blue outfit at Worth's. I don't like white. These days, everybody has white.'

Every afternoon at apéritif time Yvonne came down to our two connecting staterooms with a bottle of Cinzano, Byrrh, or Dubonnet. Dimitrij would wash out some glasses and we would have a couple of apéritifs. Dimitrij had been a pianist at the Folies-Bergères and I had worked there as an usher before I began my musical career. We exchanged reminiscences, Yvonne punctuating her stories with sprays of crystal-clear laughter. Müllenhoff always remained in the adjoining room, shocked and sulking, but Jean-Jacques came in whenever he had a chance. He would sit down on a pile of music and stare at Yvonne in deep enchantment.

It was inevitable that our little printer should fall in love with Yvonne, just as in a very bad movie. He stayed up all one night printing a special music program for Yvonne and next morning shoved it under her door. It contained the following poem:

> Oh! comme tu nagéais, jeune, ardente et féconde,
> Dans ces flots immortels chers à la volupté!
> Comme tu fleurissais sur la neige de l'onde!

Yvonne thought it was a beautiful poem and cried as she read it to us in my stateroom that afternoon. When Jean-Jacques came in, she kissed him gently on his eyes. Jean-Jacques blushed and almost died of happiness. That night he printed a special menu for Yvonne which said, under 'Café — Thé — Instant Postum':

> Plongez, de larmes arrosées,
> Dans l'océan mystérieux,
> Je t'aime, Yvonne, je t'aime!

But in his Euphoria he printed the lines on all the other menu cards also, which caused quite a stir among the Saigon matrons at breakfast.

The evening before we arrived at Djibouti, where Yvonne was to get off, Jean-Jacques was worse than ever. He ruined the 'Fledermaus' waltz by beating two-eight time, and did not take his eyes off Yvonne dancing by in the arms of other men. After the dance he waited for her. They walked up and down on the promenade deck where the lights were dim. Not wanting to intrude, I reminded Jean-Jacques to carry my violin down to the refrigeration chamber, as usual, and went to bed.

I did not sleep much that night, the heat being intolerable, and I came up on deck early next morning. The violin case was still lying on the piano, exactly where I had left it. I opened the case and gasped. All that was left of my instrument was a pile of thin wooden boards, dead and desolate. In the humid, intense heat the glue had melted and the violin fallen apart like a house of cards. It had been a medium-priced Bavarian (Mittenwald) violin, but it was not that that mattered. It was like the sudden departure of a very dear person. It was, in fact, a tragedy.

Jean-Jacques broke down and confessed. He had walked on the promenade deck with Yvonne, holding her hands and feeling 'the passionate rhythm of her heart.' She kissed him — and the world had spun in a whirl of crazy spirals. He cried and said he was going to jump overboard, life without Yvonne being not worth living, and then he told me that the poems were not his. He had copied them from Leconte de Lisle's *Poèmes Barbares,* which he had found in the library. Only the line, 'Je t'aime, Yvonne,' was original — and true.

I told him to shut up and we went down to look for another violin. In the crew's quarters we were offered two harmonicas, one guitar, one saxophone, two banjos, and one piccolo, but no violin. The purser told me to find a violin in Djibouti or not to come back to the ship.

The *Porthos* dropped anchor off Djibouti shortly after dusk, and a flotilla of launches assembled around her. First to pull up to the gangway was a large, beautiful boat flying the tricolor, and carrying the port authorities and two other figures, an officer in smartly tailored shirt and shorts, and a distinguished-looking gentleman in a Palm Beach suit who held an enormous bouquet of red roses. He climbed aboard, was introduced as the Governor's secretary, and presented the roses to Yvonne with the compliments of her fiancé, who unfortunately was unable to come to Djibouti and was awaiting her in Addis Ababa. One of the Saigon matrons whispered, her voice dripping with venom, 'Probably Persian roses, brought this morning by special plane in an ice-filled box.' Yvonne kissed us good-bye and was whisked off in the official launch. An hour later the rank-and-file passengers were allowed to go ashore, and we musicians followed them.

The moon shone palely in the heavy, moist air. The hot sand on the causeway radiated the day's heat. We walked past the salt mines and little Danakil gamins sleeping in the sand. Müllenhoff, in splendid isolation, stalked behind us carrying a cane with an ivory knob and wearing a high, old-fashioned, tropical helmet. He had bought it in a port, which, he remarked grimly, would sometime again be in Deutsch-Ostafrika. In the French district of the town two barefooted shadows, wearing white trousers and torn shirts, emerged from the darkness and, in seven different languages, promised us 'les plaisirs de nirvana' if we consented to follow them. It was hard to get rid of them, so I asked them if they had seen anybody with a violin. They muttered a few choice maledictions and departed.

Place Ménélik was a ghost square as always — a disorderly conglomeration of tall, dead, blind buildings, where phantom-like silhouettes moved silently under the arched colonnades. The lights of Pierre's cavernous shop were on. There you could get Scotch whiskey, French brandy, American gin, and Spanish sherry at fantastically low prices, Djibouti being a free port. The only problem was getting the verboten bottles aboard ship, but this could hardly defeat a man reared in customs-wise Central Europe. I happened to know that our cabin steward was a pal of the customs official. We bought a dozen bottles of Cognac and whiskey. Then I asked Pierre where I could get a violin. He gave me a quizzical look. 'Did you lose your helmet while walking across the square in the sun?' he asked. He shrugged and sighed in deep disgust. 'Tout le monde est cinglé à Djibouti!'

At the near-by café, I inquired again but nobody had heard of one. The nearest violin east of Suez was reputedly at Addis Ababa, where they had a night-club, but the next train would not leave for two days. We went to the Officers' Club, the railroad station, and half a dozen other places, and finally came back to the café, exhausted and still minus a violin, where we found Müllenhoff behind a battery of Munich Löwenbräu beer-bottles, lecturing two men at the nearest table on Germany's frustrated colonial ambitions. His audience was staring dully into space, their apathetic faces showing a third-degree cafard, like characters out of a Somerset Maugham story. A scratchy phonograph played 'Valencia.' We sat down and ordered drinks, but somehow even the ice in the whiskey-and-sodas seemed warm that night. Jean-Jacques went to make a telephone call. He came back greatly excited. 'Yvonne's coming. I called her up at the Governor's palace. They are giving a gala dinner in her honor, and I had to talk to a colonel and two private secretaries before they let me talk to her. She is an official guest at the palace until she leaves for Addis Ababa.'

Yvonne arrived half an hour later, looking cool and flower-like in a print dress. 'Was I glad when you called me up, Jean, *cheri!*' she cried. 'I thought I couldn't stand the boring crowd up there any longer. Allons, let's celebrate.' We did. After the fifth glass of champagne I told Yvonne about my violin problem. She began to search in her handbag and brought out a wrinkled envelope. 'Rosie will help us,' she said. 'She used to work with me at the Casino de Paris and at the Folies before she got married and came to Djibouti with her husband. Rosie's wonderful. Always knew about special sales and where to get a sable coat, second-hand.' We all got up and went out.

The driver of the only visible taxicab, a scar-faced, black-bearded Italian, looked stunned when Yvonne gave him Rosie's address. 'Are you sure you want to go there, Madame? Oh, it's all right for the signori, but you . . .' Yvonne told him to get going, and he shrugged and said, 'Oh, va bene. As they say in Naples, "Some people carry lava up to Vesuvio."'

After a few minutes, the car stopped in front of a big, white house near the beach. Several automobiles were parked at the entrance. Two men were wandering about, whom we recognized as the persistent characters who had promised 'les plaisirs de nirvana.' They were delighted to see us, though slightly taken aback at the sight of Yvonne. We walked in, Yvonne's high heels making clipped sounds on the flame-colored tile floors, and found a dimly lighted patio, with rows of small tables, a piano, and a long bar. Six or eight couples were dancing a tango played by a pale, bald-headed pianist. Nearly all the men were French colonial officers. The girls looked pretty and were better dressed than most girls in 'bars' east of Suez. A luscious, plump, Rubens blonde, who was sitting behind a National cash register behind the bar cried out and ran toward Yvonne. In the middle of the dance-floor the two women fell into one another's arms, crying, laughing, and chatting all at once. We were introduced to Rosie, who in turn beckoned to the pale piano-player, her husband Vuillaume. Rosie left one of the girls, a petite apache who spoke pure argot, in charge of the bar and led us upstairs to her apartment. Through the jalousies we looked out at the sea and the brightly illuminated *Porthos*. There was an immense wooden bed, a massive table, chairs, bookcase, and dresser, all brought from her parents' farm in Normandy, she explained. On the wall above the bed hung oval-framed pictures of her family and a little crucifix. And in the corner, lying on a rocking-chair, was a violin case.

Dimitrij and I both saw it at the same time, and leapt upon

it. There was a violin inside, all right. Only three-quarter size, covered with dust and colophane, the bridge broken, two pegs and three strings missing, to me a lovelier sight than Heifetz' Stradivarius. Rosie said that a few months ago, when business had been booming, a violin-player had played with Vuillaume, but he got a bad attack of the cafard and had to be shipped back to Paris. She sighed as she said 'Paris.' 'The pieces of the violin are held together by small nails, so the instrument won't fall apart in the heat,' Rosie went on. 'It sounds terrible. Like a drunken parrot whistling in a Turkish bath. Please, take it away, so we won't have to look at it any longer.'

We had a fine party. Vuillaume brought up two bottles of champagne, Rosie and Yvonne reminisced about the Folies-Bergères, and Yvonne, holding Jean-Jacques' hand, told Rosie about her fiancé at Addis Ababa. Then she took out of her handbag the poems which Jean-Jacques had given her and read them aloud, and both women cried softly while Jean-Jacques kissed Yvonne's fingers, one by one.

The siren of the *Porthos* reminded us that it was time to go back. Everybody kissed everybody. Rosie refused to take any money for the violin. 'It was such a wonderful night,' she said. 'I wish you'd all come back when the *Porthos* passes through again. I want you to feel at home here.'

It was dawn when we left. We picked up our whiskey and Cognac bottles at Pierre's and at the pier gave them to our cabin steward, who got them through the customs without difficulty. Müllenhoff arrived, three bottles of Löwenbräu clumsily concealed in his pockets. We looked on coolly as the beer was confiscated and Müllenhoff fined fifty francs. The siren of the *Porthos* wailed three times, urgent and forbidding, and we jumped into the ship's launch. I carried the violin case as cautiously as a baby. Jean-Jacques cried and Yvonne kissed him and said she would come down to Djibouti to meet us on our way back, and that Jean-Jacques should stop crying and act like a grown-up man.

The launch pulled away and Yvonne waved, while Dimitrij held Jean-Jacques by one arm — just in case. The launch tossed up and down in the choppy harbor and the whiskey and Cognac bottles, which the steward had stowed under the seats, rolled all over the place. Müllenhoff shook an angry fist at receding Djibouti and started to sing 'Die Wacht am Rhein.' Jean-Jacques jumped up, seized Müllenhoff's helmet and threw it into the water, and 'Die Wacht am Rhein' came to an abrupt end. Dimitrij gently patted Jean-Jacques on the back and said, 'Fine, mon petit. You've acted like a real man. Too bad Yvonne couldn't see that.' Jean-Jacques nodded, his eyes still wet, but now there was a faint smile on his face.

Chapter 15

MUSIC FOR THE STEWARD

THE *Porthos* suffered from a serious servant problem. As a rule, French stewards were employed in the dining-rooms and bars, and Annamites in the staterooms. Unfortunately, the Annamite boys went ashore at every port and did not bother to return. They said they did not like the food, the quarters, the treatment, or the pay. Furthermore, they believed laziness was a virtue, and did not think that any male should work more than ten weeks a year. Those who deserted the ship in such Indo-Chinese home ports as Saigon, Tourane, and Haphong frequently sent their more active wives and daughters as 'deputies.' The purser and the headwaiters had a terrible time explaining to the ladies that all jobs aboard were For Men Only. Things got so bad that there was only one steward left for five first-class cabins and none for the second-class passengers who had to do up their staterooms themselves. Once in Saigon the purser had all gangways guarded by armed sailors, but the little Annamites simply jumped into the water and swam ashore.

On one trip, when Artie, Etienne-Marcel, and I made up the orchestra, we started out from Marseilles with a cadaverous Annamite steward, who amused himself by playing hide-and-seek with our slippers and putting the bass fiddle into the bathtub. None of us was an orderly musician (a rare phenomenon, anyway), and, by the time we reached Port Said, our two connecting first-class staterooms looked like a setting for a Kaufman and Hart comedy. The Annamite did not bother to make our beds, which were always littered with music sheets, dirty socks, empty bottles, and ties. We woke up in the morning with little pieces of resin in our ears and went to bed falling over our tropical helmets which the Annamite, with bizarre whimsy, always put upside down in the middle of the floor. We were never ready in time for our concerts because part of our equipment, a few pages of music, or one of Artie's shoes were missing. The floor of the staterooms sloped slightly to port and sordines, pegs, strings, and other irreplaceable items rolled down under the bunks, and were never heard of again. The Annamite steward was descended from a long line of famous basket-weavers from Pnom-Penh, Cambodia. To keep his hand in, he produced little ashtrays and match-holders, using my discarded violin strings. Two days before reaching Singapore, the Annamite was gone. So was my entire supply of new A and D strings. Until Singapore, those of the passengers surviving the heat and gin-slings were slightly surprised to hear me play nothing but Bach's 'Air on the G String' at every performance, morning, afternoon, and evening.

One morning, halfway between Singapore and Saigon, we came down to our staterooms after the apéritif concert. The cabins were vacuum-cleaned, the beds made, the dirty laundry had disappeared, and there was a new bulb over the mirror. The bathroom was spotless, and fresh towels hung from all the racks. The bathtub was filled to the brim and a little Annamite was peacefully lying in the cool water, whistling Dvořák's 'Humoreske,' and smiling at us. He sat up and introduced himself as Nam, seventh son of one An-Ba of Tourane, Indo-China. He said he had decided to work for us as cabin steward, because he was crazy about music.

Nam refused to be quizzed about when he had come aboard. All we found out was that he had worked, in quick succession, half a day in the kitchen, the dining-room pantry, for the second-class maître d'hôtel, and in the doctor's cabin. He did not like any of those jobs and quit. This was not difficult. To the European eye most Annamites look alike, and with eighty stewards it was almost impossible to check on the individual men.

Nam got dressed, cleaned the bathtub, and started polishing the brass knobs on the portholes, an unheard-of refinement. My colleagues got so excited that they proposed keeping Nam under guard inside the rooms. Artie said he would not mind carrying down his food so nobody could steal this jewel from us. Nam gave us a gentle, nostalgic smile and said it was no use to hide him because he was too well known among the other Annamites aboard. 'I am,' he said, bowing with poise, 'une personne bien connue. My uncle is a member of the Superior Council at Saigon. My grandfather was an adviser to Emperor Tu-due of Tongking.'

Nam was frail and small, with a melancholy, effeminate face and a finely shaped head. He had shiny, black hair and very fine hands. Like most Annamites, he chewed betel all the time. Barefoot, dressed in an immaculate, white steward's uniform, he slipped noiselessly in and out of our cabins, always there when needed. He mixed Martinis and whiskey-sodas, helped Etienne-Marcel with his tie, and was the first steward who did not ruin my white shoes with cleaning fluid. We were the only people aboard the *Porthos* who had fresh water with plenty of ice in our thermos bottles every night, fresh linen twice a week, and — much to Artie's delight — a ladder always ready for the upper berth. Before, Artie frequently fell down trying to get into bed in bad weather. Nam's fame as perfect steward spread fast and the maître d'hôtel, the purser, and finally the captain himself tried to steal him. Nam was the only person aboard to refuse the captain's order and get away with it. He simply threatened to 'go off' if he were not allowed to work 'pour les musiciens.' That settled it.

Among other things, Nam took care of our musical library. This was one of the orchestra leader's main duties, but after Suez, when the heat became intolerable and every superfluous movement meant utter exhaustion, I had not the strength to look after the sheets. They had been given to me in Marseilles, neatly stacked in six or seven files. By the time we reached the Gulf of Aden, we could not play the 'Barber of Seville' overture because it was minus the violin part. The two middle pages of 'Schön Rosmarin' were gone, and such an important piece as the third-act prelude to 'Lohengrin' could not be played because Nam's predecessor had torn the piano-part into strips. He had stuffed them into the cracks around the door to prevent the arrival of a certain tenacious species of bugs which, in honor of the *Porthos*, were called 'The Musketeers.'

Nam spent long hours putting the music sheets back into order, speculating on torn-out, isolated pages, always placing them into the right spot. He never told us where he had learned how to read music. He was polite, efficient, clean. He kept taking baths in our tub and always left his tiny wooden sandals behind the shower curtain. He slept in a little corner on the floor of our rear cabin, where we stored our instruments.

One evening before dinner, when I was coming down the corridor, I heard strange and horrible sounds emanating from our cabins. Nam was standing in front of the mirror, holding my violin under the chin, trying to play it the way he had seen me do it. Totally deaf to the ugly noises which he produced, he watched himself in the mirror with the fascination of a Moslem staring at the Great Mosque in Mecca. The violin was much too large for his small hands and he had to stretch out his forearm to hold it up. He blushed and smiled in his shy way and finally made a confession. He had come aboard because he hoped to be near the musicians and 'learn about music.' He wanted to play the violin, the piano, and the clarinet. His family had no appreciation for this outlandish desire. 'They would be horrified to know that I'm working here as cabin steward,' Nam said. 'I told them I was offered a scholarship and a free trip to France by the Ecole Française d'Extrême Orient. My people are very proud of their great past. But they are poor today. Most Annamites are poor since the French moved into Cochin-China. I couldn't afford to take music lessons in Saigon.'

Artie, a man of sometimes radical opinions, told Nam to cut out these delusions of grandeur. 'You are getting worse than the Russian émigrés in Shanghai,' Artie said. 'Soon every one of you will pretend to be an Annamite nobleman.'

Nam looked so deeply hurt that, in an effort to cheer him up, I offered to give him violin lessons. I did not regret it. Nam was an amazing pupil. He worked so hard that I often feared he would drop. At a little pawnshop in Shanghai, we bought him an inexpensive violin. Nam was overjoyed. 'Merci!' he said and, once more, 'Merci!' He practiced without tiring for hours, until the passengers complained. Nam then took his violin to the bow of the ship, where he played innumerable extended tones on all four strings as I had shown him. His bare feet beat time to the rhythm of the waves breaking against the hull. By the time we arrived in Yokohama, Nam was able to play simple Ševčík finger-and-bow exercises; in Hong Kong he played the first nine bars of the 'Marseillaise' and not too badly either.

He did not miss any of our concerts. He came up on deck every morning from eleven to noon, when we played for the apéritif crowd, and from eight to nine for the evening concert. He stood behind the piano and stared at me intently, trying to memorize every movement of my fingers. He made an arrangement with the first-class bartender to help serve drinks and clean up the tables during intermissions, making his presence on deck legitimate. When he liked a piece, he would raise his right thumb and forefinger and smile at us in grateful appreciation. His favorite piece was Dvořák's 'Humoreske.' He frequently asked us to play it. He would stand there and listen transfigured, his head tilted to the left.

Shortly before we arrived in Saigon, Nam announced that he would not be with us during the *Porthos's* stay in the harbor, because he had to see his family. He packed his violin and promised to be back 'in time.' We protested and threatened and pleaded, but there was nothing we could do. When the *Porthos* was towed to the pier in Saigon, Nam was gone.

'He'll never come back,' Artie predicted gloomily. Etienne-Marcel nodded his head and sighed. We went down to our neat, tidy staterooms. The water-bottles were full and the bedspreads were tight and smooth. Etienne-Marcel lay down, but got up at once, straightening out the covers. Somehow the room seemed desolate and empty. Artie pointed at the mirror and said, 'That's where he always used to study himself when he played. His bowing was quite amazing. The other day he told me he was about to learn the third position.'

Etienne-Marcel rubbed his white beard and said, 'Il était très gentil. I wish we could play once more Dvořák's "Humoreske" and see him raise his thumb and forefinger.'

For a long time no one said anything. Then Artie sighed again and suggested we all go to the hotel and have a drink. Etienne-Marcel said he didn't feel like drinking. Artie and I went ashore. It was almost midnight, but the heat was still heavy and humid. Our ricksha-coolies gasped as they ran, big, dark sweat-stains appearing on their light-blue garments. The boulevards were bordered by trees and the open-air cafés on the Rue Catinat looked very French with their little tables and wicker chairs, but the *Matin* and *Le Petit Parisien* in the newspaper kiosks were thirty days old and the goods in the stores were covered with mildew.

The bar of the Grand Hotel was dim and wonderfully cool. Several white, wraithlike figures showing the symptoms of advanced tropical decay were slowly sipping whiskey-sodas. In the rear of the room the hotel's four-man orchestra was playing Toselli's 'Serenade.' The 'cellist got up and came over. It was Ralph Hohenfels, who had made a trip with me as 'cellist aboard the Messageries Maritimes liner *d'Artagnan*. He was a tall, impressive-looking man in his forties, who carried himself in a military manner. He had been a major in a famous Kaiser-Königliches Dragoner Regiment, one of Austria-Hungary's most exclusive outfits in the last war. After the armistice, he faced the collapse of his world rather calmly. He went to Paris, gave 'cello lessons and at night played at the Grand Boulevard cafés. He never accepted any engagement on Mondays, his day off, when he played chamber music with three Sorbonne professors. After eight years of placid living, Hohenfels suddenly got restless and took a job aboard the Messageries Maritimes liners. We went to Tunisia, Réunion, Madagascar, China, and Japan together. On our trip on the *d'Artagnan* a beautiful Russian girl came aboard in Singapore. Her name was Tanja and she was traveling to Saigon with Batoff, her father. Batushka, as we called him, looked like the perfect anarchist — black beard, bushy eyebrows, burning dark eyes, sinister and silent bearing. Those close to him knew that he was a kindly, bashful person, who liked to read popular-medicine books and to play golf. He wanted to live in England, which, he said, was one vast golf course, but he would not leave his daughter alone. Tanja had a modeling job in a Saigon dress shop. Hohenfels fell in love with Tanja and jumped ship in Saigon.

Hohenfels ordered drinks for us, and we sat down next to the decaying colonials, who were visibly irritated by our high spirits. Hohenfels shrugged. 'I've become the town's Public Outcast Number 1,' he said. 'They can't forget that I was their enemy in the Great War. And they were shocked when I married Tanja, last June. They are terribly afraid of her father. They think Batushka's going to form a sabotage ring here in Saigon which one day will blow up the Opera. Poor old Batushka! He is so much afraid of fire that he doesn't even use a cigarette lighter.'

Hohenfels called the waiter and we had more whiskey. He took his straight. His fingers were trembling. 'The doctor talks of tropical neurasthenia and high blood pressure,' he said, in answer to my questioning glance. 'Actually there's nothing wrong with me that a short walk wouldn't cure. Walking from the Place de l'Opéra to the Madeleine, breathing that wonderful mixture of acacias, Pernod, and gasoline.' He stared into space. 'Last night I dreamed I was playing Schubert's "Forellenquintett." You have the craziest dreams in Saigon. Where would I get here a bass-player for the "Forellenquintett"? There isn't one anywhere between Singapore and Shanghai.'

Artie said: 'There is a good one aboard the *Porthos* and he'd love to play the "Forellenquintett." And our orchestra leader will play the viola part.' Hohenfels let out a high-pitched yodel, which, he explained later, was the former attack cry of his Kaiser-Königliches Dragoner Regiment. The phantoms at the adjoining tables hastily paid their bill and left. Hohenfels spoke to his musicians and went out to make a few arrangements. He came back in great excitement. Tomorrow evening — the *Porthos* was sailing at midnight — Ralph's orchestra was scheduled to give a concert classique at the ballroom of the hotel, in honor of the Société Franco-Annamite, to which many prominent natives and the colony's leading officials belonged. Instead of Bizet's 'L'Arlésienne' suite, which was the main feature of the program, we would play the 'Forellenquintett.' He even got me a viola from a physician and amateur musician in Saigon. I cautiously ventured the opinion that this change in program might not meet with unanimous consent. Hohenfels shook his head. 'On the contrary. The hotel manager here is a Swiss who likes good music. Naturally, we can't pay you anything, but you three men will be guests of the hotel, American plan. You get the best rooms. The food is excellent.'

'I don't eat much,' Artie said. 'How about letting me have free drinks instead?'

I protested, but the Swiss manager said that was all right with him. We decided to have a rehearsal at ten the following morning. By that time the Swiss manager agreed that I had been right in protesting. We found Artie sleeping under a table in the air-conditioned bar, in no condition to play the piano part of the difficult Schubert opus. We carried him upstairs to his room with the assistance of Tanja, Batushka, and Etienne-Marcel, who had arrived in time for breakfast. There was no rehearsal. Etienne-Marcel and Batushka went to play golf. Tanja took the day off and joined her husband and myself on a motor trip to the Confucius temples of Cholon, the Chinese quarter.

That night there was a colorful crowd at the ballroom of the big hotel, Cambodian women in blue and maroon silk dresses, loud half-caste men, French officers in white uniforms, tired patrician-featured French women in Parisian gowns. Also present were a few Japanese in atrocious cutaways. Tanja was escorted by her father. Batushka had on a long black coat and more than ever resembled the late Rasputin. They sat down in the fourth row. They were greeted by a few Annamites, but all the French people ignored them.

The headwaiter beat a large Chinese gong and the audience sat down. Except for Tanja and her father there was a general spirit of fraternizing. Annamites were flanked by French officers, and French women discussed the latest Paris fashion news with native ladies. A high government official, representing Monsieur Pierre Pasquier, the Governor-General, took his seat in the first row, next to a dignified old Annamite in a mess-jacket. I noticed that a number of seats in the first two rows were left vacant.

Hohenfels' four-man hotel orchestra played the 'Marseillaise' and a couple of short pieces. Then Artie, Etienne-Marcel, and I took our places at the platform, together with Hohenfels and his violin-player. It seemed unreal to be playing Schubert's 'Forellenquintett' for the Saigon audience, the Annamite women with their jet-black teeth, the dazzling French officers, the heat and the smell of tuberoses, hibiscus, and of nuoc-mam, the fish-sauce that one smells everywhere in

Indo-China. The large doors were open. Our pianissimi were drowned by the sounds of the tropics from outside, the shouts of the coolies, the pad-padding rickshas and noise of the crickets. Hohenfels was burning with excitement. He played very well; his tension seemed to have gone. There was much applause after the first movement. We got up and bowed to the audience. By now the ballroom was crowded. Not one seat was left vacant. The first two rows were occupied by what seemed to be a group of socially prominent Annamites, members of the Superior Council. I heard Artie softly whistle through his teeth. 'Look at the third man from the right in the second row. I'll go on the wagon if it isn't Nam.'

I looked over. The lights in the auditorium were dim, and it took me a few seconds to get used to the half-light. Then I saw Nam. He sat in the second row, next to a French captain. He wore a stiff shirt and a white mess-jacket. He smiled at me, his unmistakable, gentle smile, and raised his right thumb and forefinger. The captain respectfully bowed toward him and Nam nodded and said something with an air of unaffected dignity.

'Nom d'un chien!' Etienne-Marcel said, whipping his bow through the air. 'He's a little prince all right. And we imbeciles treated him like a shoe-shine boy. No wonder he walked out on us.'

There was considerable applause after the quintette. Nam got up, holding up his two fingers and smiling at us, as he had always done after our concerts. The old Annamite next to the high official in the first row turned around, giving Nam a severe, disapproving glance. Nam sat down. People kept applauding, and Hohenfels said nervously, 'What now? We haven't got any encores.' Etienne-Marcel pointed down to where Nam sat and said, 'I think we have one. You fellows all know Dvořák's "Humoreske" by heart?' Hohenfels and his violin-player nodded, somewhat flabbergasted. 'All right, then,' Etienne-Marcel said, and the three of us, Etienne-

Marcel, Artie, and I began to play. The others fell in after four or five bars. I glanced down at Nam. He sat on the edge of his chair, tense and rigid. The French captain was talking to him, but Nam did not answer. His eyes were wide-open and his head was tilted slightly to the left.

When the concert was over, we tried to find Nam, but we were stopped by a frosty old colonel who took us to the official representing the Governor-General. Everybody wanted to shake hands with us. When we were able to break away and look for Nam, he was gone. It was getting late and we had to hurry back to the ship. We said good-bye to Hohenfels and Tanja, and Etienne-Marcel and Batushka made an appointment for another game of golf, next year, when our bassist would be back. Back aboard the *Porthos*, we ran down to the staterooms. We stopped on the threshold with a foolish feeling of disappointment. Etienne-Marcel's bed was unmade, the water-bottles empty, music sheets all over the place. We stood there for a while, glum and angry at ourselves. Artie said it was time to play the 'Marseillaise' and we went on deck. We looked down to the pier where people were swinging handkerchiefs and wishing bon voyage.

'He might have come down to the harbor to say good-bye,' Artie said. 'After all, we didn't treat him badly. He got a violin and all the free time he wanted.' Etienne-Marcel whipped his bass bow through the air, silently staring at the pier that slowly receded into the night.

It was very hot, and we stayed on deck while the *Porthos* was plowing slowly down the jungle-bordered Don-nai River. At dawn, when the deck chairs were heavy with dew, we went down to our staterooms. The music sheets were put away and the water-bottles were full of ice. Nam's little wooden sandals were standing in the bathroom behind the shower curtain. He himself was fast asleep in the corner of the floor of the rear cabin. He had on his white steward's uniform. Instead of a pillow he had his small violin case under his head.

Chapter 16

PHOTO FINISH

PRACTICALLY nobody aboard the *Porthos* ever saw Yang, the ship's laundryman. Yang belonged to the Legion of Invisibles — the stokers, engineers, electricians, machinists, bakers, butchers, refrigerator men — who lived and worked deep inside the ship. They had the anemic complexion that comes from never getting any sunshine. They came up on the forward deck for a while after dinner, smoking their pipes — most of them were taciturn pipe-smokers — standing with back toward the railing, staring up at the well-dressed people on the brightly illuminated promenade deck in a wistful and, it seemed, somewhat envious way. In the quarters where they lived, the corridors had no rugs, rubber mats, indirect lights, or paneled walls. Pipes ran all along the ceiling, and there were pools of oil and the smell of sweat-stained overalls and the monotonous, stamping rhythm of the turbines.

Yang's laundry was a small, dark hole at the foremost part of the ship between the brig and a storeroom, down on D deck, five decks below the promenade deck. There was no air and the heat was always very bad. People might be wearing their overcoats up on the sun deck, but in the infernal regions of D deck the men were staggering, stripped to the waist, the sweat running down their eyes. There was a big kettle for the steaming-hot water, a kettle for cold water, where the laundry was being rinsed, a washboard, an ironing-board. The porthole high up in the wall was always closed, D deck being only three feet above the waterline. Even in good weather the waves could be seen splashing against the thick glass of the porthole. A half-burned-out bulb spread a dim, yellowish glow.

Yang worked in the middle of his hole. He was short, fat, and always cheerful. He had a round, friendly, open face, and an immense bald skull, and when he bent over the kettle, his naked torso folded into an accordion of fat. He came from Canton in the South of China where, Yang explained, most people were short, fat, and cheerful. He had nine brothers, seven of whom were in the laundry business in such far-flung places as Shanghai, New York, Los Angeles, Port Said, Colombo, Panama City, and Bogotá. Yang was recognized within the family as an expert in lady's underwear. His lingerie memory was amazing. Sometimes there were over three hundred women passengers aboard. (Yang laundered only for the ladies.) The cabin stewards collected the laundry in paper bags and delivered it to Yang. Some of the pieces had no initials or first names; most were unmarked. Yang never used any laundry marks, yet there was never a mix-up. He remembered and judged underwear the way other people remember faces. He could tell you whether a woman was serious, quiet, gentle, frivolous, or catty from her deshabilles and négligés. He would point to some undies, saying, 'That's a hot cooky,' or 'This one is a dud.' He spoke a funny kind of English, a combination of American slang, pidgin English, and cockney, which he had picked up in the various big seaports.

I had met Yang on my second trip aboard the *Porthos* when Artie spilled hot chocolate on my last dress shirt and I had to have it laundered that very afternoon. When I came down, Yang was ironing a dainty, pink-lace something, humming what sounded like a Chinese melody. 'The woman who wears this is a swell babe,' he said, pointing at the piece. He pronounced it 'bi-be.' He turned around and said, 'Take your shirt back. I'm not in business for gents.' Then he saw my camera. He gasped. On that day I had taken some pictures and was carrying my Leica. 'I wish I owned one of those,' Yang said, and sighed. He told me that photography was his true vocation. He owned a cheap, small box camera, but he had got good pictures with it and was an enthusiastic fan. At night he turned his laundry into a darkroom. He had snitched a couple of plates from the kitchen which he used as developing and fixing-bath trays; he put a piece of red paper around the bulb and hung up some ladies' underwear over the door. The heat was terrific. He had to go for some ice to keep the gelatine cover on the films from dissolving.

I asked Yang how he would like to work in the ship's darkroom. He sighed again and gave me a sad smile. I went up to the purser. It was agreed that Yang could use the darkroom and do processing work for the passengers. Yang was overjoyed. He washed my shirt and promised to take care of the musicians' laundry. After that he came up once a week to pick up our stuff, an unheard-of honor. Yang squatted down in our cabin and for a while the conversation would switch from nightgowns to exposure meters. He would ask to see my camera and give it a loving, sad look, just holding it and staring at it.

On that trip we had several members of the diplomatic set aboard, a Swiss consul-general, a Jap minister with Oshi, his pretty, sexy, Paris-educated daughter, a mildly mysterious Russian chargé d'affaire who snubbed his colleagues and played poker with the crew at their quarters, and a French attaché by the name of Alphonse, tall, well-groomed, handsome, a junior Talleyrand, immensely popular with all women passengers. He was an excellent dancer and bridge-player. Even the three British spinsters, who were spending the journey knitting in their deck chairs, spreading rumors

MC

and gossip, gave him a smile when he passed by. Oshi, the Japanese flower, fell for him like a withering cherry blossom, but Alphonse did not care. He was gay and charming, playing deck-tennis with the Swiss and helping the British spinsters wind balls of yarn, but he spent most of his time taking pictures. He had two still cameras and one sixteen-millimeter movie camera. Every night he processed his films at the ship's darkroom, ably assisted by Yang. A beautiful photo-friendship sprang up between Alphonse and Yang, full of focus-secrets and shutter-speed intimacy. They worked long hours at the darkroom, speaking a practically unintelligible code of circular confusion, bromoil process, Contessa Nettel, Fresson method of printing, Rolleflex, Compur-shutters. Sometimes the attaché would go down to D deck, take off his coat and shirt and sit down on the ironing-board at Yang's laundry, talking photography.

Alphonse's favorite photographic model was the Alsatian-born wife of the German ambassador who traveled in stateroom Number 1 and was the doyen of our itinerant diplomatic corps. Cabin Number 2 was occupied by the Japanese minister and Oshi, his daughter, and Alphonse traveled in Number 3. The Alsatian was slim and vivacious with beautiful Titian-red hair. She was seen with Alphonse everywhere, which gave rise to certain rumors, ships being gossipy little communities. People were divided on the issue. The younger ones said they did not blame her. Her husband, the ambassador, was a tall, bony Prussian from Potsdam, who had an aristocratic name, complete with 'von' and hyphen, and the cold stare of an angry swordfish. He was much older than his wife, collected Malayan daggers, and for entire days played billiards with the Japanese minister. He had long, skinny fingers and sharp nails and I think it was Etienne-Marcel who called him the Spider. The greatest moment in his life was when Kaiser Wilhelm, after an exuberant stag party, kicked him in the seat of his pants. This, the ambassador would explain, casually adjusting his monocle, was an expression of

His Majesty's most profound sympathy and a great honor. It was known that the Spider was very jealous of his wife and liked to dance with her every night. So did Alphonse. Alphonse preferred tangos, while the Spider liked the old-fashioned waltzes. We liked Alphonse and played mostly tangos, which probably accounted for the Spider's remark that in the good old times, when his Junker father and grandfather on their estates were enjoying the *jus primae noctis* over all newly married women, we musicians would have been flogged on the market square and broken on the wheel.

The passage through the Red Sea was a red-hot, steaming hell, and by the time we reached the monsoon-tossed Indian Ocean, most passengers were feeling pretty low. The Spider was seasick and stayed in his stateroom, which did not keep his wife from posing for Alphonse. The attaché took countless pictures of her, in shorts on the sun deck, in a white evening gown silhouetted against the setting sun, the light beautifully caught by her hair — Alphonse and Yang discussed this shot for days — or leaning against the mast, standing in a lifeboat, kneeling in front of the funnel, and sitting on the railing with her legs dangling. They were very shapely legs. The British spinsters were happily gossiping, and Oshi, the Japanese girl, told everybody that the Spider had made a terrible scene in his stateroom one night and told his wife that he would break every bone in the attaché's rotten body. Alphonse did not care. He went on, happily taking snapshots of l'Alsacienne by day and developing them with Yang at night. Every evening after eleven, when the dancing was over, we musicians went up to the darkroom and sat down on near-by deck chairs. Presently Yang and Alphonse would dash out of the darkroom, holding the dripping films against a light bulb, exclaiming excitedly. Etienne-Marcel looked through the film and said, 'Can't see a thing,' and the two photo fellows would launch a violent protest. In the end they would compliment each other on their photographic artistry. 'Alphonse is a smart operator,' Yang said, pronouncing the word 'oper-i-tor,' grinning as though he were promised a Chinese forty-course feast.

The Spider and his wife gave a party, on the eve of our arrival in Shanghai, where they were to get off, for the captain, the ship's officers, and the diplomats aboard. The Russian was pointedly seated between two junior officers, below the salt, and after the meat course he got up and left. The party stayed in the dining-saloon until ten and then came up on deck to dance. Most of them seemed to have eaten and drunk too well. The Swiss jumped up and down, slapping his thighs, Alpine-fashion, yodeling all over deck. The Japanese fell down on his face and the Spider was red and noisy. Alphonse sent us a bottle of champagne; after that we played nothing but tangos and he danced with l'Alsacienne. She put her head close to his chin and when they danced by our platform, he kissed her bare shoulders. Oshi gasped and the German ambassador, who was about to demonstrate once again how Kaiser Wilhelm had kicked him, sat up straight and got still redder in the face. The Swiss hastily ordered more champagne. The British spinsters looked disappointed, having hoped for a juicy little scandal. At that moment Yang came out from the promenade deck. He had on his parade dress, black silk trousers, and a white jacket, and he was carrying some photographs.

'Monsieur Alphonse was to meet me at the darkroom at eleven o'clock,' Yang said, glancing discreetly at the Frenchman who was still dancing with l'Alsacienne, holding her tight.

Etienne-Marcel shrugged. 'Mon vieux,' he said, 'you'll have to learn the facts of life. There comes a time in the life of every man when he doesn't care about shutters and shadows.' The old bass-player thoughtfully played with his long white beard. He sighed and said, 'I wish I were young once again. *I* wouldn't spend my nights in a darkroom.'

Yang left and we played a last tango for the attaché, packed up our instruments, and went across the empty promenade deck. Yang was standing in front of the darkroom, sad and forlorn. There was nothing we could say to cheer him up. We went down to the bar of the tourist class, where we were sure to get drinks even after closing hours. We were having our third whiskey, shortly after midnight, when the first-class maître d'hôtel came in. He was a fat man, and he was out of breath. He had on his pajama bottoms and his white blouse, unbuttoned, and his hair was uncombed. He had obviously been gotten from bed. 'The Spider's gone berserk,' he said, very excited. 'Tried to break into Monsieur Alphonse's cabin. He threatens to kill him and l'Alsacienne too.'

Artie remained at the bar, but Etienne-Marcel and I ran upstairs. On our way we were joined by a few confused, scantily dressed passengers. There was a crowd in front of stateroom Number 3, which belonged to Alphonse, and a terrific racket. The Spider hammered against the door with a heavy alpenstock, which is popular among mountain-minded German pedestrians. He was drunk. His face had a glossy finish and the veins were pulsating on his forehead. 'Open instantly, du gottverfluchter Schweinehund!' he shouted. 'Open, or I'll beat you to a meatloaf!'

The purser, aided by two cabin stewards, tried to get hold of his arms, but the stewards were reluctant to use force, afraid of an international incident. The Spider was a strong man and shook them off like flies. Somebody behind me said, 'When those Boches get drunk, they'll murder you. Poor Monsieur Alphonse!'

I turned around and saw that it was Yang. He whispered, 'I'll be back,' and disappeared. The Spider continued to beat against the door. Everybody looked aghast. The door of Number 2 was opened and the Jap minister came out, followed by Oshi. The girl had on a beautiful silk kimono. She looked at the Spider and whispered to her father. Both of them went back into their stateroom and closed the door. The Spider was raging. 'Open up!' he yelled, kicking the door. 'I'll count, eins, zwei, und ——'

The door of stateroom Number 3 was opened. Alphonse came out, calm, casual, and well-groomed as ever. The Spider pushed him back inside the room and broke in. We all followed closely behind him.

The room was in perfect order. L'Alsacienne was not there. The Spider stopped by the bed and sniffed. 'Mimosa,' he said. 'Her perfume. Where is she? Where?'

Etienne-Marcel squeezed my arm in utter delight. 'A perfect performance,' he whispered. 'Better than at the Comédie Française. And free of charge.'

The German turned against the door to the bathroom, which was closed. 'Aha!' he yelled. 'In there. Open up.' He raised his alpenstock again, but Alphonse stepped in front of the door. 'You *can't* go in there, Monsieur,' he said. His voice had still a diplomat's intonation, soft and urbane, but somehow he sounded grim and resolute. For a few moments the quiet of the room was so intense that I could hear the sound of the engines, faint and muffled in these luxurious latitudes. There was a commotion at the door and Yang made his way into the room. He carried a small laundry basket and stepped behind the bed. I thought he had dropped something and I saw him beckon toward Alphonse.

'Open the bathroom, du französischer Lump!' the ambassador yelled. His face had a grayish hue. The cabin stewards looked at the purser, who was about to give them the sign to jump at the German, international incident or no. Suddenly Alphonse pointed at the floor by the bedside, where Yang had been awhile ago. The Spider bent down and came up with a black-lace négligé. It had the label of a Tokio store and, in small white silk letters, the name 'Oshi.'

The German looked down at the name and started. He swallowed and bowed from the waist, stiffly and very Prussian, saying, 'I apologize, sir. Must have been acting like a schoolboy. Bedauere. Will you forgive me, please?' He bowed once more, turned around on his heels, and walked out of the room, without so much as looking back. We heard him go into his stateroom and close the door.

For a few moments no one spoke. Then the purser, polite and businesslike, asked Messieurs les passagers to clear the room. Only Alphonse, Etienne-Marcel, Yang, and I stayed back. Etienne-Marcel whistled 'Ain't She Sweet?' Yang picked up the néglігé of the Japanese girl which the Spider had thrown on the bed. He placed it back in his basket and quietly left the room. There was a sad, hurt expression on his face. He walked down the corridor toward the darkroom.

Alphonse took his silent handkerchief out of his breast-pocket and wiped his forehead. 'Grand Dieu!' he said. 'That was a close one.' He looked out into the corridor, where everything was quiet now, and came back, and opened the bathroom door. The wife of the ambassador came out, smiling, pretty, and wholly unperturbed. She said, 'Chéri, I'll be up on the sun deck. I'll be waiting for you. The usual place.' Then she was gone.

Alphonse stared after her, in a funny, absent-minded way. He went to a drawer and took out his camera, a film pack, and a small bottle of hypo. He turned to Etienne-Marcel and said, 'Will you go up on deck and tell her that I can't come, mon vieux? Just tell her that I can't come. C'est ça.' He smiled and said, 'I think I forgot all about another appointment I had.'

Alphonse went down the corridor toward the darkroom.

Chapter 17

THE COSMOPOLITE

IN THE SPRING of 1930, the *Porthos* was making her regular Marseilles–Algiers run. One night in Algiers I was called to the captain's cabin around six.

'We are sailing back to Marseilles at eight,' the captain said. 'Owing to a switch in the schedules we've been chartered by the Anciens Combattants de la Grande Guerre, who have had a convention in Algiers. Get ready to play all the songs of the Great War. The Marshal is fond of the old patriotic songs.'

The captain sounded pardonably thrilled. Like all good Frenchmen, he venerated the Marshal, Henri Philippe Pétain, Marshal of France, legendary hero of Verdun, successor to Foch in the French Academy. The captain had a framed photograph of Pétain on his desk, beside the picture of his family.

I told the captain that our little orchestra of three was hardly prepared to deal with such an emergency. As an internationally mixed outfit, we had only a nodding acquaintance with French folk-song. Pedro, our 'cellist, who referred to himself as 'a pupil of a pupil of Pablo Casals,' was a lethargic, spineless mañana character from Barcelona, and

Artie, the pianist, was from Yonkers. As orchestra leader, I was supposed to be a Frenchman, but, owing to a momentary shortage of French violinists and the then excellent political relations between France and Czechoslovakia, I had got the job. Our musical library, supplied by the steamship company, contained all the important overtures, fantasias, opera arrangements, dance music, even an assortment of chamber music — everything but France's patriotic songs. Musicians aboard a French liner were supposed to know them by heart.

'You'll get the old songs in Algiers,' the captain said. 'Be sure to bring "La Marche Lorraine" and "Le Chant du Départ." They are favorites with the Marshal.'

The captain was a likeable man with a buccaneer's black beard and a great love of good music. He once moved an Argentine multimillionaire out of the ship's best de-luxe suite to make room for Maurice Ravel. The Argentine reportedly owned a hacienda larger than Alsace-Lorraine, with the Department of the Seine-et-Oise thrown in for good measure, but the captain ruled that Ravel was to have the suite, and that was that.

I said, 'Three foreigners playing for a patriotic celebration? What will the passengers say to that?'

'They won't mind. We French are cosmopolites.'

'And the Marshal?'

The captain extended both arms in a gesture of sweeping grandeur. 'The Marshal is a great European. Ever since 1917 he has been fond of foreigners.'

When I came out of the captain's cabin, the decks were swarming with cheerful, mustachioed Anciens Combattants, the French equivalent of the American Legionnaires. They were wearing blue Basque bérets and chewing dead cigarettes. One group was singing a song which, I noted with some apprehension, I had never heard before.

I found my colleagues in our two connecting first-class staterooms, which we had been assigned by the music-loving captain, contrary to regulations, which provided for second-class accommodations only. Pedro, dressed for the evening concert, was, as usual, fast asleep on his berth. Artie was reading a paper-bound history of the Marseilles underworld. I told them to go ashore and dig up some patriotic songs.

'What's wrong with "Hallelujah" and "Always"?' Artie said, the Youmans and Irving Berlin hits of the season being his current favorites.

I explained that they were swell, but hardly appropriate for the Marshal.

'I don't like Pétain,' Artie said. 'Joffre didn't like him either. You know what he calls him in his memoirs? A dyed-in-the-wool defeatist. Foch hated Pétain. And Clemenceau complained of his pessimism.' Artie had an amazing store of unexpected information.

I hastily closed the door, hoping that no one had heard the blasphemous statement. I told the boys that we faced deportation aboard the *Azay-le-Rideau* if something went wrong. The *Azay-le-Rideau*, a dilapidated liner making the dreary Indo-China run, was the steamship line's floating Devil's Island, as far as the company's musicians were concerned. Her purser, a violent man who had conceived a special dislike for string instruments, was said to have thrown musicians into the ship's brig because they 'played too loud.' Twice he had threatened to shoot the orchestra if they did not stop playing the 'William Tell' overture.

We went ashore. Algiers' few music stores had closed for the day. The night-clubs, where we hoped to borrow some stuff, were not yet open. In one place I got hold of 'Ah! Ça ira, ça ira, ça ira,' the famous revolutionary song suggesting the immediate hanging of the aristocrats to the nearest lamp-post — a suggestion we feared the Marshal might not wholeheartedly approve of. Somewhere in the Kasbah, Pedro unearthed a ditty called 'Desire,' by a local composer, with lyrics hardly suitable for the occasion. We returned to the *Porthos* with dire forebodings.

The evening concert in the dining-saloon got under way without accident. We interrupted the 'Manon' (Massenet, not Puccini) fantasy when the chief steward informed us, his voice trembling, that the Marshal was about to enter. We played the 'Marseillaise,' this being a ship's regulation. Everybody stood at attention.

The Marshal was escorted by the captain. He carried himself amazingly erect for a man of seventy-four. His gait was resolute; his clear gray eyes, the domed forehead, the firm chin, the thin lips, gave the impression of Spartan severity. After the national anthem was played, he sat down at the captain's table and we went on with 'Manon.'

Presently the stewards were carrying in champagne. The diners looked hot and happy. Undoubtedly the time for songs was fast approaching. Three men in high spirits came over to the platform and asked us to play 'La Marche Lorraine.' I cast a respectful glance in the direction of the Marshal and said we had orders to go on with the regular evening program. The Frenchmen gave us a questioning glance and went back reluctantly to their table. It was hot under the lights on our platform and my shirt was wringing wet, but we kept on playing, without pause, so the audience would have no chance to start singing.

Disaster struck while we were playing César Franck's 'Danse Lente.' There is a lot of pianissimi in 'Danse Lente,' and some men in the rear of the vast dining-saloon must have thought we had stopped playing. They began singing 'Le Chant du Départ':

> La victoire en chantant nous ouvre la barrière,
> La liberté guide nos pas;
> Et du nord au midi la trompette guerrière
> A sonné l'heure des combats.

The martial melody reverberated across the dining-saloon, rang through the open doors, and surged over the ship's decks. By the time they had reached the chorus —

La République nous appelle,
Sachons vaincre ou sachons périr,
Un français doit vivre pour elle,
Pour elle un français doit mourir

— the stewards, sailors, cooks, even some of the Annamite cabin boys were singing with the passengers, while we musicians, the only three persons aboard who did not know the song, were trying in vain to catch up with the melody. Just as the second chorus was about to be concluded, Artie got the general idea and wound up with a thundering chord. This saved the situation for the moment, giving the impression that we had been playing all the time. There was a terrific ovation and the audience launched into 'Madelon.'

'What's that?' Artie said, looking at me in bewilderment.

'Madelon.'

'Who's she?' Artie was always eager for facts.

'Didn't you ever hear the song?' I asked, in despair.

'Nope. Not in Yonkers.'

'For God's sake, keep on playing,' I said between my teeth.

'Playing what?'

'Make some noise. Keep in pitch and tempo.' I closed my eyes, dizzy with the feeling of approaching catastrophe. The people were roaring —

Elle rit, c'est tout l'mal qu'ell' sait faire,
Madelon, Madelon, Madelon!

— but my feeble attempts to accompany the singers on my violin were boldly frustrated by Artie. Bored stiff with a song they did not play in Yonkers, Artie took up the chorus of 'Hallelujah,' fortissimo, while Pedro, sinking back into his favorite state of dreamy half-consciousness, plunged into what sounded like Brahms' 'Cradle Song,' a piece he liked because 'you can play it in your sleep.'

Our audience began to shout. A red-haired giant with the rosette of the Legion of Honor on his lapel came up to the platform. 'Tiens, what kind of music is that?' he said angrily.

'Don't you men like "Madelon"? Go ahead, let's have "Sidi-Brahim," if you know what's good for you!' He swung his fist and shouted at the top of his voice,

> Debout, debout, debout,
> Mort aux ennemis de la France!

An old colonel at the table of the Marshal raised his glass, shouting, 'Vivent les chasseurs à pied!' The Marshal himself seemed to be enjoying the general paroxysm. Leaning back in his chair, he vigorously beat the time with a spoon, his bushy white mustache swinging in rhythmical motion. I remembered that 'Sidi-Brahim' was the song of the chasseurs, but none of us three knew the melody. In the middle of the patriotic enthusiasm, we were standing quiet and helpless, a trio of unhappy pariahs.

'So you don't *want* to play it?' the red-haired Hercules shouted. 'Saboteurs, hein?'

The horrible truth dawned upon me. They could not assume we did not know the song; why, every French child knew it! They thought we did not *want* to play it.

The man began to roll up his sleeves. Other ex-warriors rushed forward for a frontal attack. There was not going to be any penal trip aboard the *Azay-le-Rideau* to Indo-China. We would be hanged at the masthead, at sunrise, as radicals and enemies of the Republic.

I looked for help. Our protector, the captain, red-faced and nervous, was talking to the Marshal, apparently trying to explain the situation. Then somebody at his table shouted 'silence!' and we heard the soldierly, staccato voice of Pétain, 'Foreigners? Am I to understand that an American, a Spaniard, and a Czechoslovak have been hired to play for this patriotic occasion?'

A hush fell over the dining-saloon, interrupted only by the popping of a champagne cork. Then there was a wild battle-cry. The mob moved in for the kill. Somebody was swinging an empty bottle. I looked at the Marshal. Had he not preached the slogan, 'Spare men, don't spend them'? Had he not attacked the late Marshal Foch for his 'murderous losses'? Now or never was the moment to spare men.

The Marshal sat there, silent. There was only one thing to do. In a case of emergency — be it fire, collision, abandon ship, or a marshal of France — a salt-sea musician plays the national anthem. With fierce despair, we launched into the 'Marseillaise.' The mob rallied and came to attention.

When the anthem ended, we bolted from the dining-saloon and ran up to the dark, deserted boat deck. Our conversation, as I recollect it, was gloomy. At midnight, the captain, on his way to the bridge, found us there. 'Nom de Dieu!' he said. 'For a moment you had me worried. The Marshal thought you were trying purposely to give an unpatriotic demonstration. But you don't have to worry. I told him that you are excellent musicians. The Marshal,' the gallant captain concluded with emphasis, 'is a true cosmopolite at heart.'

When we arrived in Marseilles, we were ordered off the *Porthos* and aboard the *Azay-le-Rideau.* The company official indicated that a 'high authority' had demanded our 'exemplary punishment.' That night we played the 'Marseillaise' as the *Azay-le-Rideau* was being towed away from the Joliette Pier. The signal light over Notre-Dame-de-la-Garde receded into the misty dark and we were off for Indo-China.

Chapter 18

THE LAST WALTZ

WE MUSICIANS were far from being the only exiles aboard the lamentable *Azay-le-Rideau.* The liner's captain was a heavy-set, gray-haired, frequently unshaven misanthrope of the Ivan-the-Terrible type. He had served a long term aboard the *Azay-le-Rideau* for running one of the company's luxury liners aground near Port Said. The first mate was known around Singapore as a junior-grade runner-amuck; the ship's doctor had to give up a flourishing practice in Marseilles when the local police checked up on him. Our immediate superior, the purser, was a chronic alcoholic who considered musicians an especially noisy species of beetle. Some crew members had bulging objects in their pockets; others looked like prematurely released inmates of a psychopathic ward. Everybody hated everybody else's guts. Arguments and fights were a daily occurrence.

The *Azay-le-Rideau* had been a Hapag steamer before she was handed over to the French as a measly reparations payment on the Dawes Plan. That was a beautiful day for the Hapag people. Every ship has its special variety of rats and insects, but the hostile fauna aboard the filthy *Azay-le-Rideau* would arouse the scientific interest of the Rockefeller Foundation. There were common cockroaches behind the washbasins, grayish ones near the portholes, and a domesticated, Wagnerian species whose natural habitat was the piano and who came out only during the 'Lohengrin' or 'Tannhäuser' fantasies.

There was always trouble. Two days after Suez, the engines broke down in the middle of the Red Sea. The ship stopped, listing to port like a goose with a hangover. For forty-eight hours we were immobilized. The heat was unbearable. Mr. Hartford, an asthmatic, half-deaf, retired tycoon from Delaware, thought it was hotter than Wilmington, or for that matter, Death Valley.

The passengers were a dull collection of French officials and army men, Japanese businessmen, three Paris demimondaines hoping for a lively season in Saigon, and a group of young English clerks and bookkeepers, who had jobs with Singapore firms and preferred a French boat to the stuffy, black-tie British P. and O. liners. The only piano aboard stood on the promenade deck, under a roof formed by the sun deck above. There were wicker chairs and tables and two decrepit potted palms, and the bar was right next door. At night a lively crowd of moths, mosquitoes, and nervous Red Sea flies hovered around the light bulbs.

Playing music in this hothouse was slow death. I had to use four metal strings; my bow hairs did not keep the resin. The instruments were covered with moisture, and the keyboard of the piano was slippery. Frequently we had to play from memory as the sweat ran down into our eyes, blurring the music. The passengers lay in their deck chairs, sipping iced drinks and wishing they were dead or in Alaska. Nobody liked to listen to the sound of music, anyway, so we took long rests between pieces while we stood at the rail. There at least was some fresh air. Far across the sea we saw Mount Sinai, its craggy silhouette outlined in the pale moonlight. Pedro made the fitting observation that the *Azay-le-Rideau* should be chartered by the management of Hell for the transportation of lost souls. The ensuing gloomy silence was interrupted by the captain's bark. He had sneaked up on us in the dark and wanted to know why we did not perform our musical duties. Artie pointed out that music was the last thing the passengers wanted.

'What do you think they want?' the captain asked sharply.

'Free drinks with plenty of ice,' Artie said.

This bit of advice was not appreciated. 'Ces Américains,' the captain said, with contempt. 'All they think of is drinks and more drinks.' At that, Artie hotly defended the honor of his country. In no time the two men were engrossed in a bitter argument which ended arbitrarily with the captain's shouting at Artie to shut up and go back to work. From that night on, war was waged between the captain and the orchestra.

In Colombo the Five Ferraris came aboard. They were a dynasty of Italian acrobats, prominent mainly on the Bombay circuit, where the customers were not as blasés as at the Cirque Médrano in Paris. The Five Ferraris consisted of Father Ferrari, his three sons, Giuseppe, Gino, Giacomo, and a daughter, Lucia. Father Ferrari was six-foot-three inches tall. His sons were all smaller and each of a different height. They always walked in formation, like organ-pipes, which was funny and no doubt partly accounted for the Ferraris' popularity with the Orientals. Mamma Ferrari, no active member of the show, combined a gross weight of three hundred pounds with the dignity of the late Dowager Empress of China. She did crochet-work and watched over Lucia, who was seventeen, blonde, and beautiful.

The Five Ferraris soon turned the tourist-class deck into a circus arena. They practiced every morning in black tricots, and made magnificent caprioles and backward somersaults, without touching the ground. The finale was a living pyramid with Father Ferrari as base and Lucia as top. By that time most male passengers and many officers and crew members had arrived to have a look at Lucia, who was quite a sight in her tight-fitting black costume. On the third morning Lieutenant

Lavallère, a mild-mannered, shy, handsome officer at the wireless station, came down. He saw Lucia and fell in love with her at first sight. This fact would never have become known, Lavallère being a silent man, if it had not been for Artie, a radio-fan who spent much time at the wireless station. Artie brought the news that Lavallère had been severely reprimanded by the captain for signing three messages with 'Lucia.' 'He's transfigured,' Artie said. 'Sits there and his fingers unconsciously tap out L–U–C–I–A. I think we ought to help that guy. He's too shy to talk to her.'

Every night Lavallère came down to the dance. He sat all by himself in a remote corner and watched Lucia dance with the English clerks. Lavallère never asked her for a dance. He did not know the modern dances, he explained, only the waltz. Lucia had been quoted by several persons as being a waltz-hater. Lavallère just sat there and kept staring at her.

'It breaks my heart to look at that guy,' Artie said. 'He's growing thinner by the hour. In an emergency he would tap out L–U–C–I–A instead of S–O–S. And I'm sure Lucia likes him. The other night she smiled at him as she danced by.'

The evening before we arrived at Saigon, where most passengers would get off, there was a concert, after which Lucia, as the most popular girl aboard, made the customary collection for the musicians. We watched her go the rounds of the passengers. She crammed a heap of bills into her handbag. After the collection we played dance music. Lavallère was at his table in the rear, alone, as usual. Suddenly Artie got up. 'Ladies and gentlemen,' he said, 'we are going to play "Tales from the Vienna Woods." This is for Mademoiselle Ferrari and Monsieur Lavallère.'

The people applauded and we began the waltz. Lavallère looked flustered. Pedro stepped onto the dance floor. He took Lucia's arm and gently led her across the floor toward Lavallère's table. I thought the lieutenant would drop dead with happiness. He took her into his arms, cautiously, as though she were made of soapbubbles. He danced very well. They looked into one another's eyes and smiled. Artie had a Santa-Claus look in his eyes and played the refrain over and over again. Suddenly the deck steward walked across the dance floor and whispered into Lavallère's ear. The young officer blushed deeply. He led Lucia back to her table, gently kissed her hand, and left. We finished the waltz. I stepped down from the platform and looked around the corner. At the far end of the dimly lit deck I saw the captain talking to Lavallère. The young man saluted and went upstairs.

After the next dance Artie went up to the wireless station. He came back in a great flurry. 'Lavallère's been ordered to his quarters,' he said. 'The captain says that junior officers are not permitted to dance with the passengers. Hasn't anybody here ever heard of Abe Lincoln?' Artie was now quite excited. He had the American love of addressing large crowds. 'What's this ship anyway — a galley?' Artie shouted. The passengers were stunned. Lucia grew pale and the Ferrari brothers jumped up, ready for action. I quickly started 'Ain't She Sweet?' Fortunately, some people began to dance.

After the dance we went up to the wireless station. Lavallère sat outside in front of his room. He stared at the Southern Cross and sighed deeply. He said he had a date with Lucia. He was to meet her under the funnel. Now he was restricted to his quarters.

We stared across the sun deck. Near the funnel a shadow seemed to be moving. Lavallère sighed again. Artie could not stand the heartbreak. 'You go over there,' he said to the officer. 'We'll wait here. If somebody comes, I'll say you went below for a minute, or got the scarlet fever, or something. Come on, hurry up.'

Lavallère hesitated. There are certain things which a junior officer of the merchant marine does not do, even when he is desperately in love, he said. By way of a reply, Artie pointed across the deck. The lonely shadow over there seemed to be vanishing. Lavallère shrugged and left, giving us a last desperate glance. Artie stepped into Lavallère's room and saw the officer's cap. He put it on, gave it a rakish angle and looked at his picture in the mirror, with obvious satisfaction. 'Not bad,' he said. 'Someday I ought to get myself a job with this outfit.'

'*What* outfit?' a horrifying voice shouted. We turned around and almost fainted. 'Where is Lieutenant Lavallère?' the captain asked grimly. There was a cold gleam in his eyes. We were silent. This was no time for fast repartee. There is no telling what a madman may do. We were sure the captain had a razor on his person. Perhaps one in each pocket.

'I'll put you in irons! All of you!' Ivan the Terrible shouted. 'No shore leave in Saigon! From now on you'll work ten hours a day instead of five! Get out of here and stay at your quarters!'

We went down to our quarters. On the main deck we ran into Mr. Hartford, the ex-tycoon from Delaware. He adjusted his hearing aid, embraced Artie, and boomed that we were just in time to celebrate. This was, he said, the seventeenth anniversary of his divorce, a happy day that called for champagne. Mr. Hartford always found a pretext to celebrate. We went to the bar and had a bottle of champagne and another one. After that we forgot all about the captain and being restricted. Artie told Mr. Hartford about our war against the *Azay-le-Rideau.* The ex-tycoon solemnly put his hand on Artie's shoulder. 'There's only one thing to do,' he said. 'Strike. Don't play any more.'

I pointed out that you don't strike aboard ship.

'All right, then,' Mr. Hartford said. 'Why don't you throw your violin overboard? You can't play without a violin, can you?'

Artie said: 'It's no use. Two seamen have violins and the damned pharmacist carries a 'cello along and ——' Artie stopped in the middle of his sentence and jumped up from his chair. 'There is only one piano aboard,' he said, in a soft, alien-sounding voice. 'Without a piano there won't be ten hours of music, as the madman said. In fact, there won't be any music at all.'

A solemn silence followed these words. The magnitude of the suggestion was crushing. It was a hot night. The bartender opened a third bottle of champagne.

'If the captain finds out about this, we'll be fired in Saigon,' I said. 'What are we going to do there?'

Artie shrugged magnanimously. 'We can open an opium den. Everybody smokes opium in Saigon. And if we fold up, we can always join the Foreign Legion in Tongking.'

Mr. Hartford fussed with his hearing aid and said, would somebody *please* speak up and tell him what it was all about? When we explained our plan, he nodded gravely. He got up and picked up one of the chairs. He lifted it, testing its weight, and suddenly threw it overboard. Everybody got very excited. Pedro threw a table and another chair after Mr. Hartford's chair, 'for a mermaid who wants to furnish her room,' and I joined in with all the glasses, match-holders, ashtrays, and bottles within reach.

Mr. Hartford and Artie were already busy with the piano. Mr. Hartford said the price of such a bad, old piano did not amount to anything in American money, and that he would gladly pay for it. We had another glass of cool champagne. We pushed the piano toward the railing. The bartender and the deck steward looked on, in utter consternation. Mr. Hartford breathed hard and almost lost his hearing aid. Artie suggested that we should cover the instrument with a flag, a piano being worth almost as much as any human being and considerably more than some of them, but no one seconded the motion. We lifted the piano. It was only an upright Pleyel, but after all the drinks it seemed as heavy as a concert grand. A final effort and the instrument rolled over the railing. There was a short metallic protest and then the chords emitted what sounded like an almost human last cry. There was a big splash. Pedro, a devout Catholic, took off his Basque béret and moved his lips. Perhaps he said a prayer. There was nothing else to say. We went down to our rooms and lay down.

When the ship arrived at Saigon, we were called into the captain's office. The skipper said we had exactly one hour to get twelve hundred and fifty francs for the drowned piano. We went down and looked for Mr. Hartford, but he had already left. Artie smiled confidently. 'Let's find Lucia,' he said. 'There must be enough money in the collection. Lucia earned lots of money last night.'

We found Lucia and Lavallère on the foremost part of the deck, high above the bow. Lavallère had his arm around her. They were gazing down into the water far below. They had been standing here last night when the captain looked for Lavallère. They didn't see or hear us.

'Chérie,' Lavallère said, 'don't worry about me. I'll get transferred to another vessel. I'll be back in eight weeks. I'll be with you.'

'Darling,' Lucia whispered.

Artie cleared his throat. The couple turned around and smiled. Lucia touched Artie's cheek. 'Artie, you were wonderful last night,' she said. She opened her handbag and thrust an envelope filled with coins into Artie's hand. 'Here are the coins, about two hundred francs. Did you find the paper money? I counted almost eleven hundred francs. I put it down inside the piano so nobody would steal it overnight.'

A wave broke against the bow and I felt the fine, cool spray. Artie's mouth was wide-open and I guess mine was too, for there was a strange taste on my tongue when I swallowed.

'Chérie,' Lavallère said, and sighed.

'Darling,' Lucia said. They looked into each other's eyes, oblivious of the big bad world. We turned on our heels and tiptoed away.

Chapter 19

BIG BUSINESS

MY BUSINESS CAREER began one day in the early thirties in Paris when Marcel, a French pianist and a member of our orchestra aboard *La Bourdonnais,* invited me to join him on a trip to Panama. Marcel had excellent connections in the headquarters of the Compagnie Générale Transatlantique. Somehow he managed to convince one of the directors that a musician, after twelve months of faithful service to the company, deserved a break. The director, harboring the erroneous notion that Marcel was out for glory, obligingly offered to get him the ribbon of the Legion of Honor. Marcel turned down this offer, saying that all he wanted was a reduced-price trip on the French Line steamer *Guadeloupe.*

The *Guadeloupe* sailed from Le Havre to Colón, in the Panama Canal Zone, via the French, British, and Dutch West Indies, Venezuela, and Colombia — a fascinating itinerary and the only French Line route which Marcel had never covered. Not that he cared about exotic sights and Baedeker asterisks but it would be wonderful to travel, for once, as a passenger instead of as a musician. No working hours, no orders from a music-hating purser, no fat ladies, eager to reduce, for whom you had to play dance music after the customary evening program was over.

Marcel, who did not like to travel alone, wangled a reduced-price ticket for me, too. I had had magazine stories and newspaper articles published, and Marcel convinced his friend the director that the daily newspaper which, aboard the French Line steamers, was edited by the radio officer and distributed every morning, needed a streamlined, professional touch and that I was the man to supply it on the *Guadeloupe.* Marcel himself got the job of 'Spanish interpreter.' I knew he could not speak Spanish, and I asked him how he could possibly expect to act as interpreter.

'I have my own method,' he said, 'and I won't study the language in ten easy lessons. The average ship's interpreter needs only a few stock phrases. These I'll memorize and speak with perfect pronunciation.' He took a wrinkled slip of paper out of his pocket and read aloud: '"Nosotros lo investigaremos en seguida (We'll investigate at once). No era una chinche, Señora, lo que era fué un botón pequeño de su blusa (That was not a bedbug, Madame, but a small button from your blouse). Señor, déjese usted de estar molestando a la señora con sus atenciones (Sir, please stop bothering the lady with your attentions)."' He stuck the paper back in his pocket and looked at me triumphantly. 'You see, I'm all prepared for my job.'

Marcel said that we were to get a seventy-five per cent reduction on third-class tickets, with the oral understanding that we were to travel as first-class passengers, and showed me a letter from the director to the *Guadeloupe's* purser, requesting that every consideration be given 'à mes deux bons amis.'

Marcel was a medium-sized fellow with short legs, a confused mass of light-brown hair, and the face of a vivacious cherub. He wore sloppy black clothes and a stiff straw hat, tilted well down on his forehead. The straw hat was a tribute to Marcel's idol, the then-great Maurice Chevalier. After a good dinner and a glass of 'fine,' Marcel would get up, push the hat over his left ear, thrust out his lower lip, and sing a risqué version of 'Dites-moi, ma mère, dites-moi,' his voice even coarser than Chevalier's, if such a thing was possible.

He was probably the only musician in Paris who admired the teachings of Dale Carnegie and devoured all available books about American salesmanship, business management, efficiency methods, and related subjects. He was a businessman at heart, and I was never able to find out why he became a musician, though he was an excellent pianist. 'I'm a sad case of split personality,' he would say. He had inherited from his father a house in Dunkerque and a small annuity, and he had an account with the Crédit Lyonnais, on the Boulevard des Italiens. He was more interested in the bank's monthly statements than in seeing his name featured on our music programs. When we were in New York between trips, Marcel would spend hours wandering around the financial district. Or he would go to Macy's and talk to the floor managers until he drove them crazy. A visit to the offices of the National City Bank or of the Pennsylvania Railroad filled him with the holy excitement that musicians usually experience when allowed to sit in at an orchestra rehearsal under Toscanini.

Three days before our departure, Marcel and I went to pick up our tickets at the French Line head offices, 6 Rue Auber. There we ran into L., a friend of mine from Prague, who was vice-president of a leading malt-and-hops export firm. Bohemia, home of the delicately aromatic, pale, *real* Pilsner, Smíchov, Budweiser, Tomáš, and Českomoravské beers, grew and exported the most famous malt and hops in Europe. L. was on his way to the United States and Canada. When he heard of my projected trip, he got quite excited and asked me if I would like to look after his firm's interests in the West Indies and Venezuela, where he did not have any representatives. I replied that I knew practically nothing about malt and hops, and was about to add that I knew even less about business methods when Marcel kicked me in the ankle and interrupted me to say that I was considered a business genius by my Paris friends.

'Don't be a fool,' Marcel whispered when L. was called aside for a minute. 'This may be the great chance of your life. Do you want to die as third violinist aboard the *Ile de France*? Take L.'s offer and do what he wants you to.'

My friend came back, took my address, and said he would have to leave now, but I would hear from him. Three days later, on the morning of our departure, I received an air-mail package from L.'s firm. It contained several samples of different sorts of malt in small tin boxes, a contract letter, and detailed instructions about how I was to represent the firm on my trip. My assignment was to visit the breweries in each stopping-place, have a couple of beers with the brewmasters, inquire about their health, wives, foibles, and special wishes, and to sell good will in general and malt in particular. Also enclosed was a check for two thousand francs 'for unforeseen expenses.' On any sales I was to get the usual commission.

Marcel was triumphant. 'You're in,' he said. 'You're on the royal road to sales commissions. You'll get rich and play music exclusively for your own pleasure — string quartets and beautiful violin sonatas. No more Berceuse de Jocelyn and Toselli's Serenade for those imbeciles on the promenade deck.'

In Le Havre we had some difficulty in finding the *Guadeloupe*. Beside the *Paris* and a big German luxury liner, which were in port, the *Guadeloupe* looked like a tugboat. At the gangway we were met by an arrogant steward with shiny shoes and hair, who cast a disgusted glance at our third-class tickets and immediately discovered an interesting vacuum three inches high above Marcel's straw hat. Marcel got angry and told the steward that we were company inspectors (who frequently traveled in third-class incognito) and that the steward should consider himself fired. We used the momentary confusion following this harsh announcement to run down to the purser's office where Marcel presented his letter from the director. In no time we were installed in a first-class stateroom with private bath. True, it was an inside room, on B-deck, near the iron ladder leading down into the engine-room, and the shower in the bathroom did not work. Our table in the dining-room was in a drafty spot next to the entrance, and the table waiter, who knew us from *La Bourdonnais*, never bothered to clean up the breadcrumbs before he served the dessert; but just the same, we felt the marvelous way soldiers feel on the first day of a furlough. We were free, and easy. My duties as editor of the daily news-sheet hardly took thirty minutes a day. Marcel, as the Spanish interpreter, had no work at all, there being no Spanish passengers aboard.

Three days out of Le Havre, the *Guadeloupe* ran into moderately bad weather and Marcel and I immediately became sick. On our previous trips as musicians we had been through much worse storms without ever being seasick; crew members cannot afford that luxury. But now we were passengers, spoiled brats, and Marcel rang for the cabin steward and ordered tea with lemon and dry toast, and when the tea came, he complained that it was cold, and besides, he'd positively said tea with milk.

As soon as we recovered, Marcel set out to meet what he called the right people — people, that is, with business connections. There were only a few, among them a Mr. Lyons from Birmingham who represented a big British textile concern and was traveling with his Russian wife, Tanja, and their Pekinese, Fifi. The Lyonses led a hectic married life, which was the preferred conversational topic of the female passengers. Every other night Mr. Lyons would beat up both Fifi and his wife and move into an adjoining empty stateroom. This would be followed the next morning by a reconciliation scene on the promenade deck. Marcel was the only person aboard who did not pay any attention to these fascinating events. When he spoke of Mr. Lyons, he always pointed out that the Englishman got half a dozen radiograms a day, that every message meant more sales commissions, and that I should live up to Mr. Lyons's high professional standards so that some day I too would go around with that slightly smug smile that comes from having more customers than merchandise. 'They *beg* him to sell them his stuff,' Marcel said wistfully.

Also among the right people, according to Marcel, was Jake Constanza, Jr., from Los Angeles, who was successfully trying to spend a large part of the money his father was making by supplying optimists with oil-drilling equipment. Mr. Constanza, Jr., was a young, lanky, pleasantly lunatic character with nervous gestures and a falsetto voice. He traveled around the world, he said, for the express purpose of stealing hotel towels, but Marcel and I suspected that Mr. Constanza, Sr., had sent his son around the globe with a silent prayer that Junior would get stuck somewhere between Bucharest and the Christmas Islands and never return. Constanza, Jr., showed us photographs of his collection of 1552 towels, all stolen from hotels in Europe and the Near and Far East. He was currently working on Middle and South America. When he arrived in a town, he told us, he would go to a hotel and take a room, and pay for it in advance. If his schedule permitted, he slept there before he departed with a towel hidden under the shirt; otherwise he simply went up, took a towel and left. If he could not get a room, he went up just the same, walked into any room that happened to be open and took a towel. It would have been simpler to ask for a towel at the reception desk and pay for it, but that was, as Junior pointed out, against the rules of the game, which also demanded that the prize should be a bulky bathtowel, not a hand or face towel.

His best items came, not from the Ritzes and Plazas, where they do not bother about a missing towel, but from third-rate hotels. Once he was badly beaten up by the proprietor of the Hôtel Moderne in the old port of Marseilles. The proprietor was an ex-wrestler to whom the loss of one towel was a major tragedy, there being only a dozen in the hotel. Another exciting incident had occurred in the Hamburg harbor district at the Hotel Grand Admiral Tirpitz, whose manager sent for the police and had Constanza, Jr., jailed because he hated amerikanische Jungenstreiche. Such, Constanza, Jr., said with a sigh, were the risks of his adventurous game.

With Marcel and Constanza, Jr., on hand there was never a dull moment during the ten-day trip from Le Havre to Point-à-Pitre, Guadeloupe. Both were active members of half a dozen committees, organizing raffles, deck-tennis and shuffle-board tournaments, community singing, and amateur theatrical performances. At the Saturday night dinner, when everybody had a few drinks too many, Marcel, under the pretext of looking for a ring, crawled under the long table in the middle of the dining-saloon and interchanged the shoes which most of the ladies had pushed off their feet so they would feel more comfortable. Then he and Constanza, Jr., had a grand time watching the consternation of the female passengers as they put out one foot, then the other, feeling around under the table, and discovering that their shoes simply would *not* fit.

When we reached Fort-de-France on the island of Martinique, Marcel and I took a cab and went to the local brewery, where, in accordance with my instructions, I asked for the brewmaster. Brewmasters everywhere are either Bavarians or Czechs. The man in Fort-de-France was a fat, bull-necked character with bloated lips like sliced Bratwuerste and a disconcerting manner of belching after every fourth word. He was from München-Gladbach in Germany, and he told me bluntly that a compatriot of his had been in Martinique a few weeks ago and sold him all the malt they needed. He brought three glasses of beer. Marcel drank his and said it tasted very much like Seine water near the sewers. We took a hasty departure because the brewmaster lacked the customary Bavarian sense of humor and shouted that we should go zum Teufel. My business efforts in the ports of Port-of-Spain, Georgetown, and Carúpano were equally discouraging.

Everywhere a compatriot of the brewmaster seemed just to have passed through and made a handsome sale. I got plenty of free beer, which has its points in those tropical latitudes, but that was all. Marcel tried to cheer me up. 'Look at Mr. Lyons from Birmingham. He's worked hard for eighteen years. All he does now is to sit back and count his commissions.'

In La Guayra, Venezuela, I received a cable from my Prague malt-and-hops firm. I was to visit a big brewery in near-by Caracas, the capital, and see the proprietor, whom I shall call Señor Carlos. The cablegram added that Señor Carlos knew of my arrival and was in the market for a large quantity of malt. The deal was practically set.

From La Guayra a winding, macadamized autostrada, one of the continent's great highways, leads up to Caracas. Marcel, Constanza, Jr., and I made the trip in a ramshackle Ford. In Caracas I went directly to the brewery. Marcel and Junior were to meet me there later after what Marcel called 'a study of the local drinking habits.'

At the brewery I asked for Señor Carlos, but was taken in hand by Pan Vlček, a stocky, rotund, ash-blond Czech with a friendly, open face. Before we had finished the first glass of beer, we discovered that we had four mutual acquaintances in Prague; after the second glass we moodily looked back upon warm nights at 'U Fleků,' Prague's famous beer-hall, and the unforgettable fillet mignon at Piskaček's, prepared with sour cream in fashion of game. Vlček and I had been, it turned out, opposing fans at soccer games between Sparta and Slavia, the most popular clubs in Prague, a few years ago, shouting against one another and uniting our vocal efforts only in abuse of the umpire. Vlček said that the brewery was in dire need of a large consignment of malt. All I had to do was to have lunch with Señor Carlos. 'Be sure not to discuss business with him,' Vlček said. 'Señor Carlos is very strict about the fine points of Caraqueñian courtesy. Just let him do the talking and be nice. At the end of the meal he will take out a letter and sign it, and you leave with the order. Good luck. Nazdar!'

Señor Carlos was a handsome man in his early thirties. He wore a custom-tailored blue flannel suit and there was a dainty scent of lavender around his neck. He had the natural, easy elegance of a Castilian grandee. He offered me a seat in his office and discussed André Gide, local politics, Debussy, alleged American imperialism, the preparation of vol-au-vent Toulouse, and the latest Picasso, never even mentioning such trite subjects as beer or malt. His office was full of oils, books, Oriental rugs, and heavy mahogany furniture. Señor Carlos said that he would be honored to take me to lunch. I bowed from the waist, and we went outside and got into a black, shiny American limousine. We passed rows of houses with small balconies and enormous doors with heavy iron knobs, and then crossed the beautiful Plaza Bolívar. The car stopped in front of a quiet, expensive-looking hotel. In the dining-room, which had an air of dimness and refinement, distinguished Caraqueños were having their midday meal in an intimate, unbusinesslike atmosphere.

A French maître d'hôtel took the order. Señor Carlos's French was excellent, but he did not speak English. 'I can't even pretend that I feel sorry about it,' he said, with a faint, diplomatic smile. The food was splendid, the wines exactly right, and Señor Carlos was a charming host. We were having our dessert and I was wondering how I would spend the money from my commission when the maître d'hôtel approached our table, followed by Marcel and Constanza, Jr. I saw that my two shipmates had made a rather thorough study of the local drinking habits. Marcel wore the waggish smile that usually preceded one of his bright ideas, and Junior was somewhat voluminous around the waist; no doubt he was already in possession of a Caracas towel for his collection.

They sat down without being invited. Marcel said that

they had been told about our luncheon place by a little Czech at the brewery. Constanza slapped Señor Carlos's shoulder and told the maître d'hôtel to bring four double whiskies, straight, and make it snappy, brother. The maître d'hôtel looked as though he had eaten something bad and Señor Carlos's eyebrows went up a quarter of an inch. At that point a sturdy, determined-looking man came in from the lobby and whispered into the ear of the maître d'hôtel. The maître d'hôtel looked horrified and raised his hands in a despairing gesture. Both he and the sturdy man stared hard at Constanza's middle.

Junior got up from the table. 'They've found out about that damned towel,' he said to Marcel. 'Quick! Let's scram!'

The sturdy man came up and put a hand on Junior's shoulder. Junior grew pale and so did I. Señor Carlos gave me a questioning glance.

'Señor Carlos doesn't understand English,' I said, because I had to say something and could not think of anything else. This was a grave mistake. Marcel patted Señor Carlos's cheek and said, 'Buenos días, cómo estás, Señor. I'm the ship's official interpreter. Address your complaints to the purser. Nosotros lo investigaremos en seguida (We'll investigate at once).'

The maître d'hôtel drew a deep breath and said, 'Gentlemen, there seems to be a — a misunderstanding. The hotel detective just saw this gentleman' — he discreetly directed his eyes toward Constanza, Jr. — 'come out of Señora Tovar's room with a bathtowel in his hand. If the gentleman would explain . . .'

A waiter brought the four double whiskies, straight, which Junior had ordered. Marcel gulped one down and said, 'No era una chinche, Señora, lo que era fué un botón pequeño de su blusa (That was not a bedbug, Madame, but a small button from your blouse).'

Somewhere behind me a startled diner knocked over his glass and it fell to the floor and broke. Señor Carlos got up, put down his napkin, and said that we might better straighten this out in the office of the manager. His tone was glacial.

We went to the manager's office, the detective firmly holding Constanza, Jr.'s, shoulder. In the office Junior broke down and with a gesture of disgust pulled a towel from under his shirt — a heavy bathtowel with the hotel's name on it. Everybody was very quiet for a moment. Then Marcel said, 'Señor, déjese usted de estar molestando a la señora con sus atenciones (Sir, please stop bothering the lady with your attentions).'

Señor Carlos smiled, which was certainly another fine point of Caraqueñian courtesy. He said he had to leave — an urgent business appointment. His chauffeur would take us back to La Guayra in his limousine. He bowed with grandezza and wished me a good trip. That was the last I ever heard of him, or, for that matter, my Prague malt-and-hops firm. It was the end of my business career.

Chapter 20

A DARING, IMPERTINENT SCENT

THE GREAT ambition of all French Line musicians in the early thirties was to get a job aboard the *Ile de France.* Before the *Normandie*, the *Ile de France*, as the flagship of the Compagnie Générale Transatlantique, was the pride of France, and every cabin steward, seaman, officer, cook, musician, waiter, or bartender working on her basked in the feeling of having 'arrived.' The liner's captain, the late Georges Burosse, was an excellent violinist. I had made several crossings with him when he was captain of *La Bourdonnais*, and during bad weather, when most passengers were too sick to dance or listen to music, he used to bring down his violin and play the Bach Double Concerto, or a Schubert or Beethoven piano trio with us. Two months after Burosse was made captain of the *Ile de France*, I was hired as second violinist, on his recommendation.

The orchestra on the *Ile de France* consisted of nine musicians. We had our own completely separate first-class quarters at the end of a corridor on B-deck: four double rooms, and one single cabin for the orchestra leader, a small dining-room with pantry, and a rehearsal room which was used for card-games and drinking parties, since nobody wanted to have rehearsals. The musicians had the prosperous blasé look that comes from saying Hello to the celebrities of two continents and occasionally accompanying such passengers as Kreisler, Paderewski, Pablo Casals, Lily Pons. The most popular member of the orchestra was a little Swiss by the name of Pierre, an excellent 'cello and saxophone player. Everybody called Pierre the 'Petit Suisse,' which is the name of a French cream cheese, usually eaten with sugar, but Pierre did not mind. He did not mind anything. He was soft-spoken, with an innocent earnestness to his wide-open eyes. He wore his black hair long and brushed back. He was a very kind-hearted fellow. In the stateroom which we shared, there were always people in need of money, good advice, or both; men who worried about their future in America; unescorted girls planning their Paris vacation; wives looking for their husbands; passengers who had lost all their money in card-games. Between concerts, when most musicians took sun-baths at the swimming pool, were treated to free drinks, or flirted with pretty American girls, the Petit Suisse worried his head off about other people's troubles, ran errands, straightened out family troubles, or collected money for an impoverished steerage passenger.

On my second trip to New York aboard the *Ile de France*, Pierre's chief protégé was Granelle, a Paris barber, short, sleek, and smelling of brilliantine. Granelle traveled tourist, but spent most of his time on the first-class deck and at the bar.

He explained that he was on his way to Manhattan, where a famous hotel had offered him the job of chief hairdresser. He was a fast talker, full of stories about his adventures as coiffeur in the most exclusive hotels of Deauville, Cannes, and San Sebastian. His stories were always funny and on the risqué side.

The second evening out, Granelle told the Petit Suisse a lachrymose story which involved an old, sick mother, a divorced wife, various other ailing relatives, and some unlucky business transactions. It conveyed the picture of a generally unhappy life, and at the end of his speech Granelle borrowed fifty francs from the deeply moved Pierre and departed. The next day I came into our stateroom after the apéritif concert. Pierre sat in an armchair, apparently borrowed from our dining-room. He had on a white sheet from his bed, and Granelle was giving him what he called a super-de-luxe hair-cut, 'musician-type, hardly noticeable, parfait.' When I told him that French Line regulations prohibited his working for money, Granelle broke down and made a confession. The hotel in Manhattan, where he was supposedly offered a job, was merely a product of his imagination. So were the exclusive hotels in Deauville, Cannes, and San Sebastian. Granelle had never barbered outside of the Buttes-Chaumont district in Paris. As a sideline, he had sold perfumes, hair tonics, and face-creams, which he concocted himself in the back room of his little shop. 'The police didn't think the face-creams were any good,' Granelle said, thoughtfully. 'But you know those *types*. Always think the worst of you.'

Granelle denied that there was any causal connection between the opinions of the Paris police and his trip to America. He had an uncle in Brooklyn who owned a barber shop and had promised him a job. 'America is the only country where a débrouillard can get rich quick,' Granelle said. 'I've *got* to make some money. All I own now is my barber's equipment and a few bottles of perfume which I bought in Paris, wholesale.'

In the afternoon the Petit Suisse went around taking off his Basque béret and showing everybody what a perfect job Granelle had done on his hair. From then on, most musicians came into our room to get a 'parfait' haircut. The orchestra boycotted the ship's official barber, a gruff, ill-tempered character, who refused to give us the customary fifty per cent discount which we had on laundry, beverages, dry-cleaning, and deck-chair rentals. This barber had no sympathy for aesthetes who wore their hair longer than the average citizen. A few months ago the barber had practically ruined Bonetti, an elegant Italian fiddler of the schmaltz type. Bonetti impressed his female audiences with his long black curls and his sentimental tremolo and did not bother much about accurate phrasing. One day at the ship's barber shop, Bonetti dozed off while the barber gave him a haircut. When the violinist awoke, most of his beautiful hair was gone. So was most of his irresistible charm. The ladies were not entranced by a Prussian close-crop. Poor Bonetti was through.

Granelle liked it so well in our cabin that he stayed all day, and when I came down that evening, there was a small table near the porthole on which the barber had spread out his equipment — a clipper with nickel-plated handles, two pairs of shears, a razor, a comb, two hairbrushes, a neck brush, a half-broken shaving bowl, shaving cream, and men's talc. Two horsehide straps, a sharpening and a finishing one, were hanging from the armchair. Granelle, dressed in a white barber coat, was giving the parfait treatment to an assistant maître d'hôtel. The ship's pastry cook was lying on my bed, waiting to get a haircut before he went back to his ovens. I tried to get them out of the room, but the Petit Suisse made a pathetic speech about every man's right to work and make a living. I said, 'All right, but does he have to make a living at night, in our cabin?' Granelle stopped his parfait work and gave me a sad look. The pastry cook sat up on my bed and ominously winked. I took my pillow and went into the adjoining cabin. It belonged to the pianist and banjo-player and had an extra upper berth. The Petit Suisse slept in the stateroom of the orchestra leader, which was vacant as the leader had an all-night appointment with a lady passenger in first class. Granelle kept working in our cabin until midnight and then went to sleep in his tourist-class stateroom.

I was not surprised to find Granelle at work the next morning when I came in for my shaving equipment. A friendly, white-haired meat-packer from Chicago, known around the sun deck as a prominent shuffle-board player, was getting a haircut and a dandruff-remover treatment. Two other prosperous shuffle-board men in navy-blue jackets and white trousers were waiting their turn, smoking, looking at the pictures in *La Vie Parisienne* and *Froufrou*, which Granelle had supplied as appropriate entertainment. The barber recounted a spicy story about a Paris music-hall queen and a former Finance Minister, and the room was full of laughter. Up on deck I got hold of the Petit Suisse, who was actively campaigning among the passengers for Granelle for barber and making haircut appointments for the rest of the day. I complained, but Pierre put his hand on my shoulder. 'Don't you see — we *can't* throw him out!' he said. 'Where else could Granelle give haircuts but in our room? He's a nice fellow. Charges only six francs, half as much as the barber shop upstairs. And he needs the money badly.'

In the afternoon I caught Granelle charging a customer ten francs for a haircut. He smiled charmingly and explained that this price included his extraordinary lotion treatment, adding in the same breath that the Petit Suisse and I could have anything, *anything* from him, free of charge. The equipment on the table had markedly increased. There were new bottles of hair tonic, brilliantine, skin lotions, dandruff-remover shampoos; the small cabinet above the washbasin contained perfume bottles, which Granelle sold to his customers at prices only slightly below the exorbitant ones charged in the ship's barber shop.

Business was booming. Most of the customers were men of the prosperous-executive type. They liked the unusual, colorful atmosphere of the musicians' quarters, the risqué French magazines, which one would not find at the barber shop upstairs, and, above all, the secrecy. Before the customers were admitted to the barber's chair, they had to take an oath of silence. It was, as a hosiery manufacturer from Boston pointed out, almost as exciting as in the good old days when you had to knock at back doors and walk through dark corridors to get a rotten drink. The people did not mind the uncomfortable chair, the lack of large mirrors, marble washbasins, fresh towels, electric-powered clippers. The customers had their hair shampooed in the two small cabin basins and dried under the natural air current coming through the porthole. There was a scarcity of sheets; the Petit Suisse stole some from the neighboring staterooms, and Granelle managed to get a dozen from the chambermaid, who also came from the Buttes-Chaumont district in Paris. Granelle hung up a poster of a pretty girl in love with a tube of toothpaste; next to it he put on a large white paper with the latest New York stock-market quotations, which were shown in our — Granelle's — stateroom even before they appeared in the ship's daily newspaper. This precious information was supplied by the Petit Suisse, who had a friend at the wireless station.

There were so many customers that Granelle increased the price of 'simple haircut' to nine francs, and of 'complete haircut' (shave, shampoo, scalp treatment) to nineteen francs. Most people ordered the works. Soon our quarters smelled like a perfume factory. All doors were open and the wind carried locks of hair across the corridor into the musicians' dining-room. The musicians threatened to complain to the captain unless Granelle moved out at once. Granelle told them a mournful story about his ailing relatives. The Petit Suisse seconded his plea, until everybody agreed to let Granelle stay on, musicians being soft-hearted.

On the fourth morning Granelle appeared with a shapely brunette, whom he introduced as Madame Germaine, an artiste in the field of manicure. Germaine traveled in the tourist class where she had met Granelle. 'She told me she was a manicurist,' Granelle said. 'I told her to become my partner. All this place needs to be really swanky is a good manicurist.' Germaine put her nail files, scissors, cuticle removers, nail polish, and oils down on my bed, and for five francs gave Granelle's customers a parfait manicure. The barber put her in charge of the perfume counter. She would put a drop of Lanvin or D'Orsay perfume on her rather low neckline and let prospective customers test it as a sample.

'You must breathe in deep to get the real bouquet,' she said in her throaty voice, idly playing with an immense ring on her finger. 'This is a daring, impertinent scent. Half an ounce, forty-eight francs. You can pay in American money.' The elderly customers breathed in the daring, impertinent scent and closed their eyes. After that they were so confused that they offered both French and American money. Between manicures and perfume sales talks Germaine flirted with the banjo player, and in the rehearsal room danced with the orchestra leader to the music of a portable gramophone. She also wanted to dance with the Petit Suisse, but Pierre was too busy running errands for Granelle, checking stock quotations, race-track results, acquiring fresh linen sheets and additional customers.

Some men came for a haircut early in the forenoon and stayed on all day long. They said it was more fun than deck-tennis tournaments, raffles, dances, movies. Even the senior members of the orchestra could not remember ever having seen anything like it. The banjo-player said, 'It's amazing that the barber upstairs hasn't found out yet about this setup. Some day that éspèce de salaud is going to raise hell.' The banjo-player shook his head and added, philosophically, that there was no better place for small crimes than aboard a luxury liner during the rush season when there were more passengers than cockroaches aboard.

In the end it was not the ship's barber who 'discovered' Granelle, but a resolute, elderly lady with horn-rimmed glasses and a decidedly masculine manner of speech. She appeared the morning of the last day at the unfortunate moment when her husband, one of the white-haired shuffle-board players, had his right hand on Germaine's knee while she was giving his left a parfait manicure. Granelle put on his most seductive smile, but for once his Parisian charm was a sorry failure. For about ten minutes the ever-present noise of the engines seemed to have ceased. There was nothing but the bass voice of the enraged lady. She confined her husband to their stateroom and went straight up to the captain to complain bitterly about what she called the immoral things going on at the musicians' quarters. Captain Burosse, well informed about the Petit Suisse's philanthropical schemes, promised her a severe investigation which naturally never took place. Granelle took away his things and Germaine packed her equipment into a leather kit. Granelle gave the Petit Suisse a big fatherly hug. 'You've been swell,' Granelle said, his voice dripping with a ham actor's phony emotion. 'God bless you, mon petit. Remember, when I'm a big shot among the New York coiffeurs, you'll come in any time and get the parfait musicians' haircut.'

When the *Ile de France* passed the Statue of Liberty, Granelle came down to our cabin. He had on a blue flannel suit with discreet white stripes, a blue silk shirt, gray tie, light-gray hat, and a fresh carnation in his buttonhole. He carried two parcels, wrapped in brown paper, tied with heavy strings. He asked the Petit Suisse to carry the parcels down to the pier.

'They contain my equipment,' Granelle explained. 'Shears, clippers, brushes, my coats. My uncle, the coiffeur from Brooklyn, may wait for me at the pier and I don't want him to see my equipment. It's a surprise for him.' Granelle hastily put down the parcels on Pierre's bed and patted the boy's shoulder. 'I'll meet you at the pier.' He smiled and was gone.

There was the usual confusion when the *Ile de France* docked at Pier 57, at the foot of West Fourteenth Street. Women nervously opened their bags, everybody was looking for somebody, while porters, policemen, excited relatives and friends were blocking all traffic. I got my debarkation card and went ashore. The Petit Suisse came down the gangway with one of Granelle's parcels, explaining that it was quite heavy and he would have to go back for the other one. At the customs space marked by the big letter G, there was a large crowd. Granelle and Germaine stood in the middle by a long table, surrounded by half a dozen customs men. One took perfume bottles out of Granelle's bag, while another counted them and made notes on a pad. Granelle gesticulated wildly and looked around, perhaps for his uncle, who was not there. His voice was high-pitched and I saw the sweat on his forehead. He didn't look like a débrouillard now. 'I'm no smuggler,' he said. 'These flaçons are . . . are . . . for my personal use. All of them, believe me.' The customs man with the pad said, 'Sure. They'll last you until you are eighty,' without taking his eyes off his pencil. Someone next to me whispered, 'They've both been arrested. Tried to slip through with hundreds of bucks' worth of perfume.' I tried to warn the Petit Suisse, who pushed through the crowd without seeing what went on at the table, but it was too late. He was already there and put down his parcel, smiling good-naturedly at Granelle. Germaine exclaimed. Two customs officials tore off the wrapping. A white barber coat fell out, a brush, a clipper, and about two dozen carefully wrapped perfume flaçons.

Granelle turned toward the Petit Suisse. 'You fool!' he said, breathing fast, his lips trembling. 'You damned, damned fool!'

The Petit Suisse was released only after half an hour's cross-examination. I had to call the orchestra leader, all our men, the purser, and finally the captain, to exonerate the Petit Suisse. The boy did not look at Granelle and Germaine when they were taken away by the customs men. He went back aboard with us, pale, silent, his mouth twitching. Granelle's second parcel was still on Pierre's bed. We had forgotten all about it. We opened it. There were about twenty small bottles — Coty, Houbigant, Roger and Gallet, Chanel, Worth, Renoir. The Petit Suisse wanted to throw them into the water, but he was overruled by the vote of eight angry musicians. Under the direction of the orchestra leader the bottles were equally divided among all musicians, with the flaçon containing the daring, impertinent scent going to the Petit Suisse.

Chapter 21

THE CRUISE OF THE *CHENONCEAUX*

OCCASIONALLY I wonder who thought up the silly saying that the French are not fond of travel. Any ship's musician knows that the French like to get around as much as the next fellow, though only on French territory and aboard French ships. The pleasure cruises of the Messageries Maritimes steamers were always sell-outs. Most of them were arranged for the Christmas season, going to Syria and Palestine for 'Les Mystères de Beyruth,' 'Noël à Bethlehem.' During the Easter holiday the cruise ships went to Egypt, Tunisia, Algeria for 'Pentecôte à Djezira el Maghreb.' There were also summer cruises through the Mediterranean or up the Atlantic coast to Le Havre, and some courageous expeditions even ventured into forbidden territory as far as Hamburg and Stockholm.

The Messageries Maritimes had only two luxury liners, the *Champollion* and *Mariette Pacha.* During the rush season the management put their regular mail boats on cruise work. On Good Friday of 1931, the *Chenonceaux*, a fourteen-thousand-ton liner on which I was working, was due to sail on a special nine-day cruise, advertised as 'The Wonders of the Blue Mediterranean,' from Marseilles to Oran, Algiers, Corsica, Genoa, Monte Carlo, Nice, and back to Marseilles.

We had just returned from a trying, ninety-five-day journey to the Far East when we were told that the *Chenonceaux* would stay at Marseilles only three days instead of the customary three-week layoff between trips. The crew was in the mood for blood. On top of it all we discovered that the ship had been chartered by eight hundred members of France's largest federation of high-school teachers, which increased our misgivings. The *Chenonceaux* had never been on a cruise. We felt about cruise-ship personnel the way crack streamliner engineers may feel about streetcar conductors. Our officers, seamen, cooks, stewards, musicians, cabin boys, veterans of exotic, long-term trips halfway around the world, were horrified at the thought of paddling about the Mediterranean, catering to the whims of tourists. On our trips to the Orient we had an easy-to-please clientèle, mostly businessmen, colonial officials, and dry, disgusted military men who traveled at government expense and did not bother with large tips. They expected no special service.

'Playing for a bunch of school-teachers,' Maurice, our 'cellist, said in disgust. 'Dieu d'un dieu, they will ask me when Beethoven became deaf and whether Joseph, Johann, Richard, and Oskar Strauss were brothers.' Maurice, an old friend of mine from the days of *La Bourdonnais*, had not long ago switched from the Atlantic to the Far Eastern route because the pinard aboard Messageries ships was better. Now I worked as orchestra leader and Maurice as 'cellist. The leader has certain duties which Maurice was never sober enough to perform.

Maurice belonged to the vanishing species of musicians who play moderately well even when not entirely sober. Artie, our pianist, could not even play 'Chopsticks' when he had a couple of whiskies, which happened frequently. Between these two alcoholics I was leading a sorry, concert-to-concert existence. There was trouble every day. Artie almost lost his job because he gave the crew lessons in United States crap-shooting. Once in Hong-Kong, Maurice hoisted the yellow quarantine flag which is raised in case of contagious disease aboard. The British health authorities, lacking Maurice's macabre sense of humor, promptly put the *Chenonceaux* in quarantine for five days until they became convinced that the whole thing was a gag. Fortunately, they never found out who had done it.

Maurice began his day with one bottle of red wine and by ten o'clock was on the next. He managed himself fairly well during the eleven-o'clock apéritif concert and only an occasional trembling of the bow would give him away. To avoid this danger, we eliminated all musical pieces with long, extended 'cello-notes (Bach, Haendel, and Schubert's 'Ave Maria'). Every three or four months Maurice had what he called his critical spell. He collected a dozen bottles, wine, brandy, Bénédictine, Calvados, Pernod, rye, rum, Scotch, champagne. He placed the bottles on the left side of his bunk, put on his pajama-bottoms, and went to bed. He reached for the bottle which was nearest and started drinking. There was no way of getting him out of bed before all the bottles were lying empty on the right side of his bed. This usually took him from three to four days. Luckily the ship's doctor was our friend and told everybody that poor Maurice was suffering from his seasonal attack of the estivo-autumnal or malignant malaria. 'Pauvre garçon, he's flat on his back again,' the doctor would say. 'Caught it in Indo-China. Will never get rid of it.'

Twenty-four hours before the *Chenonceaux* sailed for the Easter cruise, Monsieur Bonhomme, the cruise director, came aboard and moved into the office of the headwaiter. Monsieur Bonhomme was said to be in charge of all restaurant, cabin, kitchen, and deck personnel, by order of the steamship company. He was tall, sun-tanned, slick-haired, and walked with the springy gait of a ballet-dancer. He reminded me of all the gigolos who make a living by fascinating disappointed, well-to-do ladies. He introduced himself as a French-Canadian efficiency expert from Montreal. He said he

KING

had worked as cruise director on big German and American liners, but the third-class bartender still remembered the time he and Bonhomme were employed in a little boîte near the Halles at Paris.

Within an hour Bonhomme managed to disrupt the *Chenonceaux* completely. He 'streamlined' the table arrangement in the dining-saloon, which he called 'outdated'; he had 'inappropriate' books, such as Céline's 'Voyage au Bout de la Nuit' and Marguerite's 'La Garçonne' taken out of the library; he changed the shifts of the cabin stewards, and rearranged the kitchen setup. He ordered small white signs hung up in the corridors and on deck, with arrows pointing 'To the Library,' 'To the Dining-Saloon,' 'To the Swimming Pool,' and so on. Bonhomme thought this was a fine bit of efficiency. Three hours before sailing, he called the three orchestra members into his office. He had certainly done a thorough job of redecorating an 'outdated' room. The walls were covered with pictures of the Mediterranean in color, a panoramic view of Paris, French, Italian, British, and Canadian flags, and a large cross-section of the *Chenonceaux*, covered with many tiny flags such as are used on military maps.

Bonhomme greeted us with perturbing deference, turned to the ship's plan and pinned three green flags on the spot indicating his office. The three green flags were the musicians, he pointed out. He had to have 'control of his men' at all moments, to know where everybody was. There were white flags for the cooks, blue ones for the waiters, red ones for cabin stewards, and green ones for musicians and deck personnel. Covering the whole wall behind Bonhomme's desk was a large sign, 'ARE YOU HAPPY?'

Bonhomme swiveled back and forth in his chromium chair. He handed me a typewritten memorandum. It read:

DIRECTIONS POUR MESSIEURS LES MUSICIENS

1. Messieurs les musiciens will work from eight to nine A.M. (breakfast concert, dining-saloon); eleven to noon (apéritif

concert, promenade deck); three to four P.M. (afternoon concert, tourist-class saloon); four to five P.M. (afternoon concert, first-class saloon); seven to eight P.M. (dinner concert, main dining-saloon); nine to eleven P.M. (dance on promenade deck), see Number 2.

2. No old-fashioned dances, such as valse, polka, galop, are to be played.

3. Messieurs les musiciens will refrain from all social contact with the passengers. They will talk to the passengers when addressed by them, and on musical subjects only.

4. Monsieur le chef d'orchestre will report to the cruise director every morning at 9.10 with (*a*) a list of selections played the day before; (*b*) a draft of the next day's program; (*c*) a copy of (*b*). The copy will be sent to the ship's printer after approval by the cruise director.

5. There will be no drinking during working hours.

6. Monsieur le chef d'orchestre will be held responsible for his men. He is to know where they are every minute.

The document was numbered M–1 and signed, 'A. Bonhomme, directeur.' I was stunned. According to our contract we were to work five hours a day, not seven. The breakfast concert at the eerie hour of eight was sheer madness; the whole memorandum was a collection of insults. I passed the sheet on to Maurice and shoved back my chair in anticipation.

Maurice did not explode. He read the order, gave it to Artie, and leaned back with a sardonic smile. We watched Artie, whose face took on the color of moldy cottage cheese. He was about to jump up when Maurice kicked him in the shinbone and motioned him to keep quiet. The cruise director, all sweetness, asked if there were any questions. Maurice said, Mais non, everything was perfectly clear. I was given a carbon copy of the order, and had to sign the original which Bonhomme placed in a green folder, of the same shade as the musicians' flags on the map.

We went out into the corridor. Artie seized Maurice by the lapels and pushed him against the wall. 'Are you going to stand for this outrage?' Artie asked. 'This is worse than a chain gang. Worse than death, for that matter. "No drinking during working hours." You know what that means?' By way of an answer, Maurice pulled out a flaçon of brandy and offered it to Artie. Each of us had a drink. I needed mine very badly. A lady passenger passed by and gave us a shocked look. Maurice smiled and offered her the bottle. The lady gasped and fled. We went over to a large bulletin board marked 'CRUISE NEWS' which had been put up near the main stairway by Monsieur Bonhomme. There was a list of passengers, a pamphlet by Monsieur Bonhomme, 'Le mal de mer n'existe pas,' and the hour-by-hour entertainment program for the next day. It began with a lecture at eight-thirty A.M. by a Professor de Milhau on 'Athens, Carthage, Rome — A Warning to France,' and ended, '9–11 P.M.: Modern Dance Music by the Ship's Orchestra.'

We went on deck. More passengers began to arrive. They had the excited, somewhat frightened look of children around a lion cage. Most of them were matronly women with bony, severe faces. They carried umbrellas, folding deck chairs, books, maps, dark glasses, raincoats, and field glasses. Maurice greeted them near the main stairway, introduced himself as the ship's 'cello-player and casually remarked that the lifeboats were on sun deck, but that there were not anywhere near enough for everybody. The passengers swarmed all over the ship. They took over the library and the music saloon and feverishly wrote postcards showing a discouraging view of the *Chenonceaux*, telling the deck steward to mail the cards in Marseilles. They went around asking which side was starboard, where the wireless room was, and why the *Chenonceaux* did not have more than one funnel? A diminutive, old man, with a beautiful white beard and the rosette of the Legion of Honor, said to me, in a thin, trembling voice, 'Is there any danger of icebergs, M'sieu?' Numerous passengers went up to the captain's office to complain that someone had stolen their life-belts. The cabin stewards were running around, carrying fresh water, towels, hot tea, extra chairs, new light bulbs, and mimeographed sheets signed by Monsieur Bonhomme containing the program for the day. A mathematics professor settled down in the bar and delightedly told everybody within hearing distance that his wife was already seasick.

Monsieur Bonhomme stood in front of his office, shaking hands with everybody like a senator in his home district. His energy was terrifying. While the *Chenonceaux* drifted through the Vieux Port, six lectures were being given on 'The Mediterranean, Hunting Ground of the Conquerors,' and related subjects. The passengers busily took notes and looked up historical data in their guidebooks. Few bothered to step out on deck to look at the harbor of Marseilles and the coast now fading into the bluish afternoon mist. Artie sat at the bar with a Falstaffian man whom Artie introduced to us as Professor Roget. They drank brandy, the professor quoting Alcaeus, Epicurus, Vergil, Horace, and Ovid on the wisdom of drinking. He was a friendly fellow, with pillows of fat all over his body. He suggested that we all move to the main saloon, where a firm-chinned, rugged woman was giving a talk on 'Hygiene Aboard Ship.' We sat down in front, and after a while Artie stood up and asked if he might give the audience a few pointers on how to avoid being seasick. The sea was perfectly calm, but everybody said, 'Yes, please.' Artie, casually introducing himself as a veteran musician of many years' ocean travel, stepped up on the platform in front of the piano and advised the audience to eat as much as possible, stay below, and throw away all seasickness pills. 'Eat plenty of heavy food, lobster, thick sauces, and pâté de foie gras. Plenty of pâté de foie gras. Keeps your stomach busy and prevents nausea.' Artie spoke slowly with the urbane approach of an expensive dietician. I saw that he had put his right hand behind his back. He grasped the edge of the piano. Slowly his body began to rotate in a clockwise direction, like a gyro, forward, to the right, back, to the left, and so on. Watching him closely one could not help feeling that the ship was badly rolling. It was one of Artie's lesser after-dinner stunts, but it seemed to work, as several people got pale and left in a conspicuous hurry.

By dinnertime the ship was pitching a little and the dining-room was deserted, with only a few brave ones fighting that certain feeling in the pit of the stomach. The cabin stewards reported that most sick passengers were staying in their cabins and refused to go up on deck, though Monsieur Bonhomme's pamphlet, 'Le mal de mer n'existe pas,' which had been distributed in every stateroom, told the people to stay up on deck and avoid heavy food. Some passengers demanded pâté de foie gras and crême de volaille, of all things. After the evening dance we spent an hour at the bar. By midnight all decks were deserted. We went past Monsieur Bonhomme's cabin. The door was closed and there was no light. Maurice said it was time to go to work.

We took down all the signs pointing 'To the Dining-Saloon' and replaced them by 'To the Bathroom' signs. Then we switched around the 'To the Dining-Saloon' signs. They now led straight down to the engine-room. The 'Swimming Pool' posters were replaced by 'Office of Cruise Director.' We mixed up all other signs, 'To the Library,' 'To the Barber Shop,' 'To the Wireless Station.' It was easy work, the signs being held only by thumbtacks. One man stood guard at the end of the corridor while two others worked. By one A.M. all the signs were completely mixed up all over the ship. The Père Racine, the night watchman, an old, staggering, spitting character, caught us while we tried to carry away the large bulletin board. We explained the situation, whereupon the Père Racine gave us a hand, pointing out that Monsieur Bonhomme had forbidden him to go to the icebox and get a sandwich whenever he felt hungry. 'Espèce de cochon,' the Père Racine said. Raiding the icebox was a time-honored privilege of the night watchman. We took the bulletin board up on deck and threw it into the swimming pool.

We went to bed, tired but satisfied by a good night's work.

The Père Racine woke us up at half-past seven. Artie threatened to kill him, but finally got up, though he did not comb his hair or wash. We followed the signs 'To the Bathroom' which guided us right to the dining-saloon. Behind us were two ladies who wore dressing-gowns and had their hair all done up in curlers. They were in the middle of the dining-saloon before they realized that this was hardly the place to wash up. They fled in panic, leaving behind a few bobby-pins and a towel. The bearded gentleman with the Legion of Honor rosette, wearing a purple bathrobe and wooden clogs, came in and asked the headwaiter if he had seen his teeth. The headwaiter shook his head. He told us that people had appeared in pajamas, kimonos, négligés, and still further deshabille. 'Everybody's asking for the bathroom,' the headwaiter said, indignantly. 'Everything's going haywire on this boat since Bonhomme, ce salaud, has taken over. Efficiency, quelle blague!'

Bells rang and stewards ran through the corridors, bumping into bewildered passengers. There was the beautiful confusion popular in slapstick comedies. From Monsieur Bonhomme's office came angry voices. A lady chaperoning two small girls in bathing-suits said that she had followed the signs 'To the Swimming Pool' which led right into this office and that Monsieur ought to be ashamed of himself. Monsieur Bonhomme sat behind his desk, without his customary aplomb. Outside we saw a large group of people, led by Professor Roget. They followed the 'Dining-Saloon' signs and wound up on the steep iron ladders leading down to the engine-room. The noise of the turbines was frightful and the chief engineer, sweating in his oil-stained overalls, tried in vain to explain to Professor Roget that this definitely was *not* the way to the dining-saloon. We helped the fat professor climb back, two people pulling him from above, three pushing from below. The chief engineer telephoned to the captain to get ces imbéciles the hell out of the engine-room before they fell into the turbines. The captain went down to

Monsieur Bonhomme's office and ordered him to get this madhouse straightened out or he would throw him overboard, without a life-belt, so help him God.

It took Monsieur Bonhomme, the efficiency expert, two hours to quell the general anarchy. Stewards were sent throughout the boat ringing the little glockenspiels which were used to call people to meals, inviting everybody to follow the 'Bathroom' signs and assemble at the dining-saloon. There Monsieur Bonhomme, slightly shaken, pronounced that criminal hands had changed the signs. Everybody was to remain in his stateroom until the signs were fixed. No one, except some of the passengers, paid any attention to him. The maître d'hôtel renewed his old table arrangement, the head cook restored his smoothly working kitchen setup, the stewards went back to their old shifts, the library steward put Marguerite's 'La Garçonne' back into circulation. Everybody was happy and the whole machinery worked as smoothly as it had before the arrival of Monsieur Bonhomme. The cruise director went back to his office, trying desperately to get control of his men, rearranging his flags, and putting through telephone calls. All sorts of strange things happened. The telephone went out of order, the bells did not ring, a sudden wind dispersed the papers on his desk, the water in his washbasin ceased to run, and in the evening the door of his office got stuck while he was at dinner and he could not get back into his office. They had to call two men from the engine-room, who somehow managed to open the door by midnight. They said that Monsieur Bonhomme was horror-struck when he entered the place. Someone had monkeyed with the little flags on the ship's cross-section. The white flags (cooks) now were all at the engine-room, the blue ones (waiters) had a convention in the fuel tanks, the red ones (cabin boys) were incarcerated in the refrigeration chamber, and the green ones (musicians and deck stewards) had disappeared altogether.

That night, at two o'clock, Monsieur Bonhomme cried for

help. The Père Racine arrived after some delay and found the cruise director soaking wet, sitting up miserably in bed. Apparently the Mediterranean had come through the port-hole. Monsieur Bonhomme was forced to spend the rest of the night on a couch in the main saloon, all cabins being occupied. No one took the pains to explain to Monsieur Bonhomme that the sea was calm that night and the waves could not possibly reach up to his porthole, which was on the promenade deck. I asked Maurice if it was true that the Père Racine and the headwaiter had been seen on deck at half-past one with buckets of water. The 'cellist shrugged and smiled mysteriously.

We did not bother to get up for the breakfast concert the next morning and never again played more than five hours a day. Everybody was very sorry for Monsieur Bonhomme, who had caught cold and had to stay in bed. In Algiers we went ashore with Professor Roget, who made an immediate hit with the inhabitants of the Kasbah by giving a demonstration of a belly-dance on the street, and singing a risqué Arabian song. After Algiers, Artie and I played without a 'cello, as Maurice was having a critical spell. Monsieur Bonhomme was not heard of any more. According to reports from the promenade deck, he was still in bed, drinking hot tea, swallowing aspirins, and straightening out his little flags.

THE END